The Silve. ____

The tea had steeped long enough. I filled a cup, brought it into the living room, and turned on the lamp. The hot drink chased away the chill. As I frequently did, I looked at my silver sleigh on the mantel, admiring its shine.

Had it been that shiny last night?

Well, of course. Something seemed different, though.

A silver sleigh, eight tiny reindeer, each one unique…

Each one was exactly the same! Cookie cutter reindeer pulled the sleigh!

I sprang up. Hot tea splashed down on my woolen skirt. Hardly aware of the sting of burning, I rushed to the mantel.

The flower-and-scroll pattern had vanished as if rubbed away by a vengeful hand. This wasn't my sleigh. How could this be?

I lifted it off the mantel, noticing immediately that it was lighter. It was an imposter, a changeling. A lightweight.

Just for a moment, I wondered if magic at been at work in my home. Then I remembered the dogs' unusual behavior. I couldn't blame the supernatural for this mysterious exchange.

Somebody had broken into the house and stolen my treasured antique, the good luck artifact coveted by the women with the Christmas names. He or she had left this cheap imitation in its place, no doubt hoping I wouldn't notice the substitution.

Apparently this had happened today when the feistiest of the collies were at the groomer's. But how could anyone have known?

The thought of an intruder with an unknown agenda in the house galvanized me into action. The side door had opened normally. The front door? Hurriedly I opened and closed it again and could find no sign that it had been tampered with.

Next I checked the windows on the first floor, trailed by Halley and Sky, while Misty slipped into Sky's favorite place under the kitchen table. More strange behavior.

The windows were securely locked, but someone must have found their way inside. The sleigh hadn't driven itself off the mantel into the unknown.

It was still snowing, a fresh layer to cover the evidence of footprints. This was no impulsive break-in but a well-planned assault on our home.

Which led me to a question. Who would have the nerve to burglarize a deputy sheriff's house?

A person unaware of Crane's profession? One who didn't care because the prize they coveted was more important than any risk.

In my view, those women at The Silver Sleigh were guilty until proven innocent.

What They Are Saying About

The Silver Sleigh

Dorothy Bodoin's newest novel, *The Silver Sleigh*, is tʰ nineteenth book in Bodoin's Foxglove Corners Mystery Series highly recommend this series as definitely one not to be mis Each book is carefully crafted with intricate skill, as they follοʷ life of Jennet Greenway who moves from Oakpoint to Foˣ Corners in Michigan after her home was destroyed by a tᶜ Readers will be continually captivated by these books aʳ mixture of Victorian houses and glorious scenery and ᵃ characters that only Bodoin could create – real ones - pᵉ could meet every day with their various idiosyncrᵃ eventually meets Crane Ferguson, the love of her lifᵉ marrying him, changes her name to Jennet Fergusο challenges and mysteries befall her.

Other Works From The Pen Of
Dorothy Bodoin

A Ghost of Gunfire, January, 2015—Months after gunfire erupted in her classroom at Marston High School leaving one student dead and one seriously wounded, Jennet begins to hear a sound of gunfire inaudible to everyone else.

Dreams and Bones, May, 2014—A renovation at Brent Fowler's newly-purchased Spirit Lamp Inn turns up human bones buried in the Inn's backyard, rekindling interest in the case of a young woman who disappeared from the Inn several decades ago.

The Door in the Fog, November 2013—A wounded dog disappears in the fog. A blue door on the side of a barn vanishes. Strange flowers and a sound of weeping haunt a meadow. And a curse refuses to die. It's another typical summer in Foxglove Corners.

The Snow Queen's Collie, March 2013—During a Christmas Eve snowstorm, a white collie appears on the porch of the Ferguson farmhouse, and the painting Jennet's sister gives her for Christmas begins to exhibit strange qualities.

THE SILVER SLEIGH

by

Dorothy Bodoin

A Wings ePress, Inc.

Cozy Mystery Novel

Wings ePress, Inc.

Edited by: Jeanne Smith
Copy Edited by: Joan Powell
Senior Editor: Jeanne Smith
Executive Editor: Marilyn Kapp
Cover Artist: Pat Evans

All rights reserved

Wings ePress Books
http://www.wings-press.com

Copyright © 2015 by Dorothy Bodoin
ISBN 978-1-61309-756-4

Published In the United States Of America

August 2015

Wings ePress Inc.
403 Wallace Court
Richmond, KY 40475

Dedication

To my brother, Nick

One

The road was a narrow ribbon of white threading through dark pine forest that sloped several feet down below ground level. Little traveled, lovely, and treacherous. It looked like a glittering Christmas card, but the snow hid a layer of ice capable of sending the Taurus careening into the trees. One unguarded moment, one skid, would be sufficient to seal our doom.

We were far from home, about two hundred miles, and it was still snowing.

At my side, Leonora aimed her flashlight on the map and issued periodic warnings about black ice and sheer drops, while in the back seat, our rescue collie, Sparkle, slept, blissfully unaware of possible danger.

She was a remarkably good and trusting dog, coming with us quietly and settling on a fluffy blanket without a single backward glance.

I could see her still form reflected in the rear view mirror. Her nose leaned on the armrest, and her eyes were closed. Dreaming of a new home, I hoped.

Sparkle was gorgeous, a tri-headed white who had landed in an Ellentown shelter. No one had claimed her, no one inquired about her, and apparently no one looked beyond her muddy, matted

1

exterior to see the luminous beauty within. No one except for the imaginative young volunteer who had named her Sparkle.

I skidded into the oncoming lane, which was fortunately empty, took a deep breath, and steered into the skid until I regained control of the wheel. That was close.

"Be careful," Leonora said. "We don't want to have an accident in this wilderness. I haven't seen another car in an hour, and my cell phone is dead."

"Don't worry. I'm very aware. And alert."

That was true, for all the good it would do if the Taurus failed to hold the road. "I have to say, though, this sure isn't the easiest assignment we ever had," I added.

It had seemed ideal and even fun this morning when we'd set out on the long drive north under a cold, clear December sky.

As members of the Lakeville Collie Rescue League, Leonora and I had inherited the responsibility of transporting collies from shelters all over Michigan to our president, Sue Appleton, in Foxglove Corners, who placed them in foster homes. Having administered to one too many abandoned dogs in heart-rending conditions, I'd tried to leave the League last summer, and Leonora followed my lead. Sue had lured us back with a promise of easy projects.

Because of capricious Mother Nature, this jaunt up north had proved to be anything but easy. As we'd left the shelter, a freezing rain turned the roads hazardous before changing over to snow. Still, it was worth the effort and stress, and even the danger, to give Sparkle the promise of a new life in a loving forever home. Even though it wasn't quite the fun-filled winter adventure we had anticipated.

The windshield wipers made a valiant attempt to clear the windows, the snowflakes seemed to grow larger with each passing minute, and on the CD player the Yuletide Singers were dreaming of a white Christmas. I drove on.

After a while, Leonora said, "I'm dying for a cup of coffee, Jennet. The stuff left in the thermos is ice-cold. Let's stop at the first restaurant we come to."

I nodded, "Or hot chocolate. If we ever drive out of these woods."

An image formed in my mind, giant-sized and enticing: a tall chocolate-colored mug of steaming cocoa topped with whipped cream. I held fast to it. Wondrous hot liquid sustenance. Our reward for braving the snows of the north.

~ * ~

We filled the gas tank in Standish and shortly afterward found a small rustic restaurant that resembled a log cabin. After walking Sparkle in an adjacent field, we left her in the car with the window cracked and went inside, choosing a window booth where we could keep an eye on her.

I took off my gloves, patted the snow from my hair, and coaxed it back into its original shape with my hand. How much more appealing the snowfall was from inside this cozy haven. The restaurant boasted a fireplace, although no one had started a fire. Ambience was everything.

We lingered over our hot drinks, getting warm and comfortable, and suddenly the miles ahead seemed more manageable. With luck we should arrive home with plenty of the day still left to enjoy.

Sue would be delighted with Sparkle. None of us had expected a white collie in good health who needed only a bath and brushing to make her presentable.

"I'm going Christmas shopping tonight," Leonora said. "How would you like to join me?"

I spooned a dollop of whipped cream from the top of my cocoa and tasted it. "Oh, I can't. I've been away from Crane and the collies all day, and I'll have to cook dinner."

During the school year, I taught English at Marston High School with Leonora while my husband, Deputy Sheriff Crane Ferguson, patrolled the roads and by-roads of Foxglove Corners. Then there were frequent claims on my time from the Rescue League, not to mention the thousand chores involved in keeping a household running smoothly. Sometimes it seemed as if Crane and I hardly saw each other.

But Christmas recess was only three weeks away. Everything would be different then.

"That's okay." A teasing twinkle appeared in Leonora's eye. "I'll look for your present."

"We'll go another time," I promised and drained the cup. "Now let's head on home."

~ * ~

As we drove south, the snow turned to flurries, then to rain. I was able to drive somewhat faster. The precipitation washed the white color from the landscape until we were passing monotonous rolling countryside under dreary skies. Barns and three-board plank fences and farmhouses built far back from the road, leafless trees— the landscape had gone from Christmas-card enchanting to boring.

Sparkle, awake from her nap, quietly drank in the scenery.

"It doesn't look like we'll have snow for Christmas," Leonora murmured.

"There's still time," I said. "You know..."

"What?"

"We're just minutes away from the River Rose Collie Kennels."

"Almost home. At last."

"I'd like to drive by the place," I said. "It won't take us too far out of our way."

"Why?" she asked. "Isn't it deserted?"

I didn't have a reason. "Just a whim."

Who knew what inspired it? I hadn't thought about River Rose in months.

Once a thriving collie kennel that housed champion blue merle and tricolor collies, the fortunes of River Rose had changed when its owner, Rosalyn Everett, disappeared, leaving her dogs to fend for themselves. In other words, to perish with no one to provide food and water.

Several days later, Rosalyn had returned, claiming she'd only been gone for a few hours, grocery shopping. She appeared to believe this. By this time, her absence had been discovered and her beloved collies rescued.

Shortly afterward, she vanished again.

That was one of the strangest happenings in Foxglove Corners, which was known for bizarre and inexplicable mysteries and an occasional wandering ghost.

"Rosalyn has been gone for a long time," Leonora said.

"Since last summer."

"River Rose will be overgrown with weeds. There won't be anything to see."

"I'm just curious," I said. "You'll still have enough time to go shopping, and I'll be able to get a dinner together. Besides, it's stopped raining."

She sighed. "Let's do it then."

"Good."

I made a right turn, taking us away from our planned route into a lightly populated area. We drove past festive houses with colored lights outlining their gables and illuminating the shrubbery. Before long we reached the country road that led to Rosalyn's house.

River Rose Collie Kennels.

The sign swayed in a light wind, dripping and dispirited. Nobody had taken it down. No one except Rosalyn Everett had the right to do that.

But no prospective collie owner, ignorant of the River Rose story, would look for a puppy in the desolate structure that appeared out of the gathering fog. The property was steeped in a deep country silence. The dogs were all gone.

Rosalyn's attractive yellow ranch house was obviously vacant. It had a dull yellow shine in a monochromatic background. Windows revealing abandoned rooms, curtains no doubt gathering dust, an accumulation of dried leaves blown into a corner of the porch. Nothing stirred except the phantoms of another day and memories.

The place looked the same as it had when I'd last seen it. Behind the house, a treed lot sloped upward into dark woods, and the clouds hung low over the treetops.

"How utterly depressing," Leonora said.

"I didn't know River Rose in its heyday, but I hate seeing it like this."

I brought the car to a stop. "If Rosalyn came back, she wouldn't recognize her home."

"Well that's likely going to happen. Now we've seen it. Shall we move on?"

I nodded and started the car, taking one last look at the house. I'd been inside it once with Sue Appleton. Rosalyn had asked me to help her solve the mystery of her own disappearance. Although faced with irrefutable evidence, she clung to her story and swore she had no knowledge of her whereabouts during those lost days.

I'd failed her.

Beside the house a shape appeared. It was a collie whose silvery gray coat was dappled with dark patches. Standing still, it pierced me with a gaze so intense I could almost feel it from inside the car.

Then it was gone.

My voice came out as a whisper. "Leonora, did you see that?"

Leonora frowned. "See what?"

"A collie."

"Where?"

"Alongside the house," I said. "Next to the spruce tree. It isn't there now."

"All I see is the spruce."

I moved the gear to Park and opened the door.

"Wait!" Leonora cried. "Where are you going?"

Knowing me, Leonora should also have realized that was a futile question.

"To find the dog," I said.

Two

Sinking deep into tall grasses, I scanned the back yard. A narrow expanse of dried leaves and weeds flowed smoothly into an upward sloping tract of land bordered by woods. All of this was Rosalyn Everett's property, as I remembered. All of it had been reclaimed by nature in her long absence.

There was no blue merle collie in sight and only one place for it to go— the woods.

"I don't see any dog," Leonora said.

"Neither do I—now. He must have run into the woods."

"Isn't it strange that he didn't bark at us, though? Most dogs would."

I knew what Leonora was really asking. I'd just asked myself the same question.

Perhaps there had never been a blue merle collie with a mesmerizing stare. My wild imagination could have created the shape, colored it silver-gray, splashed on black marling, and set it before me as a living animal.

My imagination had played tricks on me before, showing me something that wasn't there. The snow dogs of Lost Lake, for instance. If ever a place was hospitable to ghostly imaginings, that place was the abandoned River Rose Collie Kennels.

But it was too soon to leap to the supernatural.

"The fog is thicker back here," Leonora added. "You can barely see the trees. It's easy to imagine animal shapes."

"Rosalyn Everett had blues and tricolors in her kennels," I said. "What if the police overlooked a collie when they took the rest of them away?"

They *had* missed a young tri, Scarlett. At the time of Rosalyn's first disappearance, Leonora and I had found her behind the ranch house hovering near death. Fortunately we'd arrived in time to save her.

Rosalyn had returned to her home for a short while, and Sue had reluctantly brought back two of her dogs, Bluebell and Dahlia. No one ever mentioned an unaccounted-for third collie.

"The dog would have been living in the woods all this time, then," Leonora said.

Which was possible, especially in the summer. An abandoned dog following his instincts and hunting small game to keep alive as his ancestors had done. In the winter, everything would be harder, even for a savvy canine.

"If there's the slightest chance that one of Rosalyn's collies was left behind, we have to look for it," I said.

"In the woods?"

"Yes, but not today." I glanced at my watch. Our detour had taken over a half hour. At this time of year, it would be dark before long, and because of the fog, I'd have to drive slowly. "Tomorrow's Sunday. We'll come back, if you can make it."

"I can. Of course."

I headed back to the front of the house and the car. It was starting to drizzle, and Sparkle would be growing restless by now and... Dear God!

She wasn't there. The front door was open wide.

"Oh, no!" Leonora cried. "I closed the door. I *did!* Do you think…?"

"Don't panic. She may be lying on the floor."

She wasn't. Reaching the car, I peered into the back seat. I saw the crumpled fleece blanket, the collapsible water bowl, and the rabbit toy Leonora had brought along for Sparkle to cuddle. But no collie.

My heart plummeted down as far as it could go. Our beautiful white rescue collie was gone.

~ * ~

"Sparkle! Come, girl!"

My voice came back to me, a hollow echo.

I had never been in a more silent place. Still, the silence seemed to have a low, murmuring voice. I couldn't make out the words, and drizzle chilled the air. I shivered and pulled my scarf tighter around my neck.

Leonora fretted constantly, blaming herself for Sparkle's escape, while I regarded the driveway, the lonely country road, and the field beyond with a sinking feeling. The fog was thinner in front of the house, visibility was fair, and a white dog would be easy to see. If she had been there.

"Sparkle!" Leonora cried. "Treat!"

It was no use. We had allowed ourselves to be taken in by the collie's quiet, gentle demeanor and docility. A fatal mistake. She'd apparently leaped over the front seat and stepped through the open door. At the moment I felt hopelessly inept. But I couldn't let Leonora continue to berate herself.

"I left the car first, Leonora," I said. "And I was the one who wanted to stop here. But you'd think if the dog wanted to go anywhere, she would have followed us, not run in the opposite direction."

"Well, now that we bungled this assignment, Sue Appleton won't trust us with another one."

"That isn't the point," I said. "We have to find the dog, but we can't look for her tonight. If only it wasn't so late."

I started the car and drove slowly back down the driveway with an occasional glance in the rear view mirror. The house and kennels were rapidly retreating behind swirling folds of fog.

"Maybe we'll come across her in the road," Leonora said.

Hope flickered, then died. Anything was possible, but woods lined the road, sending out their siren song to a dog who had most likely lived in the wild before being brought to the Ellentown shelter.

We didn't see her, and by the time we reached Foxglove Corners, I had to accept the reality of our failure. Four hundred long miles, ice and snow, stress and lurking danger. All for nothing. We'd lost our rescue and might never see her again. Furthermore there might be another collie in distress in the wasteland that was once the River Rose Kennels.

It had not been a good day.

~ * ~

We gave Sue Appleton the discouraging news in the cozy family room of her farmhouse.

"I'm sorry," I said. "If I hadn't stopped at River Rose…"

"Maybe Sparkle is back at Rosalyn's house curled up on the porch and waiting for you," Sue said.

That, I thought, was unlikely, but I resolved to stay positive. Would Sparkle sense the past presence of the dozen or more River Rose collies and be comforted? How long did it take for the scent of dog to dissipate?

"We're going back to look for her in the morning," I said.

"Did she have anything to eat?" Sue asked.

"Just a little dry kibble. She had a meal at the shelter before we left. But she won't have water."

The rain had begun to fall again, a steady, depressing pattering at the windows. There'd be plenty of water in the county. Our lost dog would get wet and even muddier.

"There's a stream on the property," Sue said. "You wouldn't have seen it. It's deep in the woods."

"If she finds the stream. It depends on which direction she takes." I stole yet another glance at my watch. "It's getting late. I should be making dinner now."

"I was going Christmas shopping, but I'm out of the mood," Leonora added.

"You girls go home and rest up," Sue said. "As a lady named Scarlett said, 'Tomorrow is another day.'"

~ * ~

I took Leonora home, then drove back to my Victorian farmhouse on Jonquil Lane. The last rays of the sun touched the stained glass windows between the double gables, and the facade glowed like a pale green jewel. Whenever I was away for too long, I yearned for home.

As I approached the house, a cacophony of barking arose from inside. Raven, my bi-black collie who lived in a charming Victorian style doghouse, dashed out to meet me.

Crane was home.

I opened the side door that led to the kitchen and walked into a confusion of paws, long noses, and wagging tails. I'd been gone all day, and my five house dogs were voicing their indignation.

Crane stood in my customary place at the stove. He had changed out of his uniform, locked his gun in its cabinet, and started to get our dinner together. Tall with frosty gray eyes and silver strands in his fair hair, he was the handsomest man I had ever met and the only one I'd ever wanted. I'd known that practically from our first encounter.

"Hi, honey," he said in a voice that held on to a southern drawl, albeit loosely. "I was beginning to worry about you. Did you run into bad weather?"

"Ice and snow north of Standish. Then rain. I meant to call you, but it got hectic."

The steaks I'd defrosted overnight rested in the broiler. He had found the bag of frozen southern biscuits, kept for emergencies when I didn't have time to bake, and set them out on a cookie sheet. There should be a pecan pie for dessert. Dinner was covered.

"The dogs had their walks and their dinners," he said. "Did you deliver your rescue to Sue?"

"Not exactly."

He looked up from the steaks, pepper mill in hand, while I made my way through my collie welcoming committee straight into his arms for our first kiss since we'd said goodbye in this very room before daybreak.

The dogs dispersed. Halley pressed her body close to mine. From her safe place under the oak table, timid Sky watched the proceedings with a wary eye, while Candy and Gemmy danced around us, and Misty, the ever-hopeful baby, tossed her toy goat at me.

My dogs were all colors— black and white, tricolor, blue merle, mahogany sable and white. Misty was white, like Sparkle, and all of them, with the exception of Halley, were rescues.

"I'll take over now," I said. "You sit down and rest." I reached for my apron hanging on a hook out of the dogs' reach.

"I can broil a steak," he said.

"I know you can." He cooked our steaks on the grill during the summer. "I'll just wash my hands, then I'll make a salad."

He shoved the broiling pan into the oven.

"While you do that, I'll make you a cup of tea," he said. "Tell me what you meant by 'not exactly'."

"We brought the dog south, then lost her. By the way, she's a gorgeous tri-headed white named Sparkle."

"How could you lose her?" he asked.

I told him about our misadventure at River Rose, using as few words as possible. At one time, I'd considered myself indispensable to the Rescue League, but pride goeth before a fall. Certainly I wouldn't do so after today.

"In the Maple Creek area?" he said. "We'll just have to find her. A white collie should be easy to spot."

"I hope she'll be safe."

I thought about unfamiliar country roads and speeding drivers. Hungry predators from the woods. Human predators searching for dogs to steal. All the misfortunes that could befall a bewildered collie in a strange new environment.

Please let her stay on the River Rose property, I prayed.

Perhaps the two collies would find each other and form a pack.

In a perfect world, maybe. I had a sinking feeling that wouldn't happen.

With the dubious help of Halley and Candy, I set about making a salad while Crane played with the other collies. I was exhausted. If I'd been alone, I would have gone straight to bed. But I always made our dinner hour a special time with tapers in the heirloom candlesticks that had belonged to Crane's Civil War era ancestress, Rebecca Ferguson, and flowers in season.

Tonight the centerpiece was a bouquet of white silk carnations with winter berry stems and greens from the farmers market which made them somewhat natural.

After dinner, Crane built a fire, and we sat in the living room drinking coffee. Good food had revived me. It usually did. Not to the extent that I felt motivated to finish reading the Gothic novel I'd started yesterday, but I wasn't on the verge of falling asleep either.

Crane folded the *Banner*. "There's another disappearance in the news," he said. "A young woman left a party alone and never made it home. So many people are dropping out of sight. You wonder where they go."

"Like Rosalyn Everett," I said.

"After being missing for so long, there's a good chance she's dead. Either dead or lost in her own world. What's going to happen to her house and the kennels?"

"Nothing, I suppose, until her fate is known, one way or the other. River Rose looks so desolate," I added. "After Rosalyn left, no one cut the grass or raked the leaves. They'll lie on the ground all winter. Well, who would have done the outside work? The place looks almost haunted," I added, remembering shadowy spaces and silence and a collie the color of fog.

A teasing glint sparkled in Crane's frosty eyes. "Maybe that collie you saw is another ghost dog."

"Leonora thinks I imagined it. I think it's real."

But I wasn't sure. How could one be certain about anything in Foxglove Corners, home of the strange?

I only knew that I was going to return to River Rose. I had two collies to find and the need to prove to myself that I wasn't inadequate when it came to collie rescue.

Even though no one had accused me of negligence.

Three

Once again I was struck by the deep silence that hung over River Rose. After living in Foxglove Corners for over two years, I was somewhat used to country peace and quiet. This silence, however, was different, and it certainly didn't convey a sense of peace.

Again I had the fancy that there were muted voices in the silence. Perhaps a hum.

And perhaps you're going bananas, Jennet, I told myself.

I could have been developing a hearing problem added to a runaway imagination.

Or River Rose could be haunted.

Crunching down the fallen leaves, Leonora and I walked slowly uphill to the woods' edge and stood contemplating the lean dark trees and the tangle of dried vegetation. Leonora carried a small bag of beef jerky. We had both called Sparkle until our voices threatened to give out.

I hadn't really expected to find her on the Everett property, even though I held on to Sue's image of a white collie waiting for us on the porch of Rosalyn's house.

"She may be miles away by now," I said with a sigh.

I could almost see her, a shining earth-bound star streaking through the countryside. Once she started running, she wouldn't stop until she collapsed from exhaustion. Who could catch a star?

"There's no dog here," Leonora said. "We're not going to tramp around in the woods, I hope."

I'd never planned to do that. "No, it's too dangerous. Anyway, if Sparkle were anywhere near, we'd know it by now."

"I wonder how long she's had the name 'Sparkle'," Leonora said. "She might think we're calling another dog."

"Most dogs hearing a human voice would come running," I said. "I know my collies would."

And they'd smell those treats from afar, even inside a paper bag.

I hadn't seen the mysterious blue merle either. Ah, well, maybe I'd conjured him out of the fog that had lain in folds over Rosalyn Everett's property yesterday. Today the sky was clear with a bright sun that banished every fragile imagining.

"What should we do now?" Leonora asked, pushing up her sunglasses.

I forced back my disappointment. "We can make 'Lost Dog' flyers and tack them onto poles in Maple Creek. That's the nearest town. I wish we'd taken a picture of Sparkle."

"Okay. That sounds like a plan. Shall we go then? This place gives me the creeps."

We crunched our way down the slope and around to the front of the house. On an impulse I climbed the four stairs to the porch and peered through a window. The living room had a lived-in look with an open book on the coffee table and a mug. A throw lay folded over the top of the sofa, and a pillow had fallen to the floor.

It was as if Rosalyn were in another room...in the kitchen, perhaps, preparing a snack. As if she hadn't walked out of her house one day and vanished into oblivion.

There I was, giving my imagination free rein again. Rosalyn wasn't in her ranch house, neither the woman nor her body. The police had made certain of that during their investigation.

"Maybe River Rose is haunted," I said, almost but not entirely serious.

Leonora glanced toward the kennels, washed in morning sunlight but still gloomy. "Don't say that till we're out of here," she said.

~ * ~

We drove in and out of Maple Creek and found ourselves traversing miles of farmland, the monotony broken by stretches of woods and ponds. At one corner, a red-lettered sign attached to the trunk of a birch tree announced 'One Mile to The Silver Sleigh.' A green arrow pointed west, the direction in which we were going.

"What do you suppose The Silver Sleigh is?" Leonora asked. "A restaurant?"

"An inn, maybe?"

"If they have food, could we stop for breakfast? I just had coffee and a doughnut this morning."

I'd had toast and juice at daybreak before saying goodbye to Crane for the day. The idea of a sandwich appealed to me.

"Let's see what it is first."

"And if there's a sleigh," Leonora added

A mile down the road, we reached our destination, a lavender and white cottage enclosed by a white picket fence. The three evergreens in the front yard were strung with clear lights, a beribboned pinecone wreath hung on the door, and a star-shaped 'Open' sign shone in the bay window. Off to the right stood a wooden sleigh filled with brightly wrapped packages.

"It's a store," Leonora announced. "Way out here in the middle of nowhere. No wonder they need signs and arrows. Shall we check it out?"

"An antique shop," I said, reading the silver letters on the window. "Well, you wanted to go Christmas shopping."

I had already turned into the driveway.

Christmas music floated out to the sparsely filled lot to the left of the store. "Do You See What I See?" Humming the melody, Leonora practically raced up to the door.

"This reminds me of Past Perfect," I said, remembering another now-closed antique shop. There I'd met Annica, my waitress-college student friend and sometime partner in detection. A vivacious redhead making up outrageous tales about the history of the antiques, Annica had turned up later working at Clovers, a small restaurant on Crispian Road.

Bells announced our arrival as we opened the door. The music was louder inside, and the scent of balsam was strong and intoxicating. The customers—quite a few for so early on a Sunday—moved silently up and down the aisles, examining the shop's offerings. Something about them seemed strange to me, though. No one was talking, not even whispering. They reminded me of figures in a dream. Or phantoms.

I gave myself a mental shake. Probably they were just listening to the song's lyrics or enjoying the melody.

"I'm going to check out the old books," I said, veering toward a tall ivory armoire, doors and drawers open and draped with silver garland.

"Look at this." Annica had stopped at a display of antique jewelry, Christmas shopping for herself, I'd bet.

Weren't we all?

My passion is reading, and my two great loves are Gothic novels and old-time books in a series. When I was a child with only a small allowance, I cherished every book that came my way and wiled away many a happy hour pouring over the titles listed on the inner pages. I couldn't have every book I wanted then. Now, however, I am able to treat myself and have an impressive collection.

Lost in what looked like the entire Beverly Gray series, I jumped when a soft voice behind me asked, "Can I help you find something? I'm Holly."

A fortuitous name, if that was her real name. I resisted the impulse to close the book quickly and replace it. I was, after all, a potential customer.

Holly wore a green jumper with a lace-trimmed white blouse and a sprig of holly in her auburn hair, obviously dressed to complement the seasonal reds and greens of the decor. I'd just been thinking about red-haired Annica. Holly appeared more subdued than my friend.

"I'm looking for a gift for— someone," I said. "This book is really old."

It wasn't one of those World War II era editions with dull blue covers and yellowing pages but apparently a first edition. In other words, a treasure.

"How much is it?" I asked.

"That one? Fifteen dollars."

A steal, I thought. "I'll take it."

She held out her hand. "I'll keep it for you at the register while you look around."

I relinquished the book and glanced at Leonora, who was trying on emerald chandelier earrings in front of a lavishly decorated mirror. With an extravagant display to tempt her, she would be a while.

Really, I thought, *I should start my own Christmas shopping.* I needed to buy a gift for my sister, Julia and one for Leonora but not today lest she see it. And of course I wanted to find that perfect present for Crane.

As usual I had no idea what to buy for him. It had to be a special present, one that said 'I love you,' something that he'd actually use and think of me when he did. If it could tie in to the Civil War, Crane's own passion, so much the better.

I didn't think I'd find it among the Victorian-inspired antiques and novelties at The Silver Sleigh.

Happily browsing, I made my way back to the front of the store and came to a standstill at a two-tier mahogany table. On the top tier, arranged on a red velvet cloth, stood a miniature silver sleigh drawn by eight tiny reindeer. Just like in the poem.

The sleigh was ornately embellished with an intricate pattern of flowers and scrolls. Each one of the reindeer was slightly different from its fellows. The differences were subtle: the position of a foreleg, the angle of a head, the size.

Of all the antiques set out in the shop, this one called to me. I cradled the silver sleigh with its reindeer team in my hands, envisioning it under my tree on a drift of artificial snow or, better yet, on the mantel, bathed in the light of a dozen candles.

I didn't see a price tag. But does price matter when you find the gift of your dreams?

Holding the sleigh carefully, I looked for Holly. She was at the jewelry display helping Leonora, who had on a different pair of earrings with sapphire stones.

Guessing she'd choose the sapphires, her favorite stone, I carried my find to the register and waited.

They arrived at the same time, Holly and Leonora, who had added a sapphire necklace to the earrings. She set her purchases on the counter and joined me in admiring the silver sleigh.

"How pretty!" she murmured. "That's no cookie cutter ornament. I wish I'd seen it first."

Holly nodded. "That's real sterling silver, you know. You'll have to keep it polished."

Leonora ran her hand along the side of the sleigh. "With all that fancy work. Have fun."

"I don't mind," I said. "How much is it?"

"Let's see." Holly opened a notebook that lay near the cash register and turned the pages swiftly. "Ninety nine dollars, not including tax."

Leonora gasped. "Over a hundred dollars!"

"Is it a real antique or a replica?" I asked.

"It dates from the early twentieth century. Nineteen thirty-seven, I believe. So, an antique."

As I hesitated, she added, "We have other sleighs—silver-plated ones or crystal or wood. They're less expensive, and all you have to do is dust them."

Should I?

I hadn't planned on spending the money I'd allotted myself for a week's living expenses on the very first day of the week, and I had plenty of lovely Christmas decorations.

But not one as exquisite as this.

"Buy it," Leonora said.

Maybe...

I would consider it a Christmas gift for myself. Christmas is a time to toss practicality aside, if you can afford to do so. And I decided that I could. After surviving a particularly harrowing year at Marston High School, I deserved it.

"I'll take it," I said. "Oh, and the book."

"Do you want the sleigh gift-wrapped?" Holly asked.

"No, just wrapped carefully."

In the light of the table top tree on the counter, the silver sleigh had an ethereal shine. It was the perfect accompaniment for the perfect holiday to come. A sort of good luck charm.

My spirits soared. It seemed to me in that moment that our Christmas couldn't possibly be anything but merry and wonderful with the silver sleigh in our house.

Four

The melodious strains of "Silver Bells" faded as we walked to the car, but the scent of balsam followed us. I took a deep breath. Could there be a hint of snow in the sharp, cold air?

"This is a wonderful little shop," Leonora said. "I'm coming back—after next payday, that is."

I opened the trunk, and we set our packages carefully inside. "Didn't you think it was a little strange, though?" I asked.

"How so?"

"The people. They were all so quiet."

"Honestly, Jennet, you're getting carried away. They were an older, more sedate crowd, probably with plenty of cash in their wallets, that's all."

"Maybe." The unsettling feelings inspired by our brief time at River Rose still clung to me. "Do you want to stop for breakfast?"

"Yes, or lunch. Then I have to get home."

"So do I."

Both Leonora and I had our own dogs to take care of, and I'd have to let Sue Appleton know the result of our search for Sparkle.

We found a restaurant down the road a way that looked promising and ordered pancakes and coffee. I wouldn't have to eat again until dinner, which presented a familiar problem. What to fix.

I should ask for a new cookbook for Christmas.

Then I remember the silver sleigh waiting to take its place of honor on the mantel. Crane and I would go shopping for a Fraser fir next week, or perhaps we'd chop down our own tree at Bluecreek Farm. I'd open the box of holiday CDs and fill the house with Christmas carols. Happily, I succumbed to the lure of the Season's Spirit. As if on cue, the first snowflakes began to fall.

~ * ~

By five o'clock, an inch of snow blanketed the ground. The silver sleigh basked in the glow of the mantelpiece candles. Crane came home with tales of icy roads and accidents, fortunately none of them fatal. He admired the silver sleigh and said I'd found a bargain, which made me feel better about the price.

I'd decided on fried chicken and cornbread and had baked a banana layer cake, anticipating a quiet candlelit dinner alone with my husband.

It was not to be.

At five-thirty, Brent Fowler, fox hunter, perennial bachelor, lover of horses and dogs and beautiful women, stood in the vestibule dripping on the *Let It Snow* doormat. Snowdrops glistened in his dark red hair, and his eyes gleamed with merriment and a touch of mischief. He carried a red poinsettia plant sprinkled with rapidly melting snowflakes.

The dogs had formed a circle around him, Misty going so far as to jump on him, while Sky wagged her tail slowly from a respectful distance. They were his particular pets.

Crane took his jacket, and Brent presented me with the plant.

"How beautiful!" I touched the candy-cane bow. "Thank you. I was hoping to have one."

But where I would keep it remained to be seen. For the moment I stashed it toward the back of the credenza in the dining room. "You'll stay for dinner," I said.

"Don't mind if I do. That smells like fried chicken."

"*Southern* fried chicken," I said, "and cornbread."

"You have all the luck, Sheriff," Brent said. "I envy you."

Crane smiled. "You should."

Brent could have his own share of luck. With his handsome features and hearty good nature, he was pursued by women in three counties that I knew of. Annica had a long-standing crush on him, and he'd won the friendship of Foxglove Corner's reclusive horror story writer, Lucy Hazen. Neither woman seemed to mind his penchant for fox hunting. I tended to forget about it myself unless reminded.

"I have a favor to ask you, Jennet," Brent said as he settled himself in the rocker with Misty in his lap and Sky at his feet.

"Ask away," I said.

"On Christmas Eve, I'm going to hitch up the sleigh and deliver presents to my kids."

He meant the needy children on his list. Every year he donned his Santa Claus suit and rode through Foxglove Corners, distributing gifts to young people who wouldn't have anything new and nice for Christmas. Every year the list grew larger.

"What's the favor?" I asked.

"The toys are mostly all bought. Lucy picked out children's books and girls' stuff like dolls and their—uh— wardrobe. Who knew dolls needed extra clothes? Anyway, I was hoping you'd wrap them for me. I'll supply the paper and ribbons and stickers and whatever else you need. You're so artistic," he added.

That was news to me.

"I can do that," I said. "How many gifts are you talking about?"

"In the neighborhood of a hundred."

"My—goodness."

"Maybe a few more."

I saw myself in a surround of toys and dolls and games and crackling paper. Misty stealing ribbons for tug-of-war, bows stuck to the collies' fur. The need to live up to my newfound reputation as a paper-and-ribbon artist. I wondered, though, why Brent hadn't had his purchases wrapped at the store.

"I'll help you, honey," Crane said.

"Camille is donating homemade Christmas cookies and fudge to go with the presents," Brent added. "Afterward I'm having a party for everyone on Christmas night."

"These next few weeks are going to be busy," I said. "Bring the toys over as soon as you can."

"Some of the smaller ones are in my car now," he said. "I'll get them after dinner."

He'd been sure of me, then. Of course he knew I'd be honored to be a part of his traditional gift giving. I'd certainly rather wrap presents than bake and decorate hundreds of Christmas cookies.

The silver sleigh on the mantel, the snowfall, winter recess in a few weeks— the Spirit of Christmas wrapped her glittering arms around me. I could hardly wait to see Brent's toys.

~ * ~

After dinner Brent said, "I'd better get those toys inside. I brought enough wrapping paper and ribbon to get you started."

"It's still snowing. Won't they get wet?"

"They're in plastic bags. Give me a hand, Sheriff, will you?"

While I cleared the table, Brent and Crane transferred a dozen large bags of toys, along with rolls of wrapping paper, from his trunk to the living room, inciting a near riot among the collies. This was a new activity for them. From their interest, I supposed they thought the contents of the bags were for them.

"Whoa!" Brent said. "You guys will have to wait for Christmas for your treats. Where'd you like them, Jennet?"

"The basement?" Crane suggested.

"Not there." I didn't look forward to carrying them upstairs. "Take them up to my study. Crane will show you where it is."

I'd recently moved my desk and best-loved books to a small room on the second floor formerly used for storage. After the holidays I planned to paint it and add a few plants. I had my eye on a Norway pine with red and pink Valentine decorations.

"I can set up a wrapping station there," I said. "It'll be fun. Kind of."

Brent and Crane made several trips upstairs moving the toys and paper to one more place while I made coffee. Back in the living room, as I filled our mugs, I felt a soft nudge against my ankle and looked down. Misty had her toy goat in her mouth. This was her way of asking for attention and play.

She'd had that goat ever since her first days in our house. Oddly enough, the other dogs respected her ownership, whereas when bones were involved, all bets were off.

Brent grabbed the goat and tossed it into the dining room, and Misty scrambled after it.

"I bought lots of stuffed animals at The Veldt in the Maplebrook Mall," Brent said. "Not just teddy bears but exotic animals. The kind you see in Africa."

And I'd be the one wrapping them. "Your kids will love them."

He seemed in no hurry to leave, reclaiming his place in the rocker. The wind had picked up, howling around the house like a crazed predator. Thank heavens for the shelter of our home and the flames dancing and crackling in the fireplace.

"What's happening on Jonquil Lane these days?" Brent asked.

"Nothing much except Leonora and I took a trip up north to bring back a rescue. We managed to lose her on the way home."

"How did you do that?"

I told him, thinking anew how utterly inadequate I'd been.

"I thought you resigned from the Rescue League," he said.

"We did, but Sue Appleton re-recruited us. She's giving us the easy assignments. So if you see a white collie with tri markings on her head running free, do your best to capture her. She's really quite striking. Leonora is going to post a few flyers in Maple Creek tomorrow after school while I meet with Sue."

I didn't mention the blue merle at River Rose who might not exist.

Brent shook his head. "Dogs need to be inside in this kind of weather. Every year you read about dogs left outside freezing to the ground. It's criminal."

Unbidden a picture of a frozen white collie formed in my mind. Sparkle could be wandering through unknown countryside in wind-driven snow, her coat blending into the landscape. Hungry and thirsty, at the mercy of some predator who looked on her as a tasty morsel. Forever lost to us. For this we had taken her out of a safe, warm shelter.

The thought of her trying to survive on her own in a snowstorm tore at my heart.

Perhaps some kind-hearted person had coaxed her into a house, in which case chances were good that she'd find her forever home without our help.

But the image of a beautiful dog encased in ice refused to leave me.

Five

On Monday I was too busy teaching my students to recognize symbols in literature or to write clear topic sentences to worry about Sparkle.

In my afternoon Journalism class, everyone knew what they were doing and most were enthusiastic about it. The December edition of the *Marston Courier* was going to be printed in green ink. It would include a special section of Christmas stories and poems, and the two staff artists were creating seasonal graphics to illustrate it.

The buzz was happy, anticipation was high, and for the first time in my years at Marston, I hoped Principal Grimsley would glance in at my industrious class glued to their tasks. He was more apt to witness some form of chaos and comment about it.

I took advantage of a free moment to gaze out the window. Lacy paper snowflakes decorated the windowpanes, and real snow, light and powdery, fell outside. It was enough to kindle Yuletide atmosphere but wouldn't turn the commute home into a nightmare.

I was happy to be installed in my old classroom again. It had been off-limits to all in the aftermath of last fall's tragic shooting. At first I'd been afraid that my room would be haunted by the sound of gunfire—or worse. It had taken all the courage I could muster to step through the door on that first day of the semester.

Nothing untoward had happened. Thank God. And here it was December. Nothing *would* happen.

The physical reminders of that day had been painted and tiled over. The windows and desks were new, the memories muted. Out in the courtyard, the white pine planted in memory of the boy who had lost his life was dusted with snow. All was calm, all was bright.

"Do you think we'll have a snow day tomorrow, Mrs. Ferguson?"

Gwendolyn Grey stood behind me, a pencil sketch in her hand. She was a third-year art student with an enviable amount of talent.

"I doubt it," I said. "But at this rate we'll have a white Christmas."

She handed me the paper. "I drew this for the poetry page. The elf looks sad, though, doesn't he?"

All the whimsical figure needed were teardrops running down his face.

"Is he too sad?" she asked.

"A little," I said. "Why don't you work on his expression? Make it mischievous or secretive in a nice way. Give him a smile."

"That's what I planned to do. I don't know why it turned out this way."

"People should be happy at Christmastime," I said. "I know many of them aren't."

At Marston we were collecting clothing and canned goods for homeless children, most of it newly purchased. Kids today were well aware of hardship in the world, possibly some of them in their own families.

"This month we want our paper to communicate 'merry'," I said.

"I just felt sad when I was drawing him. I don't know why."

I stared at the picture, then looked beyond it to the desk at which Gwendolyn had drawn the elf. That was the same place Danny had died, felled by his assassin's bullet.

Oh, no!

Lucy Hazen had commented that the very walls of the room could absorb and hold the impressions of a horrific event. If so, all the fresh paint, all the new tile and windows and furniture, wouldn't make a difference.

I couldn't let my imagination take me to that dark place, couldn't let anyone know what I was thinking. Especially my students, who had never mentioned last year's tragedy in my hearing.

"Just work on it a little, Gwendolyn," I said.

We moved away from the window, and the snow continued to fall.

~ * ~

Don't dwell on it, I told myself as we drove away from the school later that afternoon.

I tended to magnify incidents like this—no, it wasn't an incident—and turn them into an obsession.

Gwendolyn had been depressed about a failing grade on a test, a boyfriend, or a problem at home. Who knew what troubled a teenaged girl? Her mood had intruded on her artwork.

It could be as simple as that.

Or it could be something else.

"I'm going to wait till tomorrow to put up the flyers in Maple Creek," Leonora said. "I don't want them to get wet right away."

I turned the windshield wipers up a notch and checked for traffic before merging onto the northbound freeway.

"That's a good idea. Then would you like to stop at Sue's with me? We won't stay long."

"Sure, since it's my fault that Sparkle ran away."

"Both of us could have been more careful. Sue will understand."

"But Sparkle won't. She's just a dog. She couldn't know the consequences of her action."

"I'm going to picture her lying by a cozy fire," I said. "She found her forever home with no help from us."

"How unlike you to be so optimistic, Jen," she said, then added quickly, "Just kidding."

"I can't give up on her," I said.

"Neither can I. Maybe we'll find her."

I spied a salt truck ahead of me and glanced in the side mirror, hoping to switch lanes. I couldn't do it yet.

"I wonder if we'll have a snow day tomorrow," Leonora said. "I volunteered to help Camille bake Christmas cookies for Brent."

"While I'm wrapping presents," I said.

"I wouldn't trade with you. I can't make one of those fancy bows to save my soul."

"And I like to bake but not on a grand scale. Brent chose his helpers well. Will you be going to his Christmas party?"

"Yes, with Jake."

For a fraction of a second, I took my eyes off the lane. Leonora was smiling that secret smile. She had a certain radiance when she was happy. Her eyes and even her blond hair were brighter. She practically glittered. Why hadn't I noticed the change earlier?

"Deputy Sheriff Jake Brown?" I asked.

"The same."

"He made up with you in time for Christmas, then. My mother used to say that men broke up with their girlfriends before Christmas so they wouldn't have to buy a present. Then they'd come back after New Year's Eve."

"How cynical! I don't believe that. Jake and I never really broke up. He just stopped calling."

"Well, he's in the picture now. Are you still going skiing over Christmas vacation?"

"Naturally. I'm not about to change my plans for a man."

"Hmm." That was only response I could think of.

I saw a chance to pass the truck and took it, hoping for smooth sailing ahead.

~ * ~

Sue Appleton ushered us into her family room where lively flames leaped and danced in a wood-burning stove. Her four collies greeted us sedately and retreated to their favorite lying spots. We found seats close to the fire, too.

"I'm so sorry you girls made that long trip up north for nothing," Sue said

"*We're* sorry, but we're going to try to find Sparkle. Someone must have seen a white collie."

"We went back to River Rose yesterday, but there was no sign of her," Leonora added.

"River Rose?" A strange look came over Sue's face. "Did you notice anything unusual while you were there?"

"Nothing at all," I said. "It's a picture of desolation. Why?"

"I've been hearing some odd stories about that place." Sue shrugged. "Probably that's all they are. Stories."

I sat on the edge of a wooden rocker. "What kind?"

"Rosalyn's neighbor, Mrs. Sloan, has seen lights at night in the house and the kennels."

"Were Rosalyn's lights on a timer?" I asked.

"No, and there shouldn't be any lights on that property unless someone is up to no good. Unless Rosalyn came home."

"As of yesterday, she hadn't."

"I'm sure she would let us know if she was back," Sue said. "She'd want her dogs."

I glanced at Dahlia and Bluebell. The tricolor and the blue merle lay as close to the stove as they safely could. This was their home now, not that they'd have forgotten Rosalyn.

"We didn't knock on the door," Leonora pointed out. "Maybe she was inside napping and didn't hear us."

"Then where was her car?"

"It'd have to be there, wouldn't it? How about a prowler?"

Sue nodded. "Or a homeless person trying to get in. Then there's the howling. Rosalyn's other neighbor, Cecily Lane, says she hears a dog howling."

"Could that be Sparkle?" I asked.

Or the blue merle I'd seen alongside the house, the one whose existence I'd doubted and hadn't mentioned to Sue. I tried to ignore the image of a ghost woman and her spirit dog that began to form in my mind.

"If it were Sparkle, wouldn't she have come to us?" Leonora asked.

"She only knew us for a few hours, but, yes, you'd think she would have come."

Unexplained lights and a howling dog. Neither seemed unusual, but then this was Foxglove Corners.

Not quite. Rosalyn's property was north of Maple Creek. Still…

"Whatever's going on there needs investigating," I said.

Those shivery stories gave me a perfect excuse to return to River Rose, which was what I wanted to do anyway.

Six

When I returned to River Rose on a windy Saturday afternoon, I saw nothing of the strangeness I had anticipated and nothing of Sparkle. The recent snowfall had vanquished the aura of desolation, turning the yellow house and the kennel into a charming Currier and Ives winter scene.

I sat in my car with the engine running and surveyed the pristine landscape. All white with the dark woods rising on the slope behind the house. Mine was the only vehicle to travel over the driveway since the snow, and the walkway and porch stairs to the house were buried in a small avalanche.

In front of the kennel, the wind had blown the snow into high drifts. One of them resembled a sitting collie with the characteristic collie tulip ears and head tilt. A magnificent snow sculpture.

Imagining two lumps of coal for eyes, I smiled at my fancy. The next wind gust would flatten the snow dog or rearrange it into an entirely different shape.

I let my gaze sweep the property, hoping to see something that didn't belong, some trace of the white collie. I didn't call her as the only prints in the snow were those of deer. Nor was there any sign of a real dog, nor any living person.

What of the dead?

Well, they were elsewhere.

As for the moving lights, presumably they only appeared in the dark, and I didn't intend to wait until nightfall or come back later.

It didn't seem that River Rose was haunted after all. Sooner or later any deserted property would generate stories such as the ones Sue had heard. Especially a place with so grim a history.

Disappointed, I turned the car around. I wasn't happy to give up my ghost theory and realized that in all probability Sparkle wouldn't come this way again. We'd have to rely on the flyers which Leonora had posted in Maple Creek and accept reality. We might never see her again.

Determined to salvage something from the afternoon, I drove back to the road and headed for The Silver Sleigh. A generous helping of Christmas Spirit would go far to make up for what had turned out to be a wasted trip.

~ * ~

I heard the music from my car, the poignant strains of "In the Bleak Midwinter," an appropriate carol for the weather but not for an antique shop decked in Yuletide cheer. "Jingle Bells" would have been merrier, and would, moreover, have complemented the shop's name.

Judging by the cars parked in the lot, The Silver Sleigh was crowded. I found an empty place and, swinging my purse over my shoulder, set out to brave the wind. Snow blew in my face and obscured my vision as I trudged up the shoveled path to the entrance. I could barely see the wooden sleigh with its load of presents which couldn't have been wrapped in real paper.

I opened the door to the ringing of brass bells and stepped into a haven of warmth and the spicy scent of balsam. Pulling off my gloves, I breathed in the fragrance.

The aisle closest to the door held a display of Christmas ornaments, whimsical forest dioramas and delicate balls decorated with hand-painted winter scenes. In the center of the shop a live fir tree glowed with clear candle lights, rarely-seen tinsel, and decorations of every description. An old-time tree surrounded by antiques. Perfect.

Did we need more ornaments for our tree? Probably not, but it wouldn't hurt to look. I found a gold-edged oval depicting Santa Claus at a fireplace and an inquisitive collie sticking its long nose in his Santa's bag.

This one was obviously meant for me. Gently I removed it from a blue velvet box.

"Excuse me, miss…"

An attractive woman all in gray stood beside me. She wore a silver leaf choker necklace with matching earrings and had arranged her silvery-gray hair in a youthful bob. The only color about her was her bright red lipstick. Otherwise she looked like an ice sculpture set amid an incredible display of shining color.

As she wasn't wearing a coat, I suspected she was a saleswoman.

The Ice Lady glanced at the collie ornament in my hand, just as I noticed the sign: *Touch the Merchandise at Your Own Risk.*

Without preamble she said, "I wonder if I might have a word with you? In the back room?"

Did she think I'd meant to steal the ornament? Surely not. Still I felt a trifle guilty and felt something else, an inexplicable and instant aversion to the woman.

I hesitated. "What is this about?"

"It's a private matter," she said. "My name is Mrs. Cramer. Carol. I'm one of the owners of The Silver Sleigh."

A woman standing nearby moved surreptitiously closer to us, her bright eyes alert at the possibility of a disturbance.

In a low voice, I said, "I'm Jennet Ferguson."

"I know."

"How do you know? We've never met."

"My salesgirl, Holly, recognized you from the newspaper when you were in here the other day.

I sighed. On occasion, my picture and name had been in the *Banner* in connection with a mystery in which I'd been involved. With my average height and dark brown hair, I didn't, however, consider myself particularly memorable.

I stood still, holding the ornament, and waited for her to elaborate.

She said, "If you'll follow me, please…"

"Well…"

"This will only take a minute."

Curiosity overrode my instinctual dislike of Carol Cramer.

I followed as she led the way through the aisles to a tiny, dimly-lit room crammed with furniture and boxes. One corner held a desk and two exquisite Queen Anne chairs covered in old rose velvet.

At her bidding, I sat, feeling suddenly uncomfortable, my eyes on the arch that led back out to the shop—on escape, if escape were needed.

Had I just willingly walked into trouble?

"I'll come right to the point," Mrs. Cramer said. "You purchased an antique from us last week, a silver sleigh with eight reindeer attached, I believe."

"Yes, I did. I love it."

"That's regrettable. You see, the sleigh wasn't for sale. Holly made a mistake."

"Well, I did purchase it," I said, "for over one hundred dollars, if you count the tax."

"I don't dispute that. I'm offering to buy it back from you for, say, one hundred twenty-five."

No!

Had I said that aloud? I couldn't have because Mrs. Cramer wore a smug look that reminded me of a cat who has pounced on a hapless mouse.

I was nobody's mouse.

"I'm afraid I can't accept your offer," I said. Echoing her words, I added, "The sleigh isn't for sale."

The smug look evaporated. "You don't understand, Mrs. Ferguson. That particular antique belongs here in our shop. It's a symbol, a good luck charm." She paused. "It gave the shop its name."

I was astonished at the wave of possession that swept over me. I pictured the sleigh as I had last seen it on the mantel, with candles on either side. In a sense, the silver sleigh was a symbol for me, as well, a symbol of our happy Christmas to come.

That was part of what I felt. The other part was a growing suspicion too sharp to be ignored.

I didn't believe Carol Cramer and didn't trust her. There was more to the story. At present I had the sleigh, and possession is nine-tenths of the law. No one could deny or challenge my ownership.

Among my papers, I had a receipt, stamped *Paid in full*, and if I was being unreasonable, so be it.

This unpleasant encounter had stripped the antique shop of its appeal for me. I rose. "Holly said you have sleighs of all kinds in the shop," I said. "This one is mine."

Mrs. Cramer smiled. "Would you change your mind for a hundred and fifty dollars? That would give you an extra fifty to buy something else."

My suspicion grew, along with my curiosity. But I knew I didn't want to stay in The Silver Sleigh another minute. Oh, darn... I still wanted to buy the collie ornament; I was still holding it. Well, there must be another salesperson in the shop.

Mrs. Cramer said, "If you reconsider, please take my card."

She handed it to me, and I slipped it in my purse. I, of course, had no intention of changing my mind.

~ * ~

That was odd.

Back outside, I made my way through blowing snow to my car, clutching the small package containing the collie ornament. I felt as if I'd just emerged from a situation fraught with unknown peril.

Carol Cramer's story didn't make sense. If the antique wasn't intended for sale, why was it in the shop in the first place? If it were a good luck symbol, which I doubted, shouldn't it have been in a special place, showcased in a front window, perhaps? Also, Holly had found the item and its price in the shop's notebook.

The flakes were thicker and falling faster. I'd need to clear the car windows and turn on the lights for the drive home. And I'd better hurry while the roads were still passable.

As I pulled out to the road, it occurred to me that I'd left a mystery behind. A tantalizing Christmas mystery. Unfortunately I had no desire to pursue it if that meant going back to The Silver Sleigh.

Seven

By the time I reached home, the snow had diminished to flurries. The sun made its first appearance, scattering diamond dust on the fresh landscape, and the air felt a little warmer. At least weather-wise, the day could be salvaged.

I leashed Sky and Misty, called to Halley, and set out to make the first tracks in the new snow. I always felt guilty taking three dogs and leaving two at home, but Crane had insisted on walking Candy himself. In the past she had proved too boisterous for me to manage and too fond of having her own way to keep us out of trouble.

Raven dashed out of her house to join us. At the lane, she turned right on a course that would take us to Sagramore Lake. Occasionally dogs crave variety in their walks. I didn't object. Fringed with snow-draped woods, the lake in winter was a wondrous sight with water so pale a shade of blue that it scarcely seemed to have any color at all and isles of ice floating on the surface.

In fact, on a day when I didn't have four collies to supervise, I ought to come by this way and take pictures for my Christmas cards. There would be plenty of opportunities, since we were at winter's beginning. Not even that. Technically it wasn't winter yet.

As we trudged through the snow, my mind wandered back to the incident at The Silver Sleigh and Carol Cramer, or the Ice Lady, as I persisted in thinking about her.

I'd been looking forward to future visits to the antique shop. I hadn't seen even a tenth of the Christmas wares and vintage books yet. Now I felt awkward about returning and the possibility of encountering Mrs. Cramer again.

There's no reason to feel awkward, I told myself. *You bought an item the shop offered for sale. You have a receipt. If the situation were reversed, if you wanted to return an antique you purchased, they might refuse to take it back.*

Would Mrs. Cramer make another offer for my sleigh? Add another fifty or hundred dollars to sweeten the deal? Or would she ignore me? Or—happier thought—would she even be there? Maybe Holly or the other owner would be on the floor when and if I returned. I could talk Leonora into going with me for moral support. After next payday, she'd said. That was next Friday.

Maybe I'd find out what made the silver sleigh so desirable that Carol Cramer was determined to re-purchase it at a substantial loss to herself. In other words, maybe I'd solve my Christmas mystery.

I would have to see what the coming weeks brought. I still had Brent's presents to finish. I'd only wrapped three of them. Three subtracted from a hundred…

I needed reinforcements. Crane had offered to help, but he had less time than I did. Also, my husband had a myriad admirable qualities but, unfortunately, an artistic touch wasn't among them.

Raven was barking, and my other three dogs were in a state of high excitement while I was woolgathering.

Somebody was shoveling snow on Sagramore Lake Road. Snow went flying through the air onto the top of a massive mound alongside the walk. Two slight figures, one in bright aqua outerwear, the other in orange, manned the shovels. They appeared to be clearing a path just for us.

Wagging her tail, Raven dashed ahead, while Misty pulled on her leash, frantic to join her, and Halley cast me an imploring look. *Hurry!*

By then I was close enough to recognize Molly and Jennifer, our two young friends who set up lemonade stands in the summer and built snow forts in the winter. They weren't so little anymore. Cheeks rosy, eyes bright, with scarves wrapped around their heads, they were hard at work.

Raven danced around the girls, a dizzying vision of black and white.

"Collies!" Molly cried, dropping her shovel on the mound. "And Jennet! I forgot their names, Jennet." She knelt on the cleared walk, her arms around Raven's neck.

"That's Raven," I said. "Halley is my quiet, patient girl." I laid a hand on her head and tightened my grip on Misty's leash. "The wild white one is Misty, and you remember Sky. She's a little timid."

"They're so beautiful," Molly cried, trying to pet all the dogs at once, which threw them into a frenzy.

"Aren't you girls going to build a snow fort?" I asked.

Jennifer giggled. "That's for kids. We're working this year, shoveling snow. We have four clients already."

"My goodness, that's what I call enterprising."

"Well, we're in the eighth grade," Molly said.

"The last time I saw you girls, you had a mystery."

I glanced at the houses across the street, trying to remember which one came with a phantom owner. According to the girls, a young woman had moved in and promptly disappeared, leaving her outside furniture to the mercy of the elements. Molly and Jennifer were sure she'd been murdered, and they were determined to solve the mystery.

"Alicia's back," Jennifer said. "She was away for a while, then I guess we just didn't see her when she came home."

"So there was no real mystery, just one that solved itself. It happens."

"Guess what I'm getting for Christmas?" Jennifer said in a dizzying change of subject.

"Clothes? Books?"

"A collie puppy. I need money for her food and toys and stuff. Molly's helping me."

"That's a wonderful present," I said.

"My mom and me already picked her out and named her. She's golden like your other collie. But she's only five weeks old."

"What's her name?"

"Ginger. Isn't that pretty?"

"It's perfect for a little sable."

"I'm going to help train her and teach her tricks," Molly said.

"We've been reading dog books from the library," Jennifer added.

"That's a good place to begin," I said. "You have to know what to feed your new puppy and how to take care of her properly."

Good grief, I sounded like a teacher.

"Will you come by to see her?" Jennifer asked.

"I sure will. Right after Christmas."

"We'd better get back to work," Molly said, giving all the dogs a farewell pat. "We're only half through."

"I'll be back to see Ginger," I promised.

The dogs wanted to stay and play in the snow, but it wasn't their choice. As soon as we started moving, they fell in with the plan. Some of the Jennifer's joy trailed along with me as we headed to the lake. Jennifer thought she was happy now, but she couldn't imagine the joy in store for her once Ginger joined the household. Remembering my first collie puppy, I envied her.

~ * ~

Determined to make the most of every precious hour of the weekend, I hurried through my chores. In the final hours of the afternoon, I decided to reward myself with take-out dinners.

With its winter woods backdrop, Clovers reminded me of a gingerbread cottage, complete with a fall of sparkling icicles. The band of bright green clovers painted on the façade contrasted with the snow on the roof. White and green. Christmas colors.

As I stamped the snow from my boots on the doormat, I breathed in the hundred delicious scents of Christmas and looked across the tables for Annica.

The restaurant resembled a forest of poinsettias with red, pink, and white plants on the center of the tables and taller ones on the counter. Everywhere I looked, I saw red, green, silver or gold. Every aspect of Clovers exuded enchantment. Arriving here, even the most dedicated Scrooge would feel the Spirit stealing over him.

Annica had seen me. Dressed for the season in red with chandelier earrings that sparkled like the icicles outside, she strode toward me, coffee pot in hand.

"Hi, Jennet. I haven't seen you in ages," she said as she led me to my favorite window booth with its view of the woods.

"Clovers looks very Christmasy," I said.

"Our motto is 'merry and bright.' Sometimes I think we're too bright. All this color is giving me a headache. Did you come for dinner or take-out?"

"Take-out dinners. When I don't feel like cooking, I know where to come."

"You're in luck," she said. "Today's special is turkey with all the trimmings and pumpkin pecan pie."

Crane would love that, much more than another boring steak.

"I'll take two dinners and a cup of coffee for here."

"Coming right up. I'll join you. Marcy will cover for me. She owes me."

While waiting for Annica, I admired the centerpiece. Lacy figures adorned each plant. The ones on my table were a crocheted snowman with tiny stones for eyes and buttons, an angel, and a gingerbread man. I wondered if The Silver Sleigh had something similar.

Annica brought two cups of steaming coffee to the table. The coffee at Clovers was exceptional too. I'd tried and failed to duplicate it at home.

"What's new?" she asked, spooning sugar into her cup.

I took a long satisfying sip, not caring that the liquid came close to burning my lips.

"I have a couple of new mysteries."

"Again?"

I smiled. "I do seem to attract them."

I told her about Sparkle and the strange matter of the silver sleigh. The only one I didn't mention was the blue merle collie at River Rose. I'd more or less decided that I'd imagined it.

"There has to be a good reason the lady wants the sleigh back," Annica said. "What could it be?"

"I can't imagine. Something tells me not to believe her."

"If you want to go back there, I'll go with you," Annica said. "I never have time to do my Christmas shopping. Besides, I miss Past Perfect. I loved working there."

"I remember," I said. "I'll take you up on that. Whenever you're free. After school, I mean. I'm going to be busy getting the house ready for Christmas. Besides decorating, I promised to wrap gifts for Brent's Christmas Eve giveaway."

She set her cup down. "Why are you doing that?"

"He asked me."

"Well, I like that." She couldn't hide her indignation and maybe a shred of hurt. "Why didn't he ask *me*? He took me out to dinner just last week."

"He knows you're busy with work and school and everything," I said.

"So are you."

I decided not to add that Camille and Leonora were baking cookies to accompany the presents.

"You can help me wrap toys," I said. "It's fun, really, seeing the dolls and stuffed animals he bought. There are all kinds of toys and games."

"It isn't the same." She truly looked unhappy, but Annica never brooded for long. "I'd love to help you. There aren't any little kids in my family to buy for."

"It's a date then," I said. "We have two dates. To go shopping and to wrap presents."

Annica drained her cup and cast a quick look around the restaurant. It appeared that Marcy had everything under control. "Just so you remember, that shopping trip is going to double as sleuthing. We're going to solve the mystery of the silver sleigh."

"Just in time for Christmas," I said.

Eight

Two days later I met Annica at Clovers, and we drove to The Silver Sleigh in a light snowfall. Even with Annica along for support, I felt a trifle uneasy at the prospect of entering the shop again. I imagined Carol Cramer waiting for me with another plan to acquire the sleigh for herself.

I ordered myself to let go of this ridiculous fancy and enjoy the fun of Christmas shopping with my friend. After all, what could Mrs. Cramer do? The item she coveted was in my possession, legitimately purchased and safe on my mantelpiece.

The sprightly strains of "The Twelve Days of Christmas" wafted out into the snow, encouraging all who passed by this way to come inside, rejoice and be merry—and open their wallets.

Five gold rings, four calling birds...

"This is wonderful," Annica said as we navigated the recently-cleared walk. She pulled off her knitted yellow hat, letting snowdrops settle on her red-gold hair. "It's like Past Perfect without the angst."

I opened the door to the ringing of brass bells and surveyed about a dozen or so customers moving quietly along the aisles.

Like ghosts.

Why did this place always bring out the Gothic side of my nature?

"What a gorgeous Christmas tree!" Annica's eyes filled with admiration. "I'd love to have a string of those candle lights, only I'm not having a tree."

I didn't see the Ice Lady, although she might have been in the back room. A woman whose long black dress indicated her status as saleswoman was arranging figures in a manger.

Holding a shepherd, she turned around at the sound of the door chimes. Grabbing Annica's hand, I gravitated toward the collection of sleighs to which Holly had alluded on our first visit.

Holly was right. The shop had impressive groupings of sleighs of all kinds from tiny ornaments to a child-sized wicker model with an exquisite doll propped up inside. The doll wore a red satin dress trimmed in lace and a tiara on her coal-black curls. She also wore a price tag of two hundred and ninety-nine dollars. Certainly she wasn't meant as a child's plaything, but for a collector's shelf.

As for the sleighs, they were made from different materials: brightly decorated wood, crystal, and china, silver, gold, and even sequin-sprinkled cardboard. One of them resembled the sleigh I'd bought. It was silver but lacked the intricate flower-and-scroll pattern, and the eight reindeer were all the same. Cookie cutter deer, Leonora would say.

There was, however, one significant difference. This sleigh had a jaunty Santa Claus in the seat, a feature which mine lacked.

"Jennet." Annica touched my arm lightly. Too late.

The woman in black strode purposefully toward us. This time, mindful of the store's hands-off policy, I'd resisted touching the merchandise.

"May I help you?" she asked. Her eyes were a deep blue, a close match for the stones in her glittering wreath brooch.

"Just looking," I murmured.

"This is a lovely collection, isn't it?"

"I'd love to have that doll," Annica said. "Too bad I had to grow up."

"Any one of these sleighs would make an excellent gift," the woman added.

Apparently the store's policy didn't apply to her. She lifted one of the sleighs and held it up to the light of a Tiffany floor lamp behind the display.

"Take this beauty, for example," she said. "It's Polish crystal, made in the early part of the last century. You can fill it with your favorite Christmas candy and place it near a candle. Or fill it with tiny blue or red ornaments. Whatever you like."

She painted an appealing picture. I nodded, seeing the sleigh on my credenza overflowing with chocolate nonpareils.

Annica said, "My mom would like that, and twenty-five dollars is about what I can afford."

Deciding to stir the waters, I said, "I prefer silver myself. How much is the sleigh with the reindeer and Santa Claus?"

The woman gave me a strange look, a mixture of curiosity and, oddly, of triumph. It reminded me of the expression on the face of a cartoon huntsman I'd once seen. He was asking the fox if she would care to come out of her den and play.

I pushed the idea away as another ridiculous fancy.

Then the woman spoke, directing her words to me. "I believe you've been in our shop before. You purchased a sterling silver sleigh just like this one."

I suspected she was certain of her facts. Did they have a picture of me posted on a board in the back room?

"You're Mrs. Ferguson?" she asked. "Am I right?"

"That's my name."

She took a breath. "As you were informed, that item was sold to you in error. We're anxious to have it back."

Beside me, Annica fidgeted, holding on to her chosen gift. "Shall I take the candy dish up to the register?"

The woman ignored her.

"That's true," I said.

"Then I take it you've changed your mind about selling it back to us," she said.

"Not at all. I came to see if you have anything else I might like."

Her voice took on a brisk no-nonsense tone, and her stone-blue eyes grew sharper. "I'm Gloria MacBride, one of the owners of the shop. As such, I can offer you a nice incentive if you return the sleigh. We'll reimburse you at the price Mrs. Cramer mentioned, and you can choose a hundred dollars' worth of merchandise at no additional cost."

Annica gasped. I narrowed my eyes.

"That's a generous offer," I said. "May I ask why that particular sleigh is so important to you?"

"Of course." Her smile reminded me again of the cartoon huntsman. "It's our good luck charm. It shouldn't even have been on display. Holly never should have sold it to you."

"But she did," I said. "Can't you find another good luck article, one of these other sleighs?" I pointed to the sleigh with the cookie-cutter reindeer. "That one, for instance. It's silver and it's a sleigh."

"It isn't sterling silver," Gloria said. "And it's not *our* sleigh."

As if that endowed a decoration with the ability to bring good luck to a business.

I hesitated, hoping she would think I was considering her offer. Then I said, as politely as I could, "I think I'll keep the sleigh I bought. Now I'd like to look around."

During our exchange, Annica stood quietly at my side, holding the gift she'd selected for her mother carefully in her hands.

"I'm taking this one," she said.

A strident voice rang out, "Miss? Could I please have some help over here?"

With a chilly smile, Gloria MacBride turned and walked away to wait on her demanding customer.

"I am heartily tired of talking about sleighs," I said.

~ * ~

"What do you make of that?" Annica asked when we were safe in the Taurus with our many purchases stashed in the trunk.

"She really wants my sleigh—to the tune of a hundred and fifty dollars more than I paid for it. I still don't know why."

"Because it's worth even more than that?"

I considered. "There was no tag on it. Holly quoted the price from a notebook. That doesn't suggest an expensive mismarked antique to me."

I turned on the road and slowed as the car skidded on a patch of ice covered with snow. In control of the wheel again, I said, "I wonder what it would be like to travel down this road in a horse-drawn sleigh?"

"Magical," Annica said, "and just as slippery." She turned on the radio in the middle of "Frosty, the Snowman."

"Could Mrs. MacBride be telling the truth? Maybe the sleigh is just a good luck piece?"

"It's possible, but I have a suspicion there's more to it."

"There's a mystery attached to it, you mean."

"I think so. If that shopper hadn't interrupted us, I think Mrs. MacBride would have gotten even more aggressive."

"She might have raised her incentive to two hundred dollars." Annica sighed. "Imagine what that could buy! I would have found that amount hard to resist. Are we ever going back?"

Whereas at one time I hadn't wanted to darken the shop's doors again, I was eagerly anticipating my next visit. There was indeed a mystery at The Silver Sleigh, the safe kind that couldn't possibly involve me in any danger. It was the Christmas season, after all, a time to be merry and have fun.

"I still need to find a gift for Leonora," I said. "She wears antique jewelry, and I want to browse in the vintage book section."

Also I wanted to know if Gloria MacBride would make another attempt to regain the silver sleigh.

Gloria...

"Something just occurred to me," I said. "The names Gloria, Carol, and Holly. Is it just a coincidence that they're associated with Christmas?"

"The ladies may be using false names to boost holiday sales. They go with the whole package—music, ornaments, antique dolls, sleighs."

"Maybe," I said.

But possibly the Christmas-inspired names were part of the mystery. On our next visit to The Silver Sleigh, would we encounter Merry or Joy or Noelle?

"I'm definitely going back," I said. "Will you come with me?"

"You can't keep me away." Annica's wary eyes were fixed on the curving road ahead. "Only the next time let's go when it isn't snowing."

Nine

Sue Appleton couldn't wait to tell me the latest news. Rosalyn Everett's neighbor had spotted a white collie running on the River Rose property.

"At first she couldn't be sure," Sue said. "It looked like blowing snow. Then she saw the animal up close. It was a white collie."

I carried the cell phone into the kitchen, away from the friendly scuffle-growling of Misty and Gemmy.

"I'll have to go back to River Rose," I said. "Maybe we'll find Sparkle yet."

It must be as I'd once thought. The scent of canine would have clung to the kennels and Rosalyn's house. Sparkle would feel welcome there and comforted. The poor lost baby.

"There's more," Sue said. "When Mrs. Sloan drove over to see if she could coax the dog into her car, she saw a wreath with a red ribbon on the door. It's the kind Rosalyn usually bought. She thinks Rosalyn has come home at last."

"She must have," I said.

"Not so fast. No one answered the door."

"Did she see tire tracks or footprints?" I asked.

"Just deer tracks, but remember how it snowed yesterday."

I did. Snow falling on snow, spreading a thick white cover over the evidence.

"Mrs. Sloan didn't see Rosalyn's car," Sue added.

"Still, who else but the homeowner would hang a wreath on the door?"

"Only Rosalyn. I'd check it out myself, but I'm in bed with that darned flu. And I had a flu shot, too."

"I'll go," I said. "This is the first clue we've had to Sparkle's whereabouts. What happened to the dog, by the way?"

"Mrs. Sloan couldn't get close to her. She ran into the woods."

Where I couldn't very well follow her. Perhaps I'd see her running on the property as Mrs. Sloan had, or sheltering on the porch.

"Good luck, Jennet. I'm dying to know what excuse Rosalyn has this time."

"If she's there," I said.

This latter development seemed too good to be true. I did have hope of finding Sparkle, though, if not on my next visit, then another one. I didn't want her to keep living in the wild and foraging for herself as we moved deep into winter.

~ * ~

The next day in Journalism class, I planned my return trip to River Rose. The problem was finding time in my busy schedule. Both at school and at home, practically every hour had an attendant activity.

Well, Sparkle and Rosalyn's mystery were important, too. As were my own collies and Crane and all the dinners I'd have to prepare and the school work I brought home every night. Not to mention finishing my Christmas shopping and wrapping presents for Brent's children.

All of a sudden I felt overwhelmed. I understood the need for all those articles on dealing with holiday stress. Like the kids, I wanted a snow day.

A disturbance at the back of the room caught my attention. Icy air stole over me, and an indignant voice yelled, "Hey, close the window! It's freezing outside."

Jacqueline stood in the direct path of the wintry blast. "It's too warm in here."

Lynn, the indignant one, countered, "Take off one of your sweaters then."

"Mrs. Ferguson!" Two voices appealed to me.

Choose your battles.

"It's thirty-two degrees today," I said. "Take one deep breath, Jacqueline, and close the window."

Grumbling, she did as I asked and stomped off to her desk.

We were laying out the December issue of the *Courier*, deciding on the best placement for ads and art work. The two-page creative writing section was finished. I paused to admire the poems, each one accompanied by a seasonal illustration.

Unbidden, unexpected, a heavy sadness settled around me. I felt myself descending into a yawning malaise.

I would never find Sparkle alive. Tonight the temperature would fall. Like any dog left outside by an uncaring owner, Sparkle would freeze to death. She'd become part of the winter-bound earth, sealed to the ground, snow shaped in the figure of a lying collie.

What?

Where had that grim scenario originated? And why did I feel like weeping when nothing was wrong?

Look where you're standing!

I felt cold all over, and not because of the frigid air trapped in the room.

This was the place on which Danny had been shot and killed. The place where Gwendolyn had set out to draw a cheerful elf and found herself overcome with sorrow, unable to create a smile.

The haunted place.

Quickly I stepped back and moved to one side.

Don't let this happen, I prayed. *Please.*

"How does it look, Mrs. Ferguson?"

Joyce, the feature editor, looked up at me, obviously seeking approval. "Is it too Christmasy?"

"It's perfect," I said. "Think how pretty it'll be in green ink."

~ * ~

Could I continue to teach in this room and never ever set foot on those tiles again?

I remembered Lucy Hazen's belief that the very walls of this room would have absorbed the trauma and grief of that terrible day—and the floor as well.

These weren't the same tiles. They were new.

It didn't matter.

Could I remember in the course of conducting my classes to avoid walking or standing on this spot?

I'd have to.

On the way home, I told Leonora about my experience.

"Gwendolyn must have had a similar feeling," I said. "She kept drawing unhappy elves."

Leonora hesitated. "Was Gwendolyn in that American Lit class?"

"No," I said. "She's a new student this semester."

"Then why would she feel anything?"

"She's sensitive or psychic or whatever? I can't explain it."

"I can," Leonora said. "You have too much on your plate, Jen. Slow down."

"Make a to-do list?"

"Prioritize. Let some tasks fall by the wayside."

"If I do that, I'll never have that sense of loss again?"

"Loss? I thought you said you felt sad?"

"I did. Loss of well-being. Of joy."

"You're reading way too much into a passing mood," Leonora said. "How do you feel right this moment?"

The freeway lane was clear, it wasn't snowing, and the exit lay ahead swimming in a light snow fog. We were half way home.

"Happy," I said.

"Well then, hold on to that feeling. Think of everything that's waiting for you at home."

My husband, Crane, six loving collies, half a chocolate cake. And a hundred presents (minus three) to wrap.

"That's good advice, Leonora," I said. "I'm going to try to take it."

~ * ~

What tasks could I let fall by the wayside? Not dinner. I stirred the beef stew, scraping the bottom of the Dutch oven before it burned. In a half hour, Crane would be home and hungry. Not my collies; never the dogs. Not the presents. I'd promised Brent, and Annica planned to help wrap them tomorrow.

For the time being, the shopping trip to The Silver Sleigh and the River Rose mysteries could wait. Just until I got caught up.

I glanced at the collie calendar on the kitchen wall. In two weeks, Christmas vacation would begin, and there'd be many miles between me and the haunted classroom at Marston High School.

But on the calendar I noticed notations in red ink. The collies had grooming appointments at Marina's Pet Parlor. I was taking Halley, Sky, and Misty; Crane would take the others. I had a hairdresser's appointment. A dental appointment? Cancel that.

Satisfied that the stew was almost ready, the salad was made, and warm rolls were in the breadbasket, I sank into the rocking chair in the living room. Misty promptly threw her toy at me. I caught it, debated about throwing it in the washer, decided that could wait too, then tossed it into the dining room for her to retrieve.

The silver sleigh glowed down at me from the mantel with pillar candles on either end waiting to be lit. How the silver shone! I'd only polished it once the day I brought it home. For a moment, it seemed to come alive, bringing with it merriment and the peace of a quiet starlit night. And a sound of sleigh bells ringing on the frosty air—if I listened closely.

No, not bells. That was pure imagination. A lovely thought but not real.

To me, the sleigh was a symbol of happy times to come with good friends and the man I loved and the dogs who shared our home. It had been a lucky day when I'd discovered the antique shop and seen the sleigh set out in all its glory on a red velvet cloth.

For now, that was enough.

Ten

While the mysteries at River Rose technically resided by the wayside, every now and then they raised their heads and clamored for my attention.

What would be the harm in a quick trip to Rosalyn's house some day after school to see if the wreath was still on the door? If I were lucky, I might catch a glimpse of Sparkle. In any event, I wanted to see the wreath for myself.

"Let's do it," Leonora said the next day on the way home. "Then you'll know one way or the other and can stop obsessing about it."

"I'm not obsessing."

"Stop dwelling on it then."

"That's the same thing."

She was driving this week, and the roads were dry with no snow in the forecast or the sky.

"If you don't mind," I said. "It'll only take a few minutes."

"I don't have anything pressing to do tonight. Just a little school work. Besides, I'm curious, too."

"Then let's go."

I settled back to enjoy the scenery. After all this time, the picturesque Victorian houses and mysterious woods of Foxglove Corners still intrigued me. We drove through Maple Creek and before long came to the River Rose Collie Kennels sign. Fringed in icicles, it swung in the wind, a nostalgic name for a vanished enterprise.

River Rose looked the same as it had on my last visit. Snow blanketed the grounds, high drifts held together by frigid temperatures. The woods rose up on their incline to an icy gray sky. The Currier and Ives scene had gone from enchanting to unnerving.

The yellow ranch reminded me of a house lost in time.

The only change in the scene was the green pine wreath decorated with gold bells and a trailing red ribbon. It hinted that someone was inside, that the house wasn't a vacant target for burglars. As expected, there was no car in the driveway and no tire tracks other than our own.

So had Rosalyn dropped down from the sky, wreath in hand, and taken up silent residence in her yellow house?

Impossible, but no more puzzling than her never-solved disappearances.

We sat in the car, the engine idling, "Jolly Old Saint Nicholas" on the radio.

"I guess there's nothing here to see," Leonora said. "I wonder who hung the wreath."

As if in answer, a distant howl from the woods broke the eerie silence. It hung on the air, a chilling sound that seemed to have originated in a primeval time. One howl, lost and lonely; then all was quiet.

I opened the window, unmindful of the cold air sweeping into the car. "Was that a dog?"

"It sounded more like a wolf," Leonora said. "That must be the sound Rosalyn's neighbor heard."

"Wolves don't live in this part of the state," I pointed out. "At least I don't think so. Someone is always claiming to see one."

"Maybe it's one of those wolf-hybrids that escaped from his owner."

"I think it's a dog. It could be Sparkle."

"Well, we're not going in those woods to find out."

We both wore boots and jackets with warm woolen dresses underneath, not exactly hiking clothes. Also, the trees grew close together, and I'd never seen a wood without fallen branches and vines lying in wait to trip an unwary walker. It would be especially dangerous with the snow cover. Not to mention the bitter cold.

"No," I said. "I'd like to call Mac Dalby. But he would say this isn't a police matter, and he'd be right. I just hope it wasn't Sparkle."

Somehow I didn't think the dog who howled was our pretty white rescue collie.

The blue merle then? The collie I thought I'd seen once? That seemed more likely.

"I can ask Crane to investigate," I said. "And speaking of Crane..." I glanced at my watch. He would be home soon, and I hadn't given a thought to dinner. "We'd better be on our way. I think I'll come back, though."

"Why? You've seen the wreath."

"But not Rosalyn. Sue is certain she's back. She's wondering why Rosalyn didn't come for Bluebell and Dahlia."

Leonora made a turn and headed back to the road. "Well, it's all a mystery. I for one don't want to meet up with that creature in the woods, whatever it is."

"In a way, I do," I said.

Even though the memory of that howl had left me with a strangely unsettling feeling.

It felt like doom.

~ * ~

That evening Annica and I wrapped Christmas presents for Brent to distribute on Christmas Eve. With somebody to help me, the chore I'd been avoiding turned to fun. We worked in the study upstairs, supervised by Halley and Misty while Crane and the other collies rested by the fire.

It felt as if we were adrift in a sea of bright paper and rolls of curling ribbon, scissors and tape. Green, red, silver, and gold surrounded us. It felt like Christmas.

Angel stickers indicated a gift for a girl, while snowmen were to be used for boys' presents with an angel *and* a snowman for a present that would be appropriate for either sex like a plush animal or game.

"How sexist." Annica frowned as she affixed a fancy red bow to a box containing a toy stove." She reached for an angel. "Brent is so old-fashioned. Who says a little boy wouldn't love to receive this stove and a little girl that train set over there?"

I smiled. "This is what Brent wants. He *is* a little old-fashioned."

"He spent a fortune on toys," Annica said.

"Well he can afford it, and it makes him happy."

"I guess. When I was a kid, I always wanted an electric train."

"Did you ever get one?"

"Never. Santa Claus thought like Brent."

"It's never too late," I said. "You could buy one for yourself."

"Hey!" she shouted. "Get back here with that, you little devil!"

I looked up from an odd-shaped box I was trying to wrap neatly in time to see Misty make off with a stuffed rabbit. Halley watched her with what looked like disapproval.

"Catch her!" Annica shouted.

I left my package, let the paper unfold itself. "Misty! Bring it!"

She didn't stop. Not surprising for my feisty youngest one. Like white lightning, she dashed down the stars and collided with Candy, who joined in the chase, her eyes on Misty's treasure.

By the time I caught Misty in the kitchen and reclaimed the toy, it was ruined. I stared at the huge rip in the purple vest in dismay. Along with being torn, it was wet with collie drool. I couldn't give it to one of Brent's needy children in that condition. Maybe when all the Christmas madness was over, I could sponge off the rabbit and mend its torn jacket. One of my collies would love it. Probably Misty. Until then...

"Bad Misty!" I said. "We owe Brent a toy."

Misty watched me shove it to the back of the counter with her head tilted and no sign of remorse in her eyes. I had to remind myself she was still a puppy despite her size, and I'd better leave her downstairs where she couldn't get into any more mischief.

"Go find your goat," I said.

She just looked at me, then shifted her gaze to the counter.

Crane joined us in the kitchen and poured himself a cup of coffee. "What's all the commotion?"

I told him.

"Misty is still a baby," Crane said. "She wants to play."

"You play with her. We have to finish wrapping presents."

"Do you need any help?" he asked.

How surprised he'd be if I accepted his offer.

"Thanks, but we have it covered," I said.

He turned to Misty. "Come, girl."

The recent fracas forgotten, she followed him into the living room. It always annoyed me when she ignored me but obeyed Crane.

Back in the study, I found that Annica had wrapped four presents in my absence.

"Why don't we play with the system?" Annica asked with a mischievous glint in her eye. "See that toy robot? I'm going to stick an angel on it."

"Good idea, but it'll probably go to a little girl who wants a traditional doll, complete with wardrobe."

"A robot is a sort of a doll. It says on the box that it walks and talks."

I picked up a book with a beautifully illustrated cover. *Alice in Wonderland*. Probably one of Lucy's choices. Angel and snowman, I decided.

"But let's not get carried away," I said. "Christmas isn't the time to make a statement."

~ * ~

Surprisingly, in the next hour we wrapped all the toys and stacked them in a corner of the living room for Brent to pick up.

"I wish I could be there when Brent delivers them," Annica said.

"On his sleigh?"

"Yes. Wouldn't that be a perfect way to celebrate Christmas Eve?"

"Lucy usually goes with him," I said.

"Oh."

"Let's go sit in the living room with Crane. I'll make cocoa."

I hadn't had a chance to tell Crane about the howling in the River Rose woods. Now I could tell him and Annica at the same time.

I boiled water, made the cocoa, and poured it into three mugs. Annica remembered the Christmas cookies she'd brought from Clovers. With refreshments and hot drinks, we settled down to enjoy a well-deserved rest and the fire.

"Sure, I'll check it out," Crane said when I told him about the howling in the woods. "You probably heard a feral dog. He may be long gone."

"And it may be Sparkle."

"I wish I could find her for you, honey."

Carrying her cocoa, Annica walked over to the fireplace. "I love your sleigh," she said, running her finger over the fancy flower-and-scroll pattern. "Don't let that woman talk you into selling it back to her."

"Don't worry," I promised her. "It's here to stay."

Like the heirloom candlesticks that had belonged to Crane's Civil War era ancestress, Rebecca Ferguson, the sleigh had become so much more than a Christmas decoration in a short time. It seemed it had been on the mantel forever, a veritable part of our home, almost a blessing on it. I couldn't remember what I'd had on the mantel last year.

Just for a moment, I imagined the mantel with other ornamentation. A collection of vintage Santa Claus figurines, miniature Christmas trees, *papier mache* angels... Or the mantel with only candles, the way it would be if I'd never discovered the antique shop, never bought the silver sleigh.

But it didn't happen that way. Suddenly feeling the cold, I took a long sip of cocoa. It didn't make me feel any warmer.

Eleven

The next morning before my first hour students came blustering into class. I turned on the lights and surveyed the section of the room in which Danny had died.

I had dreamed about it last night, a frightening distortion of last year's shooting. Most of the dream had soon evaporated, but one aspect remained clear. When I'd stepped on the tiles, they'd promptly burst into flames.

I woke, feeling a painful burning sensation on my feet. Almost immediately it went away. Of course. It was in the dream or rather, the nightmare.

Could this possibly be a warning to me not to tempt fate?

I didn't think so.

It might make sense to avoid that part of the room in the future in case the floor did indeed have the power to alter my mood. Still, I didn't like to give in to paranoia when there was no need to do so. Also, five classes met here. The chances were good that someone sitting in the desk at which Gwendolyn had tried to draw a happy elf would need special help.

Realizing I couldn't very well avoid the haunted place, I decided to tempt fate and let the chips fall where they may.

With twenty minutes until the first bell, the hall was quiet. Quickly, before anyone could interrupt me, I walked slowly to the haunted place and came to a stop, waiting.

Nothing happened. Thank heavens. Nothing except perhaps for an all-too-natural wish for a reprieve in the teachers' lounge with a second cup of coffee.

I didn't move for several minutes, resting my hand on the desk— newly polished and smelling of lemon—and gazing at the winter scene beyond the window: an area roughly the size of a two-lane road, a high fence, and sparse woods affectionately known as the swamp. Because technically students weren't allowed on this part of the school grounds, the snow was pristine.

It was going to be all right. The curse had flared and died.

Feeling as if a weight had been lifted from my soul, I went back to my desk to prepare for the day. It was a coincidence that Gwendolyn had been unable to draw an elf with a smiling face. Ever imaginative, I had created the grim scenario involving Sparkle out of my fear for her. That fear was real, but so was Crane's promise to search the woods behind Rosalyn Everett's house.

Christmas was a time for miracles. I hoped one of them might be the return of the white collie before she grew emaciated and sickly, her snowy coat stuck with burrs, her collie spirit broken.

This settled, I opened the heavy World Literature textbook to the day's selection, an obscure Christmas story by Louisa May Alcott, and waited for the sound of thirty tenth graders rushing toward the classroom.

Rushing? In a dream world.

The bell rang. They came. For a time I forgot about the haunted place. In all, it was a satisfactory morning.

~ * ~

My reprieve didn't come until lunch time. We didn't have a traditional lunch hour at Marston but had to make do with twenty minutes, not including five minutes before and after for passing to and from the cafeteria. It was a source of never-ending amazement to me that the Administration expected us to gulp our food down in so short a time. To extend the period, Leonora and I usually brought our lunches from home and took turns eating in each other's room.

Today we sat at the long table set aside for laying out the school newspaper. Leonora had a container of fried chicken, along with iced brownies for both of us. Unimaginative when it came to making lunches, I had a brought a turkey sandwich and the inevitable bland apple.

As I told Leonora about my experiment, out of nowhere a new thought occurred to me.

Perhaps the phenomenon that Leonora referred to as the 'living tiles' was governed by time. The shooting had happened later in the day in my American Literature Survey class. I had conducted my experiment around seven-thirty in the morning.

"Suppose it's activated by time," I said.

"I don't understand."

"It's simple. The only time a person can feel sorrow or grief or whatever is when Danny was shot. He died almost instantly. It was…" I glanced at the clock. "During fourth hour."

"That doesn't sound right," Leonora said. She handed me a brownie.

I took it out of the plastic wrap and broke it in two. "I don't understand it either, but it's worth considering. This means I have to test it again," I added.

"You should let it go, Jen. You're going to drive yourself crazy."

"I don't think so. I have to be sure."

I couldn't wait to tell Lucy Hazen about my idea, Lucy being the one who had mentioned that the physical components of the room had absorbed the trauma of that day.

"Well, when it's that time, walk on the tiles again," Leonora said. "See if your mood changes. If not, then it was a one-time happening."

"For both Gwendolyn and me?"

"Like I said, I don't understand any of this. My advice still stands. Forget about it. Leave well enough alone."

Naturally I didn't.

At the approximate time of the shooting, I strolled down the aisle and paused at the haunted place. Kyle Landfield, who'd been reading a car magazine instead of the day's story, hastily shoved it under his notebook and opened his literature text—to the wrong page.

My mood didn't change. All I'd accomplished was to stir the cauldron of painful memories and give Kyle a few anxious moments.

So my time theory fell apart. In all likelihood, Gwendolyn's experience and mine were unrelated. I didn't have to fear they'd be repeated. It was strange, but then life was filled with the inexplicable.

In a haze of relief, I taught my classes and read student essays on my conference hour. The day limped to an end with the harsh sound of the last bell ringing.

During the past hour it had started to snow. I watched the wind blow a thin but massive white wave across the swamp, then gathered my books and papers and contemplated nothing more harrowing than the long commute home.

~ * ~

On my arrival, three dogs greeted me instead of the usual pack. Crane had taken Candy, Gemmy, and Raven to the groomer in Lakeville. He would pick them up on his way home.

Halley and Sky were so quiet it was almost as if they weren't there. Misty, with her zany reputation to uphold, danced around me, nudging my hand for play. I didn't see her goat, but she saw the rabbit with the torn vest, still languishing on the counter.

I distracted her with a biscuit from the Lassie canister. After eating their own biscuits and lapping fresh drinks of water, Sky and Halley lay down in the kitchen to watch the eternally fascinating procedure of tea making. Every now and then, Sky uttered a whimper which was unlike her, unless something had caused her distress.

Halley stayed still for a few minutes, her nose on her paws, then rose and began to pace. More uncharacteristic behavior.

They must be missing their sister collies, but it was strange. I'd seldom known Halley to be so restless.

I took my three girls outside and let them play in the snow, but soon Halley and Sky drifted back to the side door, waiting patiently for it to open. Candy, Raven, and Misty were the snow lovers in the pack. But even Misty was ready to leave the branch she'd unearthed. As for myself, I would appreciate a snow scene far more from inside the house.

I called to the dogs and we all trooped inside, bringing with us a prodigious amount of snow that promptly melted on the floor.

East, west, home is best, I murmured, smiling when Halley wagged her tail in agreement.

The tea had steeped long enough. I filled a cup, brought it into the living room, and turned on the lamp. The hot drink chased away the chill. As I frequently did, I looked at my silver sleigh on the mantel, admiring its shine.

Had it been that shiny last night?

Well, of course. Something seemed different, though.

A silver sleigh, eight tiny reindeer, each one unique...

Each one was exactly the same! Cookie cutter reindeer pulled the sleigh!

I sprang up. Hot tea splashed down on my woolen skirt. Hardly aware of the sting of burning, I rushed to the mantel.

The flower-and-scroll pattern had vanished as if rubbed away by a vengeful hand. This wasn't my sleigh. How could this be?

I lifted it off the mantel, noticing immediately that it was lighter. It was an imposter, a changeling. A lightweight.

Just for a moment, I wondered if magic at been at work in my home. Then I remembered the dogs' unusual behavior. I couldn't blame the supernatural for this mysterious exchange.

Somebody had broken into the house and stolen my treasured antique, the good luck artifact coveted by the women with the Christmas names. He or she had left this cheap imitation in its place, no doubt hoping I wouldn't notice the substitution.

Apparently this had happened today when the feistiest of the collies were at the groomer's. But how could anyone have known?

The thought of an intruder with an unknown agenda in the house galvanized me into action. The side door had opened normally. The front door? Hurriedly I opened and closed it again and could find no sign that it had been tampered with.

Next I checked the windows on the first floor, trailed by Halley and Sky, while Misty slipped into Sky's favorite place under the kitchen table. More strange behavior.

The windows were securely locked, but someone must have found their way inside. The sleigh hadn't driven itself off the mantel into the unknown.

It was still snowing, a fresh layer to cover the evidence of footprints. This was no impulsive break-in but a well-planned assault on our home.

Which led me to a question. Who would have the nerve to burglarize a deputy sheriff's house?

A person unaware of Crane's profession? One who didn't care because the prize they coveted was more important than any risk.

In my view, those women at The Silver Sleigh were guilty until proven innocent.

Without further thought, I whipped my cell phone out of my purse and dialed the police.

Twelve

Before starting dinner, I searched the rest of the house. As I suspected, nothing else was missing—and we had many valuable possessions that a run-of-the-mill robber would be happy to scoop up.

Our house hadn't been targeted by a regular thief. Only the silver sleigh was gone. For all I knew, it might be back at the antique shop set out on its red velvet cloth.

Lieutenant Mac Dalby, who was a personal friend of Crane's, took my report with his accustomed efficiency but appeared to be unimpressed with my story. I'd been sold an antique by mistake and the previous owner was so anxious to have it returned she'd committed a crime to retrieve it?

"It's worth only a hundred dollars?" Mac asked. "What else was taken?"

"Just the sleigh."

I tried to explain that the antique was obviously worth a great deal more than a few hundred dollars to the person who had stolen it. I added that the shop's owner had offered me more than I'd paid if I would sell it back to her.

Unfortunately, I didn't have any proof of the break-in and could give him no explanation for how it had been executed. I didn't even have telltale footprints.

Only three listless collies and a receipt.

You can't accuse a person of theft without proof. That is, you could, but you couldn't take it any further.

"You *are* going to investigate, aren't you?" I asked.

"I'll be in touch," he promised.

Translation: I was on my own. My crime was low priority.

I knew Crane would take my story seriously. After all, this was his house, too. Later that day, he turned three freshly groomed collies loose in the kitchen. They wore bright holiday bandanas with jingle bells attached and had a slight dusting of snow on their coats. All three were bursting with pent-up energy.

I smothered them with extravagant compliments and petting as they dashed around the oak table in ecstasy, then said, "We were robbed sometime today, Crane. The silver sleigh is gone. There's a cheap substitution in its place."

Before I'd finished speaking, Candy dashed into the living room sniffing at the mantel, looking puzzled. Not that she understood me or knew the sleigh above her was different, of course. The thief had left his scent behind. Her scent. I had convinced myself that one of the women from the antique shop was our burglar.

Raven and Gemmy joined her. If only they'd been here during the break-in, the story would have been different.

Hastily, moving like a seasoned lawman, Crane followed the dogs to the fireplace. Removing the sleigh from the mantel carefully, he set it on a side table. "We'll see if the thief left any prints on it."

"I touched it," I said.

"Is anything else missing?" he asked.

"Not that I could find. I called Mac."

"Why would anyone break in for a Christmas decoration?"

"Because there's something special about this one. I knew it when those women tried so hard to get it back."

"So you think it happened today?" he asked. "Did you happen to look at the sleigh last night?"

"I'll swear the real sleigh was on the mantel last night."

"I'm going to check outside," he said.

I'd already done that, but maybe Crane would find something I'd overlooked. He hadn't changed into civilian clothes yet; he still wore his gun. I was sure the intruder had long since fled with the sleigh. Well, I'd done what I could. Camille was away from home, so I hadn't been able to ask her if she'd seen an unfamiliar car or anyone suspicious loitering around our house.

Crane opened the side door, and Raven seized her opportunity to slip out with him. Being groomed must have been a particular ordeal for my outside-loving collie. Candy stayed behind at the mantel, still sniffing, until I took the chicken out of the broiler and started mashing potatoes. Then she lay down in the doorway where she had a good view of the proceedings.

I took my anger out on the poor potatoes, smashing them until bits flew out of the pan as if looking for a hiding place.

After a while the door opened and Crane came back inside, his jacket and hair covered in snow. He stamped his boots on the doormat.

"Nothing?" I asked.

"Not a trace."

"It had to be one of the women at the antique shop," I said. "Nobody else wanted it. Who else even knew I had it? Just Leonora and Annica and you."

Crane nodded. "Except they'd know you would suspect them. That tells me they're stupid."

Melodramatic thoughts careened through my head. The sleigh contained a secret message or concealed a priceless jewel.

Okay. Where? Did one of the reindeer open? I should have examined it more thoroughly. But who would even think of hidden compartments?

"If only we had proof," I said.

My sales slip would indicate that I'd purchased a sleigh. Anyone could argue that I'd lost or disposed of the item after leaving the shop.

There must be some way I could find the missing sleigh and reclaim it.

The theft had thrown my timing off. Usually I waited to put the finishing touches on dinner until Crane had showered and changed clothes. Certainly after he'd locked his gun away in its cabinet. I'd have to put the chicken and potatoes in the oven to stay warm.

He dropped a kiss on my cheek. "I hope I can get your sleigh back for you, honey. I'm going to try."

I smiled. "In time for Christmas?"

"Maybe before then. I'm going to take care of changing the locks."

"And from now on, leave at least one of our prime watchdogs home," I added with a rueful glance at Sky who was lying under the kitchen table.

After we ate, I intended to move the candles on the mantel closer together to fill in the space where the sleigh had been. A poinsettia plant would add color or maybe I could find the pair of wood carved reindeer I'd had since childhood.

I wondered if I would ever see my sleigh again.

~ * ~

After dinner when it was allowable to introduce serious subjects again, I said, "I'm going back to that antique shop as soon I find the time."

Crane looked up from the *Banner*. "Not to accuse one of the women, I hope."

"I'm not that foolish. I'll shop for sleighs and never let on that I have an ulterior motive. Who knows? Maybe my sleigh will be there."

Even as I spoke, though, I remembered that it wasn't supposed to be on display to begin with.

"You can ask Leonora or Annica to go with you," he said.

"Surely you don't think there's any danger? They have what they want. For all they know, I didn't notice the substitution."

"It doesn't matter," he said. "If you're right about one of those women being the burglar, you'll be walking into a dangerous situation."

For a moment I remembered the back room at The Silver Sleigh, dimly-lit and crammed with antique furniture and boxes. In retrospect, it was a sinister place. Did the door have a lock? I saw myself trapped inside after hours, freezing and starving and a sign in the window, 'Closed for the Season.'

I let the grim little fantasy slide away. That wasn't going to happen. Not to a customer casually browsing the antique sleigh display in the midst of Christmas shoppers with holiday music playing in the background.

Peace on earth, good will to men...

Suddenly I couldn't wait to return to the antique shop.

~ * ~

When something is important to you, make time for it.

After school the next day, I dropped Leonora off at her house. She had a dinner date with Deputy Sheriff Jake Brown which was to be the highpoint of her week. Annica had a late class in the Victorian Novel and hadn't finished *Jane Eyre* yet.

I was, as I thought I'd be, on my own.

The roads were clear, and the day was cold and dry. After making sure the house was secure and the collies were taken care of,

I drove to the antique shop only to find the parking lot empty and the store closed.

There would be no investigation, no confrontation today. Then I noticed a new display of decorative sleighs in the bay window. They rested on a blanket of white material that resembled snow. Leaving the engine running, I went closer to investigate.

I remembered seeing many of them on an earlier visit to the shop, especially the ornate painted sleigh holding the doll in the red dress. New items had been added to the collection, but I didn't see my sleigh.

Well, I wouldn't be likely to. I felt certain the stolen sleigh was somewhere on the premises, perhaps locked in the back room. At any rate, it was beyond my reach.

That meant I'd have to come back to the shop. And I would, over and over again, until I solved the mystery. Until, that is to say, it was back on the mantel where it belonged.

Maybe on my next trip, Annica or Leonora could accompany me. Maybe Mac would bestir himself to investigate; maybe Crane would have luck finding the thief. The prospect of all the maybes cheered me somewhat. In the meantime, I had a perfect way to make up for the day's disappointment—a quick stop at River Rose.

Thirteen

As soon as I turned in the driveway of River Rose, I saw the dog, a massive blue merle collie standing close to the house.

So I hadn't imagined him.

He was magnificent, a dream of a collie with a beautifully marled silver coat in an elegant position, complete with tilted head, almost as if posed for a photograph.

I reached for my purse, intending to take a quick picture on my cell phone, and left my car quietly, but when I was perhaps four yards away, he turned tail and dashed around the house and up the slope. Out of sight.

Like quicksilver.

The quicksilver collie, I thought. He must be a dog of Rosalyn Everett's breeding, perhaps one of her champions. How had he managed to avoid the police who had liberated the other Red Rose collies from the kennel when Rosalyn's absence became known?

I recalled that another collie had done so, the one Leonora and I had discovered starving and dehydrated at Rosalyn's back door. This one had apparently taken care of himself, except his gorgeous, thick coat must be a mess. He couldn't have done anything about that.

He was gone, but this was obviously his territory. In the future, I'd know where to find him.

I wondered why Crane hadn't seen the blue merle or Sparkle when he'd searched the woods.

He'd told me he had only sighted a coyote, boldly following his progress but not daring to approach him. It was big and hardy for a coyote. Maybe it was one of those crosses between wolves and coyotes known as coywolves.

Maybe the coywolf was the creature that howled in the woods. I wondered. Wolves howl; coyotes make a yipping sound. What would a coywolf sound like? Was it relevant?

All I knew was I hoped I'd never meet up with one.

There was no question in my mind of trying to coax the blue merle into my car. Even with jerky treats, which I kept in the glove compartment in case I came across a collie in need of rescue, I'd have to win his trust first, and that would take time.

Well, no matter. The last of the Red Rose collies, the quicksilver collie, was here presiding over the grounds of the deserted kennels, perhaps dreaming of dishes heaped with kibble and bowls of fresh water as he slept on his nest in the woods. And a soft hand caressing his head. I didn't know for certain but assumed that a dog who had been raised by a human would never forget his origins.

While there was nothing I could do about the quicksilver collie at the moment, I knew he couldn't stay in Rosalyn's woods throughout the coming winter months. Domesticated dogs need their people.

Perhaps he'd already turned feral? How else could he have survived for so long?

And, by the way, where was Sparkle?

Dreaming of plans for future action, I got back in the car, turned it around and headed for home. The mystery of the silver sleigh was at a temporary standstill, but the story of River Rose had acquired a fascinating new development.

~ * ~

That evening Brent descended on us, his hands full of Christmas presents already wrapped, albeit a trifle clumsily.

"Are these for your giveaway?" I asked.

"No, they're for my two favorite people, you and Crane. Merry Christmas in advance."

"My goodness. So many?"

There were six of them in various sizes and shapes. I hadn't even finished my shopping and had no idea what to buy for a man who had everything.

"I'll take them." Crane stacked the boxes on a side table. One of them jingled, which drew the dogs' attention. Misty especially eyed it longingly. I hadn't seen her stuffed goat lately or seen her carrying around any other toy.

"We don't have our tree yet," I said, hanging up Brent's heavy leather jacket.

"We will, this weekend," Crane added. "Chopped down and put in its stand."

"Crane takes care of the lights and I do the decorating," I said.

Yesterday he had carried our boxes of ornaments and decorations up from the basement. I'd found the pair of wooden reindeer I'd received as a present when I was a little girl. With tiny wreaths around their antlers, they filled in the space on the mantel where the sleigh had been quite nicely. But they didn't look as impressive as my sleigh had.

Still, they were antiques from my own past.

Crane shook the jingling box. "I wonder what's in here."

"Do not open until Christmas," Brent said with a mischievous glint in his eyes. "That one's for Jennet. I have more presents in the car for the dogs."

"Excuse me for a minute," I said. "I don't want my roast to burn."

Candy beat me to the kitchen and stood at my feet entranced as I turned the meat over and basted the potatoes and carrots with juice. Dinner *did* smell good, and, although not expecting company, I had a chocolate pie in the oven.

When I rejoined the men, Crane was telling Brent about the burglary.

"I've seen that shop," Brent said. "Never been in it, though."

"The women call themselves Holly, Carol, and Gloria," I said. "I'm sure one of them stole my sleigh. Probably Gloria, one of the owners."

Brent dropped into the rocking chair he favored and invited Sky and Misty to join him, Sky at his feet and Misty on his lap. "You've found a new mystery, Jennet. The Case of the Haunted Sleigh."

I nodded. "It's a puzzling one."

"It could be dangerous," Crane said. "There aren't any ghosts in this one, Fowler. Just a real thief."

"I'm going to visit this antique shop tomorrow and tell them I'm interested in buying a silver sleigh—for my girlfriend," Brent said.

Yes! A light came on in my mind, the traditional light bulb appearing over the head of a cartoon character.

"That gives me an idea. I'll ask all my friends to descend on the shop. Everyone's going to be looking for an antique sterling silver sleigh. Let's see, I can recruit Annica and Leonora. I'm sure Lucy, Camille, and Gilbert will agree to be part of our team. I wonder if Miss Eidt at the library would be interested."

"What will that do?" Crane asked.

"Harass them. They'll have to keep talking about silver sleighs. I'll tell them I'm going to start a collection of sleighs and never let on that I noticed the substitution. Well…" I shrugged. "It's better than doing nothing. With a little luck, we'll drive them crazy."

"Drive them crazy," Brent echoed. "Right in keeping with the Christmas spirit. I like it."

~ * ~

After dinner, after the dogs had gobbled up generous portions of leftovers, Brent brought his hundred and ten Christmas packages downstairs.

I said, "The ones with the prettiest bows were wrapped by Annica. She volunteered to help me."

"Annica's a great girl," he said. "I bought her a fancy present."

"What is it?"

"All will be revealed on Christmas Eve." He glanced appreciatively at the stack of gifts. "They look good. Like a professional did them."

"Well, some of the ribbons are store-bought."

"The kids won't notice," he predicted. "They just want what's inside, but I wanted them to look nice."

"I'm trying to guess what you found for Jennet that jingles," Crane said.

"You won't be able to." Brent ran his hand over Misty's head. She wagged her tail lazily.

The flames in the fireplace, newly stoked to life, crackled nicely. Secure in the comforts of my cozy living room, my thoughts drifted to the lonely incline behind Rosalyn Everett's house and the woods beyond and the quicksilver collie curled into a silver ball in his forest den.

"I saw the blue merle at River Rose again," I said. "There may be two purebred collies in those woods, Sparkle and Silver."

"Silver?" Brent asked.

"He has to have a name."

"All I saw was the coyote," Crane said. "And he didn't have a name."

"Where there's one, there's a pack," Brent pointed out. "They hang around my stables, too. Napoleon and Chance are always on the lookout for them."

I brought the conversation back to the quicksilver collie. "He's wary. It's possible he hasn't interacted with a human since Rosalyn disappeared, and that was months ago, back in the summer."

"What makes you think he'd be happy in foster care?" Crane asked.

"He probably wouldn't be at first, but we have some wonderful foster homes in the Rescue League. It would all come back to him, living with people, and he wouldn't have to stay in the wild all winter."

We could do that for Rosalyn, I thought. Or in memory of her, if it came to that.

"I'm willing to take another collie." Brent bent down to give Sky equal attention.

He'd already adopted a skittish blue female named Larkspur who had been rescued from a demented abuser of collies.

"I have plenty of space," he added.

And plenty of heart.

"We'll keep on looking for him," I said. 'And I'll bet some of our roast cut up would be a powerful lure. Look how our dogs loved it."

Feeling better about the silver sleigh and the quicksilver collie, I sat back to enjoy the rest of our fire-lit evening with my husband and our good friend.

Christmas is coming, the goose is getting fat...

Well, there was no goose, fat or otherwise. A turkey, probably, or a ham.

All we needed to do was deck the halls and put up our tree.

Fourteen

Our tree, a shapely Fraser fir, lay in back of the house, its trunk submerged in a pail of water that had frozen. A pail of ice, to be exact. A balsam wreath adorned our front door, and smaller wreaths crafted of red velvet hung in every window. Inside, boxes of decorations filled one corner of the dining room. Tonight after dinner I planned to transform our house into a Christmas wonderland, as soon as Crane set the tree in its stand, that is.

That was my plan. Sue Appleton's call derailed it.

"The strangest package came in the mail yesterday," she said. "It's from Rosalyn Everett."

"She's alive then!"

"I don't know. Somebody else mailed it. I didn't recognize the return address, and there was no letter from Rosalyn inside, not even a note."

"What was in it?"

"Rosalyn's kennel stuff. Pedigrees. Records of her breedings through the years and hundreds of pictures of her dogs and litters. There are records of sales, too. You have to see it."

"I want to."

I had brought home take-out turkey dinners from Clovers. Three of the dogs had been walked, and all had biscuits and fresh water.

Crane wouldn't be home for a few hours, and Sue's horse farm was right around the corner, or rather, around the lane.

"If it's convenient, I'll be right over," I said and, ending the call, went back to the closet for my jacket and boots, trailed by Candy who thought she was going for a walk.

"Crane will take you when he comes home," I told her. "Now you watch the house while I'm gone."

In spite of new locks and five large inside dogs, I couldn't rid myself of the lingering fear of a break-in, even though the thief had already absconded with the object of her desire. Still, I had to leave the house sometime, and the package from Rosalyn was a strong lure.

Rosalyn must have treasured the contents of that box. If she had entrusted them to Sue in such an unusual way, that meant she had no further use for them.

The only conclusion I could draw was that she was dead.

Or expected to be dead by the time the package arrived.

~ * ~

In the family room of Sue's farmhouse, I studied the return address on the box. Black ink. Hastily scrawled. A few smudges. A Maple Creek address; that fit, keeping in mind River Rose's location. Neither of us recognized the name of the sender: E. J. Lancaster.

In contrast, Sue's address was neat and legible.

"This is Rosalyn's handwriting," Sue said. "It matches the writing on the records. Somebody else, this E. J. Lancaster, handled the transition for Rosalyn."

"This may be our first real clue to Rosalyn's whereabouts."

"I already looked in the phone directory," Sue said. "He isn't listed. He or she. It could be Edward or Elizabeth."

"Let's pay him a visit. I'd rather call first, but it won't be possible. What are you going to do with the River Rose papers?"

"Keep them until we know, one way or the other. If Rosalyn isn't coming back, it's only right that the pedigrees go to the people who adopted her dogs."

Her foster collies, the blue and the tri, lay quietly in the room, side-by-side. Both of them stared at us, almost as if they knew our conservation might concern them.

"I already took out the pictures and paperwork for Bluebell and Dahlia," Sue said. "As far as I'm concerned, they are my dogs now—whatever happens."

In the excitement of examining the material from Rosalyn, I'd forgotten to tell Sue that I had seen the blue merle collie earlier that day. I told her. To my surprise, she said, "I'll bet that's Icemaker. There was one blue I couldn't account for. He'd be three years old now."

She flipped through a packet of pictures and drew out a glossy print of Rosalyn standing behind a majestic blue merle collie. I recognized him immediately. The dog was a mirror image of the one I'd seen at River Rose.

"River Rose Icemaker," Sue said. "His call name is Icy. What do you think?"

"That's Icy, all right. I called him the quicksilver collie."

Sue took the picture from me and set it on the coffee table. "We have to find him."

"We will, now that I know I didn't imagine him. I can't say when, though."

"What about Sparkle?"

"We have to find her, too. They may be together."

Sue sighed. "There's so much to do with the holidays coming up. These two collies need to be rescued. I'm having a party for my riding students and one for the Rescue League. There's a big family dinner, shopping… I'm exhausted just thinking about it."

I decided not to dwell on my own to-do Christmas list, which, fortunately, didn't include hosting any holiday parties. I'd take one day at a time, as I always did, and prioritize.

"First we'll have to talk to E. J. Lancaster," I said.

~ * ~

After dinner I made hot chocolate and joined Crane and the collies in the living room, carrying the mugs. He looked up, smiling, set the *Banner* down, and took his mug from me. By then I was out of the mood to decorate the tree. I only wanted to enjoy my drink and the fire.

It had strings of old-fashioned bubble lights, new this year, and they gave the living room a soft mesmerizing Christmas glow. For tonight that was sufficient.

"You've been busy," I said. "I should have been here to help you with the tree."

He laughed. "Candy and Misty helped me. They think we have candy canes hanging on the branches like last year."

"That was a disaster." I'd had to pick up bits of candy canes and chewed paper all through the house well into January.

"Besides, I'm curious about Rosalyn Everett, too," he added. "Maybe we'll finally find out what happened to her."

"If Sue and I can agree on a time to visit the person who sent the package to Sue," I said. "We're both booked solid."

My priorities, I thought. At the top of the list were the collies, Sparkle and Icy. Then came the antique sleigh and Rosalyn, whose mystery had been with me forever, it seemed. There was school, the last few days at Marston High School before Christmas recess. I was looking forward to them.

The kids were already in holiday mode. In all likelihood, Principal Grimsley would unbend just a little bit, and while parties in the room were forbidden, enterprising teachers could give their lessons a Christmas spin. Add a possible surprise gift from a student, and this was truly the most wonderful time of the school year.

"I'm happy to tell you that you're on my list of priorities, Crane," I said. "I never dreamed I'd have such a perfect husband."

How corny that sounded. But how wise to say what was in my heart.

The perfect husband set his mug down on the coffee table. "I hope so, honey. I know you're on mine."

"More hot chocolate?"

"About half a cup."

Candy, the ever-hopeful, followed me to the kitchen with Halley in her wake.

That deserved a treat. Just for my two loyal ones.

Quietly I lifted the top of the Lassie tin. Suddenly they were all in the kitchen, all clustered around me, bright eyes begging for a treat.

I'm so happy, I thought. *Everybody should be this happy. I hope it never ends.*

~ * ~

I remembered that thought the next afternoon when I responded to a student's request for help and inadvertently stepped on the haunted tiles.

Like a heavy stone, an all-encompassing sadness dropped down on me.

It was hopeless. The end. Over too soon.

Dear God!

The floor seemed to be in motion under my feet. The tiles were spinning. I was falling...going down... I reached for something to hold onto.

Hopeless. The end. Over.

"This poem doesn't make any sense, Mrs. Ferguson."

Nancy's voice held a hint of a whine. Her paper was blank except for the name of the class and the period.

Emily Dickinson. *And if I go while you're still here... Know that I live on...*

I forced myself to ignore the spinning sensation, to touch the back of Nancy's desk. I stepped to one side, and my out-of-control world righted itself.

"Dickinson is writing about death," I said, "and the afterlife. Holding on to love. Living your life."

Was I making sense? I loved that poem, knew it well.

But why of all the poetry in the American Literature textbook, did I have to assign that one today of all days?

Because I'd thought today would be an ordinary day in my class.

There'll never be an ordinary day in this classroom, I thought.

To Nancy, I said, "All you have to do is write what you think the poet is saying to you about death."

"That's creepy," Nancy said. "Why can't we read something happy?"

But she started writing.

As I walked back to my desk, the feeling of overpowering sadness rapidly drained away.

Fifteen

The rest of the day I avoided the haunted place. It was easy to do as no one else who occupied that desk asked for special help.

I found myself wondering why only Gwendolyn and I had been swept into the vortex of sadness. I had five classes a day. That meant four students who occupied the space remained untouched by whatever dark power governed the space.

How do you know that?

I didn't. I could only judge by their demeanor and behavior. No one except Gwendolyn had ever communicated the slightest distress to me.

What, then, set Gwendolyn and me apart from the others? Was there an experience in her life that would make her vulnerable to the strange power?

Impatiently, I stacked the books and materials I planned to take home. I didn't want to dwell on my brief sojourn in the Twilight Zone place. Only now, on my conference hour, I had too much time to think. The room was peaceful and warm with still more snow falling. I couldn't seem to keep my thoughts from wandering to the moments when sadness had overwhelmed me and the floor began to move.

Having made my peace with the summer's gunfire haunting, I didn't want to open the door to yet another disturbing phenomenon.

I had toyed briefly with the idea of asking Leonora to step on the tiles and see if anything untoward happened, but she was so happy now with Jake Brown that I didn't want to risk it. In fact I wouldn't even mention today's incident to her. Besides, whatever this was, so far it only concerned Gwendolyn and me. And Gwendolyn had never mentioned her thwarted attempt to draw a happy expression again.

So forget what happened. Plan an exciting seasonal assignment tomorrow for World Literature. Something different. Out of the textbook.

How about writing a poem on snow?

They'd hate that.

Maybe not. Experiment. Tell them it didn't have to rhyme which was the most frequent stumbling block for a student told to create a poem. They needed to become more comfortable with the thesaurus anyway. There was plenty of inspiration just beyond the windows.

I wrote 'Creative writing day—snow' in the appropriate space and closed my plan book.

~ * ~

"It's a perfect day with all the snow out there," Annica said. "I can leave now. Let's do it."

I'd told her about my plan to have my friends storm the antique shop with requests for a sleigh, and she could hardly wait to participate. We would be two shoppers who wanted to add to our sleigh collections.

"But if Gloria waits on us, she might remember that I have a limited Christmas budget," Annica added.

"She can't possibly remember every shopper," I said.

Except me. Gloria had good reason to remember me.

"I wonder if I can put that doll in the sleigh on layaway," Annica said.

"The Silver Sleigh seems to be more a cash or credit card kind of place. Don't you have an afternoon class?"

She shook her head and her gold earrings jingled. "Not tonight. And I finished *Jane Eyre*. Yay." A faint tinkling accompanied this announcement. "Next up is *Wuthering Heights*. I'll start it tomorrow."

"Are you wearing jingle bells?" I asked.

She touched an earring, and it jingled obligingly. "They're legitimate earrings. I love to go jingling at this time of year."

With her bright red hair and flamboyant personality, Annica could jingle with impunity. I preferred to keep a low profile.

"We could make a quick stop," I said.

I had a casserole in the freezer for tonight's dinner and had just bought a blueberry pie. I'd only stopped in at Clovers for dessert and a quick cup of hot chocolate, but Annica was persuasive. I *did* want to go back to the antique shop. It was on my list of priorities, not at the top but certainly not at the bottom, and I'd rather go with a friend than alone.

Still, I raised one last objection. "The roads may be icy."

"That never stopped us before. Anyhow, this is a nice fluffy snow. Wait here till I get my coat. I'll just be a minute."

Left to my own devices for that minute, I gravitated toward the dessert carousal, eyeing a tray of strawberry-iced brownies that Marcy had just brought from the kitchen.

"I'll take two brownies," I said. "No, make that four."

Sleuthing can be hungry work.

~ * ~

We stood outside the antique shop window, gazing at the sleighs on display and letting the snow fall on our hair. On my hair, I should say. Annica wore a green knitted hat with a row of jingle bells attached to its edges.

Music floated out on the icy air, and the myriads of lights inside the shop sent out their beacons.

Here we come a wassailing/Among the leaves so green...

I opened the door, and we stepped into light and instant good cheer. The place was crowded. We weren't the only ones braving the snow, but then the days until Christmas were dwindling down to those precious few.

I hadn't seen my stolen antique in the window, but Annica spotted the painted sleigh immediately. It had been moved to another counter.

"There's a different doll in it," she said, frowning.

The new doll wore a deep blue ball gown sprinkled with sequins, hardly a sleigh-riding outfit. A tiny tiara sparkled on her golden hair. She was a little beauty, delicate and rosy-cheeked about the size of the vintage story book dolls set out on a shelf.

"I liked the red one better," Annica said.

"Let's ask if they still have it." I wondered at Annica's fascination with the doll. Perhaps this was akin to her childhood desire for an electric train.

I looked for Carol or Holly or Gloria but didn't see them.

A young girl with long wavy dark hair stood behind the cash register. Another with the hair the color of honey arranged in the same hairstyle presided over the tree in the center, from which location she had a clear view of the people who roamed the aisles. Some of them, I noticed, were ignoring the shop's 'Touch at Your Own Risk' policy.

We found more sleighs toward the back, not grouped together but scattered among the other antiques.

"Here it is! The red doll... Yikes. It's over two hundred dollars, sold separate from the sleigh. If I didn't have to pay tuition..."

"You can find something else," I said. "There are dolls all over the place, but remember, you're supposed to be looking for a sleigh."

"Oh, yes. That's a pretty glass one." She pointed, almost clipping a fragile gold reindeer. "Or is it crystal?"

I reached for a wooden sleigh with Santa and presents lying around a Christmas tree painted on each side. If others could touch the merchandise, so could I.

The girl who had stood at the tree appeared as if by magic at my side. Her holly-and-ivy name tag identified her as Nicola. Of course. For Jolly Old Saint Nicholas.

"That's one of our latest estate sale finds," she said. "It's one of a kind. If you're interested, you'd better grab it while you can. Other people have noticed it."

Carefully I replaced the wooden sleigh on its pedestal. "I was really looking for a sterling silver sleigh, preferably with a team of deer attached, but this caught my eye."

"Sterling silver?" She pushed back a long strand of honey-colored hair. "I'm sorry. We don't have any silver sleighs in stock."

"What about your name?" I asked.

"My name? It's Nicola. Not Nickie, please. Nicola."

"I meant the name of the shop."

She shrugged. "Oh, that's just a name."

"I'm looking for a silver sleigh, too," Annica said. "I collect them."

Nicola looked from Annica to me and back to Annica. "Both of you collect silver sleighs?"

"Only at Christmastime," Annica said.

"Let's see." Nicola gave a fair impression of a girl in deep thought. "I know what you might like. Over here with the jewelry."

She led the way to a display of vintage necklaces, brooches, and earrings and removed a charm bracelet from the wrist of a bride doll. "This is pretty, and it's silver."

Each of the charms represented an aspect of Christmas: a tree, a candy cane, a star, a wreath, a bell, and a sleigh, no larger than a thimble.

"You could have it cut off the chain and wear it around your neck like a pendant," Nicola said, holding it up to the light. "It'll be unique."

"I'm not into miniatures," Annica said.

"Well then I'm afraid we can't help you." Nicola looked genuinely sorry, an act, I felt sure. "But we have lots of sleighs made from other materials. Gold, china, glass, crystal, and wood. I think variety makes a collection special."

She was probably right, but that was beside the point.

"Are you expecting any to come in?" I asked. "Silver sleighs, that is."

"Not this year. Try again next Christmas."

A loud voice boomed over the murmurings of the shoppers and the strains of the wassailing song. "Which way to the silver sleighs?"

Sixteen

"It's Brent!"

Annica's face brightened as she spied him in the doorway. She waved and he returned her smile. As he strode toward us, he towered over the other customers. With his green leather jacket and dark red hair, both liberally sprinkled with snow, he looked like a person of some importance.

I didn't think we'd come to the shop at the same time, all wanting to buy silver sleighs, but maybe that would work to our advantage. On the other hand, faced with multiple requests for the same item, Nicola might grow suspicious.

She stared at Brent with a look of instant interest mixed with admiration. Brent usually garnered such looks from women.

"Hi, Jennet—Annica," he said. "Are you guys doing some last-minute Christmas shopping?"

"I am," I said, as Annica appeared to be tongue-tied. "For myself. I collect silver sleighs and thought this would be the ideal place to find one."

"That's a coincidence," he said. "So am I. I want something special, though. A sterling silver sleigh with eight reindeer attached. Where are you keeping them, Miss...?

"Nicola." Our salesgirl came back to earth. "I was just explaining to your friends here that we don't have any left."

That wasn't exactly what she had told us.

"Did you ever?" he asked.

"I suppose so. It's kind of late in the season. The seasonal items are flying off the shelves. We do have a variety of other Christmas-themed gifts, though. I can help you find something..."

"Excuse me, ladies. Miss Nicola..." Taking her arm, Brent led her a short distance away from us. They were close enough that I could hear voices, but I couldn't make out what they were saying, which was rare in Brent's case.

He pulled a card out of his pocket. After a moment's hesitation, Nicola took it, gave him a coy smile, and hurried back to the Christmas tree in the center of the shop.

Brent strolled back to us, his eyes agleam with triumph.

"What did you say to her?" I asked.

"I offered her a little bonus if she could find me the kind of sleigh I described. Strictly under the table."

"Ingenious," I said. "How much?"

"That's my secret."

"It might just work," I said.

"She can't figure out why suddenly everybody wants a silver sleigh."

"Everybody?"

"You, me, Annica..."

"Anyone else?"

"I'm quoting her. She didn't elaborate. It might be us three or more."

I suspected I might not know everything about the stolen antique. Or maybe one of my friends had already visited the store.

"I told her I'd be back tomorrow, same time," Brent said. "Who knows? You might have your sleigh back by then."

"It occurs to me that a lot of money is exchanging hands over this one little antique," I said.

Brent patted my arm. "Santa Claus aims to please. Now that I'm here, I want to buy a pair of earrings for a pretty lady I know."

He eyed Annica's jingle bells. "Something like what you're wearing, Annica, but a little quieter. Something fancy with more sparkle. How about if you gals help me choose?"

Gals? Annica looked at me.

"The jewelry is over this way," she said.

Her voice lacked its characteristic lilt. Come to think of it, her brightness had begun to dim.

Vintage Jewelry appeared to be a popular counter. Brent found us a place where we could gaze to our hearts' content. Dazzled by emeralds, sapphires, rubies, and diamonds, I imagined that I was selecting a present for myself. That ruby ring in its intricate gold setting, for example. I'd always wanted a ruby. I slipped it on my finger and glanced at the price tag. I'd assumed the jewels were paste and was surprised to realize that they were genuine and very pricey.

Oh, to have unlimited funds!

Was that what I really wanted? I thought of the jewelry Crane had given me over the years, those treasured gifts meant just for me. No, I didn't need riches and precious stones to be happy.

The ruby ring would be nice to have, though.

Put it back.

"Emeralds would suit her," Brent said. "She has the most beautiful eyes." He picked up a chandelier creation of emeralds set in silver.

Nine hundred dollars!

"I'll take these," he said. "Are you girls finished shopping?"

"I've done what I came for," I said.

We accompanied Brent to the cash register where I discovered that the other salesgirl was named Noelle. No surprise there. We waited while Brent whipped out his charge card and told her he'd wrapped the gift himself.

Without anything else to attend to, I watched the shoppers, listened to the music—*"The Little Drummer Boy"*—and kept my eye on the door to the back room. It was closed. Secretive, sinister. Even if it were open, I couldn't think of any way to access it.

I wondered if my stolen sleigh was hidden there amid the boxes and shadows. Would Brent's bribe convince Nicola to defy Gloria and secure it for him? I also wondered where the other Christmas ladies were. Holly, Carol, and Gloria. The shop had a surprising turnover for its small size and off-the-beaten-path location.

Brent shoved the package and receipt into his pocket and addressed us. "How would you girls like to go someplace and have a drink now?"

"It's too cold," I said. "Besides, I have to go home. Crane will be sending out a search party."

"A hot drink, I meant," he said. "One of those Christmas-spiked coffees or hot chocolate. Annica?"

"Well…" She hesitated, no doubt thinking of the emerald earrings and the pretty girl with the beautiful eyes who would wear them.

"You have the evening free," I reminded her. "Remember, you finished *Jane Eyre*."

What could she say?

"That sounds good, Brent. I accept."

~ * ~

I had stayed too long at The Silver Sleigh. The dogs would be anxious. Crane would be worried. I hoped the blueberry pie in the trunk and the casserole, one of my successes, would distract him.

100

From now on, I'd resist the temptation to make a stop on the way home. Unless that stop was at Clovers.

The snow continued as I drove back to Foxglove Corners. It was still fluffy, still atmospheric. Perfect for Annica's impromptu date with Brent.

I regretted that I didn't have anything tangible to show for my visit to The Silver Sleigh. While I was waiting, I should have browsed in the vintage book section. There must be a series book with a Christmas background I didn't have.

Already planning my next trip for Saturday morning, I turned on Jonquil Lane. The lights were on, the dogs were barking, and Crane's Jeep was there, acquiring a new cover of snow. Raven dashed out to meet me as I parked behind the Jeep. She danced around my boots as I made my way up to the door, carrying the box with its enticing blueberry scent and slipped inside with me.

Barking merrily, she shook, then with an elegant play bow, invited the other collies to run through the house with her.

"I was starting to worry about you, honey," Crane said. Pulling me into his arms for a snowy kiss, he added, "Did you get held up at school?"

"No, I stopped at Clovers for this..." I laid the box on the table. "Then went to The Silver Sleigh with Annica. Sorry I'm late."

He took my coat, and I transferred the casserole to the oven. "Dinner will be ready in about a half hour."

"I fed and walked the dogs," he said. "Snow makes them hyper."

I brought rolls out of the freezer and started to make a salad. Sky detached herself from the roughhousing collies and lay down at my feet.

"You have a letter," Crane said, pointing to the stack of envelopes and catalogues on the counter. "It looks interesting."

I left the lettuce and tomatoes and picked up a long brown envelope, bulging with its contents. It had three stamps on it, more postage than was necessary. It was as if the sender wanted to ensure that it reached its destination intact.

I recognized the handwriting and the name on the return address.

"It *is* important," I said, "and totally unexpected."

I ripped open the envelope, and a key clattered down on the table. I read:

Dear Jennet,

If you're reading this, what I feared must have happened. Sue Appleton tells me you've solved a few mysteries that baffled the police. I hope you can solve one more—the mystery of my murder."

In the midst of the vibrant life that flowed around me, I held the letter so tightly that I crumpled the edge. I became aware of Crane's gray eyes focused on me, of the cold in a kitchen that had been cozy just a few minutes ago.

I reached down to touch Sky's head. She was so soft, so warm, so alive.

"This is a letter from the dead," I said. "It's from Rosalyn Everett."

Seventeen

"Listen," I said and read the first paragraph again, this time aloud.

Crane's reaction was predictable. I'd said the dangerous word. Murder.

"I don't like the sound of that," he said.

"Let's see what she says." I read on.

Lately, I've become aware that somebody is trying to kill me. There've been three suspicious accidents. They might have been innocent, but I don't think so. I've made a few enemies over the years. After the first accident, I started keeping a journal of suspects' names and descriptions of the problems between us. A few of them involved collie people.

At the time I didn't take them seriously. Now I wonder if someone I crossed in the past is plotting against me. I feel this threatening presence everywhere, even in my own home. It grows stronger every day.

If you're reading this, I must be dead. Sue has a key to my house. The key I enclosed with this letter opens the top right drawer of my desk in the living room. You'll find the journal there. I trust you can bring my killer to justice. If you do, be assured you'll have my sincere gratitude and blessings from the grave.

It was signed Rosalyn Everett. There was no date on the page. She could have written this letter anytime and in any location. If she felt threatened in her own home, that might explain why she chose to disappear and make up that story about losing time.

How strange it all was. How creepy. I folded the letter and slipped it back in the envelope for safekeeping.

"Well," Crane said. "What's your first impression?"

"It wasn't what I expected. I hoped Rosalyn would tell us why she disappeared. Where she'd been. Where she is now."

"In her grave," Crane said. "Second impression?"

"That she's as nutty as the proverbial fruitcake. Should I say 'was'?"

"Depending on if you believe her."

"At this point, I don't know."

"She sounds paranoid," he said.

"To say the least. It would make more sense if she'd gone to the police with her suspicions and asked for protection. Not wait until it's too late and write a letter to someone she hardly knew."

"I don't know what the police would have done," Crane said. "She was so vague."

"Maybe the person who forwarded the letter can shed some light on the matter."

"What are *you* going to do, Jennet?" he asked.

I picked up the key. My purse was the safest place for it. "I'll call Sue, of course. We'll go over to River Rose together. We'll have to track down the person who sent the letter. But not until after Christmas. I'm interested, but I have enough mysteries on my plate. If Rosalyn Everett is dead, there's no urgency."

Those were my future plans. My immediate priority was dinner. The casserole should be ready in a few minutes, but the salad was in the counter in pieces; and the rolls needed to go in the oven.

I placed the letter in the basket on the counter and told Crane about Brent's ingenious plan to retrieve the sleigh.

While I mixed the salad, I said, "Leonora is going to go shopping for a silver sleigh tomorrow. Sooner or later, those Christmas ladies will realize that we're on to them."

"That's when this harassment will get even more dangerous."

"So far it isn't," I said. "Brent is a generous man. I don't think he's thinking in terms of ten or twenty dollars. But if the sleigh is so important to them, I can't see a salesgirl sabotaging their plans."

"You should know one way or the other tomorrow."

"Yes."

I imagined the stolen antique shining on the mantel with all the candles lit. That would make my Christmas merry indeed.

~ * ~

In truth, I wasn't eager to discover the identity of Rosalyn Everett's so-called killer. What I wanted to know was why she had vanished, leaving her collies with no one to care for them, which would have resulted in their deaths. An unfortunate few of them had perished in spite of the rescue.

Was it true that she believed she'd only been gone for a few hours that first time, when it had been several days?

Nutty as a fruitcake. Having leapt into my mind, that phrase refused to leave.

I almost resented that Rosalyn had neglected to address that mystery and instead tossed another one into my lap.

To be sure, I was curious to read her journal but was willing to let it wait.

Finding the quicksilver collie, River Rose Icemaker, and coaxing him into a foster home were more important.

And Christmas is coming, the goose is getting fat...

~ * ~

On Friday we had a half day of school, then over a week of glorious free time. I would be able to put the finishing touches on the house's holiday décor, go Christmas shopping, and perhaps pay another visit to The Silver Sleigh. I had faith in Brent's powers of persuasion and his bribe but believed that heaven helps those who help themselves.

Last night I had dreamed of the silver sleigh. Well, it wasn't my lost antique. It was real, the size of Brent's sleigh, able to carry three or four people or one Santa Claus and his sack of gifts.

The dream sleigh was made of silver with the scroll-and-flower pattern I remembered. And were there eight reindeer pulling it?

Yes! I'd forgotten the deer. They looked like the ones that wandered around our house, driving the dogs to a frenzy as they searched for food, but they were silver as well, life-sized animals to pull the sleigh.

The elegant silver sleigh stood in a deep snowdrift outside the kitchen door. It shone in the moonlight, looking as if it had just been polished.

Waiting for me.

~ * ~

Sue Appleton was unimpressed by Rosalyn Everett's revelations.

"I don't believe a word of it," she said.

This might be a long conversation. I took the cell phone into the living room and made myself comfortable in the rocker. Halley followed me and nudged my free hand for a reassuring pat.

"You don't think someone was trying to kill her?" I asked.

"I doubt it, but she could have convinced herself of that. This isn't the woman I thought I knew. First she abandons her collies; then she concocts this melodrama. If Rosalyn is truly dead, though, then may she rest in peace."

"So you don't want to help me investigate?"

"I didn't say that. Just not now. I don't have a single hour to spare."

"After Christmas then," I said.

"When we have time to do it properly. Is there any news about Icy or Sparkle?"

"None so far. Crane has stopped at River Rose several times but didn't see either one. Once he left cubes of roast beef on the porch. They were gone the next day. That could just mean that some hungry woodland creature gobbled them up."

"Poor Icy. Well, one day we may find him."

I said goodbye and thought again of Rosalyn's beautiful blue merle collie living in the winter woods. I hoped he'd been the creature to find the beef, hoped he had a warm place to nest and would one day allow himself to be approached.

Icy and Sparkle had to be the two most elusive dogs in Colliedom.

A new thought surfaced. What if Icy were waiting for Rosalyn to come home?

I brushed the sad thought away, while knowing it could be the answer. More than one loyal dog has waited for an owner who never comes back. Some of them on the owner's grave.

All we could do was keep looking and leave an occasional meal of the foods most pleasing to a canine.

And hope.

Eighteen

The next day the flurry of activity involved in preparing the December edition of the *Marston Courier* for sale distracted me from thoughts of haunted happenings in my classroom. The issue with its festive green ink and Gwendolyn's whimsical artwork was our Christmas present to the school and an excuse to turn the entire period over to reading the stories and features.

As a special promotion, Gwendolyn had drawn an extra holly berry on the fourth page of one of the papers. Whoever bought that copy would win a one pound box of chocolates with a large marshmallow Santa in the center.

"This is the best *Courier* I've seen in a long time," I told the class as I handed out manila envelopes to Lana, the Circulation Manager, who had drawn up a list of sellers. Each envelope contained eight quarters for change. The sale would take place during fourth hour in the cafeteria. Afterward, I would count the money and leave it in the school's safe until after the holiday.

Gwendolyn alone was unhappy. "My elf looks pathetic," she said. "It's so sad."

"I don't think so." In a reversal of our usual procedure, Gwendolyn had written a short poem to accompany the drawing.

"It makes me unhappy just to look at it," she added.

"Don't look at it, then." Maddy, supposedly Gwendolyn's best friend, had a sharp tongue.

"Read my Christmas memory if you want to see unhappy," Kimberly piped up.

"You did an outstanding job on the artwork, Gwendolyn," I said. "You all did your best work. I'm proud of each and every one of you."

I looked around the room. It was a typical class-in-winter scene. Bulletin boards reflected the season with silver paper bells and candle cut-outs. Desks had migrated from their regular rows, a privilege I only allowed in Journalism. Everybody was quieter than usual, most engrossed in reading the Creative Writing section that contained a comic strip. Outside, a light snow fell.

I treasured the rare quiet time in the midst of pre-vacation turmoil. Then in the silence I heard a muffled sound. Someone was sobbing and trying to hide it. Sara. Her *Courier* open on the desk, she was fumbling in her purse.

She'd moved her desk onto the haunted tiles! In the haunted zone.

I walked quietly up to her, careful to stay a safe distance from danger. "Is something the matter, Sara?"

She shook her head, wiping her eyes and smearing black mascara on her face.

"Are you ill?" No answer. "Do you need to be excused?"

She nodded and tore off a piece of notepaper. Quickly I wrote a hall pass for her, and she hurried out of the room, clutching her purse, still sobbing. Naturally her classmates had noticed. They stole curious glances at her as she made her awkward exit.

"What's wrong with her?" Lara asked.

Mason, always ready with an answer, usually a wise one, said, "Christmas is an emotional time."

I glanced down at Sara's desk. The *Courier* was opened to the Creative Writing section. To Gwendolyn's illustration for her elf poem. Sara's tears blurred the little creature's face.

~ * ~

"Did you find out why Sara was upset?" Leonora asked.

"No." I locked my door and we proceeded down the hall, which was understandably deserted. The last bell had rung ten minutes ago.

"She never came back to class," I said. "I sent a note to the office and one to her counselor."

As her teacher, I had to cover myself in this manner. Sara was my responsibility during that period. If she were to leave the building and (God forbid) meet with an accident, I'd be in great trouble.

"She might have a problem at home," Leonora said.

"I'll talk to her the next time I see her, but that won't be until vacation is over. Her class doesn't meet tomorrow."

We reached the cafeteria with its wall of windows. It was a little like walking through Alice's Wonderland at Christmastime, courtesy of Art Club volunteers. They had painted a scene from that classic novel, written in 1865, on each window and included Christmas symbols among Lewis Carroll's characters.

In a way, I was going to miss Marston High School during Christmas vacation. Scandalous thought! In another way, I wouldn't. Because there was an obvious reason for Sara's distress.

A scattering of teens lingered in the cafeteria, reluctant to leave the school at the end of the day. After classes, they hung out at the tables, socializing and drinking pop. No one was close enough to overhear our conversation.

"I let the kids move out of their seats in Journalism," I said. "Sara ended up sitting at *that* desk."

"Well, did the floor move?"

"Not a bit. She was reading Gwendolyn's poem, or looking at the elf she drew. Probably both."

"I meant to tell you your paper was exceptional this month," Leonora said. "And no, I'm not missing the point or changing the subject. I saw Gwendolyn's elf, and it didn't alter my mood."

"But that's what happened to Sara."

"Because she sat in that particular spot?"

"What else am I to think?" Something was bothering me, a new and disturbing thought. "When I approved the layout, I didn't notice that the elf looked unusual."

"Unusual how?"

"Sad," I said. "You know, elves should be jolly, as in A Jolly Old Elf."

"I hope you're not suggesting that the elf changed its expression by itself after you okayed it. We're talking about a kid's drawing, Jen."

Hearing Leonora's reaction, I had to admit my fear sounded far-fetched. The situation was sufficiently puzzling and frightening. Why add another layer to it?

"I'm just thinking that now we have three people who have been affected by something when they're in that place," I said.

"Change the furniture then. You're in charge. Have five rows instead of six."

"The haunted space will still be there. As an aisle."

"You're right. Then I don't know."

We reached the exit. I pulled my hood up and surveyed the snow through which we'd have to make our way. Three yards to the car, one snowy hour-long commute, then home. I could do this.

"Gwendolyn, you—and an enchanted elf," Leonora said. "I don't know what to say."

"Neither do I."

Fortunately tomorrow was a half day of school with shortened classes. Traditionally this was one of the happiest days of the school year with kids exchanging presents, candy cane messages delivered by National Honor Society members, and Principal Grimsley in his Santa Claus hat.

After tomorrow, I could move the mystery at Marston High School a few spaces down on my priority list.

~ * ~

That evening after dinner, Brent handed me a narrow green striped box. "Mission unaccomplished," he said. "It's a sleigh, and it's sterling silver. But not the one you lost."

I opened the lid and lifted out the sleigh. Light green popcorn spilled down on the rug. Misty pounced on it. Crane moved quickly to sweep it out of her way.

The sleigh lacked the delicate scroll-and-flower design on the sides or any ornamentation whatsoever, and it had two reindeer instead of eight. The cookie cutter kind.

"It's an attractive piece," Crane said. "Maybe you should start a collection, Jennet."

"I paid Nicola the bribe money anyway," Brent said. "But I suspect a trick. She knew the sleigh I wanted. I'll swear to that. They're all in it together."

"They're clever at this game they're playing with us."

"We'll just have to be more clever," Brent said. "Or is it cleverer? Jennet? You're the English teacher."

"More clever," I said. "I think. I don't have all the answers, Brent. I wish I did."

Brent picked up Misty and settled her on his lap. She gave him a sweet collie kiss. "Your puppy is getting heavy, Jennet," he said.

"Misty isn't a puppy anymore. She acts like she is, though."

He set Misty on the floor and she promptly tried to climb back in his lap.

"I haven't seen that toy goat she used to carry around lately," Brent said. "Did she outgrow it?"

"Now that you mention it, I haven't seen it either. I gave her one of the stuffed rabbits you bought for your Christmas delivery. She'd already torn it."

"Poor Misty," he said. "Did you lose your goat?"

She gave a pathetic little whimper. Sometimes I was sure she understood what we were saying to her. An idle thought drifted into my mind. Misty and I had both lost something we'd treasured. A pet store toy and an antique decoration.

So, what was the significance of that? I couldn't think of any.

"Thanks for trying, Brent," I said. "I'd love this sleigh if I'd never seen the other one."

"I'll come up with something else," he said.

"Camille and Gilbert went to the antique shop separately today. They heard the same story from Gloria. They have sleighs made of every other material under the sun except sterling silver."

"Where do you want the sleigh, honey?" Crane asked.

"Under the tree, I guess. Let me pay you for it, Brent."

Crane pulled out his wallet. "I'll take care of that."

"Put your money away," he said. "Consider it an extra Christmas gift. I'd like a slice of whatever smells so good, though."

"You've got it," I said. "Banana cream pie."

"My favorite!"

Departing from his usual habit, Brent had missed our dinner hour. I made a fresh pot of coffee and reset the dining room table. There was no reason Crane and I couldn't celebrate the approach of Christmas with another piece of pie, and while we ate we could brainstorm. This setback made me all the more determined to find the real silver sleigh. There had to be a way to do it.

Nineteen

Once winter recess vacation began, the days grew shorter, whole hours vanishing in seconds as the calendar raced toward the twenty-fifth. One visit to the Maplewood Mall was sufficient for me to finish my shopping, which included the perfect gift for Crane. In a single trip to Blackbourne's Grocers, I gathered the items I wanted for our Christmas dinner.

I was going to bake a ham and make a mountain of potato salad, enough to last us for three days. Rolls, rye bread, and a cherry pound cake would complete the menu.

On Christmas Eve, Crane and I were attending Brent's party. No cooking that day, not even a dish to bring as Brent was having his affair catered.

Amid the hustle and bustle of last-minute preparations for the holiday, Sue Appleton stopped by for a visit. She had news, brought to her from one of Rosalyn Everett's neighbors, Cecily Lane.

"I've come to the conclusion that River Rose is haunted," Sue said. "Although I don't believe in ghosts."

We sat at the oak table in the kitchen with mugs of steaming tea and a Christmas coffeecake that Camille had shaped as a wreath and decorated with white icing and green sugar. The collies sat in a semicircle near the doorway watching over the refreshments lest a wayward crumb fall on the floor.

"Did she hear the howling dog again?" I asked. "Because that was either Sparkle or Icy. Or maybe a coyote-wolf mix."

"Cecily saw a ghost, she says. She was standing at her kitchen window when she noticed a woman in a fancy white dress, no coat or anything, walking away from her across the field toward Rosalyn's house."

I paused, my fork halfway to my mouth. "This woman was wearing just a dress in the wintertime?"

The temperature had hovered slightly below freezing for several days. No one would step out of the house for even a second, let alone go for a frigid winter walk without protection from the elements.

"Cecily says it looked like a ball gown or a wedding dress. It had elbow-length poufy sleeves and a bell-shaped skirt with what looked like a shawl, but that was part of the dress. Keep in mind that this was a back view."

"So Cecily never saw her face?"

"No, but the woman's hair was dark and done in an elaborate upsweep style. Rosalyn used to arrange her hair like that for special occasions, like collie club dinners."

"How could she see all this detail from inside her house?" I asked.

"That's what's so strange. She said the woman appeared to be up close and far away at the same time. Like Cecily was seeing her through a telescope. Weird, huh?"

"Downright ghostly. So this would be the spirit of Rosalyn Everett?"

"That's what Cecily thinks. I'm inclined to agree with her."

I couldn't resist saying, "Even though you don't believe in ghosts."

"I simply can't think of any other explanation."

"Well, a spirit wouldn't need a warm winter coat," I said, looking out the window at the frosty landscape. "Anyone else would."

"Cecily hurried out to her porch and took a picture with her cell phone. All she got was a white mist."

"What happened then?"

"You know how windy it's been? The wind kept blowing the snow, and the woman seemed to vanish into it. At least Cecily couldn't see her anymore."

Maybe she never had, I thought. Blowing snow could create illusions. The mystery of her neighbor's disappearance most likely preyed on Cecily's mind. Still, I wanted to believe in the ghost. Cecily's detailed description was uncanny, as was the telescope effect. In the past I'd sensed that River Rose was haunted. In dealing with the supernatural, I would be traversing familiar territory.

I said, "That sounds like something a spirit would do. Vanish in the snow-mist."

"It means Roz really is dead," Sue said. "I'm sorry I thought that letter was just another one of her tricks. She really was afraid for her life."

Sue drained her cup and said, "Rest in peace, Rosalyn." After a pause she added, "She can't be in peace, though, can she?"

"Not if she's walking in the snow," I said.

"I have my riding students' party tomorrow and a thousand and one things to do," Sue said. "Are you busy the day after Christmas?"

I glanced at the calendar. All the spaces after December 25th were blank.

"Not that I know of," I said.

"Let's go over to River Rose and get that journal. Then we'll see if we can track down the person who forwarded Rosalyn's mail to us."

"That's what Rosalyn wants me to do," I said. "To find out who murdered her."

I cut Sue another piece of Camille's Christmas cake. "You don't sound like a non-believer to me, Sue," I said.

A faint blush stole over her face.

"I always thought there had to be a rational explanation for every mysterious thing that happened. But who else... I should say *what* else would go strolling through a snowy field in a long white gown without a jacket or hood?"

"Only Rosalyn Everett, Spirit," I said.

She was crossing a field to her property, dressed in white. Where was she going? To her now-uninhabited house or into the woods? And from what shade-begotten place had she come?

This, I told myself, was the mystery I'd been waiting for.

A nudge on my hand drew my attention downward. Candy had ventured near the table and was eyeing the small piece of coffeecake left on my plate. As for the other collies, they had moved inches closer.

I poured us more tea and, mindful of pleading brown eyes, set biscuits on the floor for the dogs. They fell on them, seeming to merge into one multi-colored crunching entity.

"It's too bad Cecily's picture didn't come out," Sue said. "Those cell phone cameras are usually pretty accurate."

"I think you need a special kind of camera to photograph spirit activity."

"You're the expert, Jennet," Sue said. "Is there any chance this wasn't a ghost but a real live woman trespassing on River Rose land?"

A refugee from a ball? Or a wedding?

I thought again of all the layers needed to survive a Michigan winter. Of a long white ball gown, no doubt made of satin or silk or some light fabric. Of a killer wind raging through the snowfields and sub-zero temperatures.

"None whatsoever," I said.

~ * ~

On the morning before Christmas Eve, I found myself in The Silver Sleigh. It was Annica's idea. Crane had expressed a wish for a turkey dinner from Clovers with all the trimmings. Coincidentally, when I arrived at the restaurant, Annica's shift was just ending. Fortunately turkey was one of the day's specials. They also had a dozen pumpkin tarts in the dessert carousel.

"Let's see if the antique shop has any silver sleighs in," Annica said. The sparkle in her eyes rivaled the shine of her crystal star eardrops.

So here we were, turkey dinners and tarts stashed in the trunk, jostling with the last-minute shoppers for space at the counters. At least twenty people stood in line at the cash register where Holly was ringing up purchases, mostly small gifts. She handed out a tiny package to each customer, explaining that it was a holiday thank-you gift from the shop.

The music was a trifle louder today.

Silver bells, silver bells... It wasn't unpleasant, though, and in the background I heard the subtle ringing of bells. It wasn't part of the music.

Attired in bright Christmas green, Nicola was waiting on a customer at the antique jewelry boutique, and the door to the back room was ajar.

At last!

I sauntered slowly toward it while Annica veered to the display of sleighs. From across the room, I saw her lifting the doll in the red dress, touching its long dark curls.

Handling the expensive merchandise! That should bring Gloria MacBride to her side.

I inched closer to the door with no particular plan and peered inside. Stacks of boxes rose on either side of a makeshift aisle that wound back into darkness. There was Gloria's antique desk, covered with papers, and the Queen Anne chairs with the old rose upholstery.

And there was Gloria MacBride coming around one of the towers of boxes. She looked like an evil spirit in a long black dress with a sparkly shawl draped over her shoulder. An antique medallion consisting of large ruby stones and gold dropped down to the low V-neckline that barely covered her ample bust.

"Come on in, Mrs. Ferguson," she said. "I've been expecting you." Her blood-red lips curved in a smile that was anything but welcoming.

Evil spirit? Vampire.

I didn't move.

"I don't want to intrude," I said. "I was just looking. Just wondering if you received any silver sleighs since my last visit."

"Now that's funny. All of a sudden, everybody wants to buy a silver sleigh. Why is that, I wonder?"

Think fast.

She had me at a disadvantage. I'd been hoping to see her again but didn't think it would happen today. Inspiration struck.

"Is it so surprising?" I asked. "Snow and sleighs and Christmas go together."

"Have you reconsidered selling our heirloom back to us?" she asked.

Don't let on that you don't have it, I told myself. *And why did she want to know that if she'd stolen it? And how should I answer her?*

Simply, I decided.

"No, I haven't."

"But now you want to buy another one?" she asked.

I was rapidly tiring of this going-nowhere word game we were playing.

She moved to the door and closed it firmly behind her.

"For my collection," I said. "I like that sleigh so much I decided to buy more of them, new ones every year."

"Every now and then people bring back Christmas ornaments after the holiday," Gloria said. "Sometimes we take them back, sometimes we don't. It depends. If you decide you don't want the sleigh after Christmas, when you're taking down your decorations, my previous offer stands. That sleigh is just a pretty decoration to you. To us, it means much more."

Gloria had thoroughly confused me with these comments. She didn't sound like she had the stolen antique in her possession, although I could have sworn...

If she didn't have it, who did? Who had broken into our house and left that inexpensive imitation in its place? And why? I had been so sure I knew where to lay the blame.

"I'll think about it," I said.

What I thought, though, was this: Could another ghostly happening possibly have landed in my lap?

Twenty

I made my escape and joined Annica, who stood enthralled in a dazzling surround of antique jewelry. The shop seemed even busier than it had when we'd arrived, and the line at the cash register was longer. Another bell song was playing.

Hark! How the bells, Sweet silver bells, All seem to say, Throw cares away...

If only I could...

Although I didn't turn around, I felt certain that Gloria MacBride was keeping a watchful eye on me. Maybe she thought I was going to help myself to one of the smaller antiques like the glittering star brooch in Annica's hand.

Turnabout is fair play, for I'd been thinking of Gloria as a thief.

"Are you ready to leave?" I asked Annica.

"Now? I haven't told anyone I'm looking for a silver sleigh yet."

"There's been a change of plans. I'll tell you about it outside."

She hesitated. "Wait, I'm going to buy a Christmas pin."

They were whimsical holiday novelties: trees, reindeer, wreaths, and snowmen sparkling with multi-color stones. Mixed in with pricier antiques, they looked every bit as appealing.

"Which one?" I asked. "They're all so pretty."

"The gingerbread man. I'll wear it at Clovers." She picked it up and replaced the star brooch she'd been admiring.

"Well, you get in line, and I'll see if I can find a good book. Something appropriate for the season."

I looked for Gloria but didn't see her, and the door to the back room was shut. Feeling as if the door to the mystery's solution had also closed, I allowed the music to coax me into a holiday mood.

Vintage and contemporary books, all Christmas-themed, lay in merry disarray on a mahogany dining room table, sharing space with red candles in crystal candlesticks, some of which had been lit.

The Bobbsey Twins at the Ice Carnival, The Secret of the Musical Tree, The Melodeon, Louisa May Alcott's Christmas Treasury—Told under the Christmas Tree...

Ah, that last was a charmer. I'd received a copy years ago but had no idea what became of it. This one was in excellent condition. I opened it, recognizing the beloved old selections. *Pegasus and the Star. The Friendly Beasts, The Fir Tree...* And the quaint illustrations. Just as I remembered.

Almost lost in the din of multiple conversations in progress, a soft voice broke through my nostalgia.

"I don't see any silver sleighs. Do you think we should buy crystal? This one is nice"

A deeper voice replied, *"No. It has to be sterling silver."*

Soft Voice again: *"I don't know where else to look. We've been all over, and we're running out of time."*

"We'll have to think of some other place. Crystal isn't an option."

Still holding the book, I glanced over to the display of sleighs, trying to determine which of the women milling around me had spoken.

Could I approach strangers, confess that I'd overheard their conversation and ask them why they wanted a silver sleigh?

Yes.

They'd think I was crazy.

No matter. Take the chance.

However, no one was looking at sleighs at the moment. Nowhere did I see two women together. How could they have blended into the crowd so rapidly, practically between one minute and the next? They might have separated as Annica and I had.

At any rate, the opportunity had presented itself only to slip through my fingers.

Annica was in line with three people ahead of her and two behind. It seemed that the front door was constantly opening and closing. People streamed out, laden with packages. Others came in, shivering and stamping the snow from their feet. The bells on the door rang and rang and rang.

A faint throbbing at the back of my head alerted me to pain on the way.

Suddenly I wanted to leave the shop as soon as possible. Should I buy the book in my hand? Yes, to add to my vintage collection. I took my place at the end of the line, remembering my first purchase at the antique shop, the sleigh.

Why couldn't I let the mystery go? It seemed as if I'd been on the trail of the silver sleigh for months instead of days. Every time I thought the solution was in sight, something came up to prove me wrong, like my suspicion that Gloria or one of her minions was responsible for the theft.

But who else had been outspoken about her desire to retrieve the silver sleigh? Therefore, who could have broken into my house and stolen a Christmas decoration from the mantel, leaving an unremarkable imitation in its place?

A new thought came to me. Was my focus in the right place? Could there be a clue in the cookie cutter sleigh? It was possible.

I gave myself a mental shake. If I kept this up, I would spoil Christmas, rip the holly and mistletoe and good cheer right out of its heart.

I knew some mysteries are never solved. Perhaps there was nothing significant about the brief exchange I'd overheard. According to Gloria, everyone wanted to buy a silver sleigh, apparently not only the people I'd enlisted to harass the antique shop ladies.

And why not? As I'd told her, snow and sleighs and Christmas went together.

So let it go.

The person in front of me stepped away from the cash register, clutching a large shopping bag crammed with packages. I pulled a twenty dollar bill out of my wallet, wondering if my modest purchase would entitle me to one of the thank-you gifts.

And I resolved to stop thinking about my stolen antique. For a while.

~ * ~

"Since we're so close, let's stop at River Rose," Annica said. "Maybe we'll see the lady in white."

I glanced at my watch. What did I have to do today? Take care of the collies. Dinner and dessert were covered.

Still, my head hurt.

Well, we'd only stay a few minutes. Maybe a few minutes breathing in cold, clear air would cure my headache.

"Based on your description of her dress, I think the ghost might be a forsaken bride," Annica said.

A bride and not Rosalyn Everett? I'd never thought of that. The ghost of a bride left at the altar?

"It's the right kind of weather for a ghost to walk," I said. "Wind blowing the snow around, light mist forming…"

"Snow fog," Annica added. "If I were a ghost I'd hate to keep walking. I'd find a cozy house and settle into some nice dark corner."

Discarding Annica's bride theory, I assumed that the lady was Rosalyn heading for her yellow ranch house—going home at last. Still, I recalled another ghostly experience I'd had in which the apparition had mostly roamed up and down the hall of the Spirit Lamp Inn.

Dark hall or snowy field. Who could know what roads and by-roads a restless spirit would walk?

Just ahead, Rosalyn's kennel sign waved in the wind, directing the traveler to an enterprise that no longer existed.

Every time I visited River Rose, it looked more than ever like what it had become: a windswept, abandoned property, overlooked by dark woods at the top of the slope behind the house. Bereft and lonely.

A haunted place.

I came to a stop in front of the house and let the car idle.

"It's so quiet," Annica murmured. "Like we just drove to the end of the world."

Something moved. Alongside the house, a chunk of snow detached itself from the landscape and dashed toward us. It took the shape of a white collie with a tricolor head. Fur whipping in the wind, tail wagging madly, she skidded to a stop at the car.

"Sparkle!"

I opened the door as Annica reached in the back for the bag of Christmas cookies she'd brought from Clovers. Thank heavens for bells sprinkled with green sugar and gingersnaps.

She handed one to me. "Give her this."

There was, however no need for a bribe. Sparkle leaped into my lap, slamming me sideways against Annica. The gingersnap tumbled to the floor, unlamented. Ears flattened, yipping joyously, Sparkle showered me with collie kisses. In return, I hugged her, making contact with myriads of burrs that had attached themselves to her snowy coat.

Our errant rescue had returned, come out of the snow, as easily as she had slipped out of my hands on that long ago day at River Rose. Long ago? While it seemed like longer, we'd lost her only weeks ago.

"What do we do now?" Annica asked.

"We put her in the back and take her home. Or..." I paused, considering ramifications, complications I'd never thought of during my search for her. Such as six collies, one husband, and a houseful of holiday temptations. "We'll take her to my house for a little while. Then to Sue Appleton's."

Poor Sue with her thousand and one chores, her riding students' party, and her family dinner. But she was the president of the Lakeville Collie Rescue League and her horse farm had been our original destination.

Annica wrinkled her nose. "She has that wet dog smell."

"Grooming is the least of our concerns," I said. "She needs food and water and a trip to the vet."

"She's really liking these Christmas bells," Annica said, taking one for herself.

"I wonder what she's been eating, and I wonder..." Before turning the car around and heading for the road, I took one last long look at Rosalyn's property. "I wonder where the quicksilver collie, Icy, is?"

"Not here or we'd see him."

All I saw was the house in its backdrop of snow and glowering woods. Still I looked. He'd be in the woods, I thought, on his own longer than Sparkle, wary and waiting for Rosalyn.

"I always thought they'd be together," I said.

With a little encouragement, Sparkle jumped happily into the back of the Taurus and lay down on the fleece throw I always kept there for the dogs. It was as if she'd never left. She might have known me all her life.

"This," Annica said as she nibbled on a cookie of her own, "turned out to be a profitable little outing. It's just too bad we didn't see the ghost."

Twenty-one

Some honeymoons are over soon after they begin.

Once home, my reunion with Sparkle took a turn for the worse. She bared her teeth at Candy, almost starting a dog fight, and sent Sky scurrying to her safe place under the kitchen table. She growled at Misty who offered her Brent's stuffed rabbit to play with.

This wasn't going to work out.

I couldn't blame Sparkle. Neither could I allow disharmony in our happy home. It was the night before Christmas Eve, and I desperately needed holiday peace and quiet.

When Sparkle pounced on Gemmy, who'd had the audacity to lap water from the dogs' pail, I locked her in my sewing room with a bowl of water to herself and a dish of kibble and called Sue Appleton.

"I have good news for you, Sue," I said. "And bad," I added, remembering that I hadn't taken my headache medication.

"I'll take the good news first."

"Annica and I found Sparkle. Rather, she found us."

I told her the details, then painted a vivid picture of the chaos the white collie had brought to our home. Sue didn't hesitate.

"I'll be over to pick her up after dinner. It's like a Christmas miracle, isn't it?"

The miracle was howling in the sewing room. Having rejoined society, Sparkle didn't care to be separated from it. I felt sorry for her, but sorrier for Sky whom I couldn't coax out from under the table.

"I'm going to take her over to Emma Brock," Sue said. "She called the other day to tell me she's able to foster another rescue. The timing couldn't be more perfect."

I closed the cell phone. Sparkle continued to howl. Candy paced through the first story while Misty settled down with her bone.

Glad that I didn't have to assemble our dinner from scratch, I took my headache pills, drank a cup of hot tea, and settled in the rocker to wait for Crane while the lights on the Christmas tree worked their magic.

I reached for the thank-you gift from The Silver Sleigh. It was a gold-plated cake server with holly berries on the handle, worth as much, I imagined, as one vintage Christmas book.

I opened *Told under the Christmas Tree* to the story of *Pegasus and the Star* and felt myself drifting away on a wave of nostalgia. How I'd loved that tale as a child! I should light the candles, and we could have a fire in the fireplace. When Crane came home.

The collies' excitement and the slamming of the door woke me. Crane, still in his jacket, still wearing his badge and gun, knelt at the tree. A box wrapped in shiny red paper lay next to the sleigh Brent had brought us.

I got up and stretched.

All of the collies had gathered around Crane. Only Sky was missing. My heart broke for her. I'd have to start working with her all over again. Someone else would have the job of taming that little white wildcat upstairs.

"What's in the box?" I asked.

"You'll find out tomorrow," he promised. "Or should we wait till Christmas?

"Let's wait. We'll be at Brent's party tomorrow." I eyed the package, stopped short of touching it. "It looks like jewelry," I said. "A new necklace? A bracelet?"

"A surprise."

Sparkle howled. She'd been so quiet while I'd dosed. Or else I hadn't heard her. Separated from my friendly pack, she had probably fallen asleep.

"What's that?" Crane demanded, looking up at the ceiling.

I told him. "But she's leaving right after dinner. Sparkle turned out to be aggressive."

"That's why Sky is hiding."

Whether Emma had any other dogs at present I didn't know. Maybe not, if she'd volunteered to take in a rescue.

"Sue will find a forever home for her where she's the only dog," I said.

"I want to meet this collie I've been searching for. I don't know why I never saw her."

"Because she looks like snow," I said.

"Will she take my arm off if I look in on her?" he asked.

"Tell her you're with me."

I watched Crane as he locked his gun in its cabinet. In the glow of the tree lights, his fair, silver-streaked hair had a mesmerizing shine. My vacation from Marston gave me time for relaxing, reading, and romance. The three *R*'s that were important to me but often fell by the wayside during the rest of the school year.

I realized I'd slept my headache away.

"I hope you're hungry," I said. "Your turkey dinner is staying warm in the oven. I got us all the trimmings and a surprise for dessert."

"What is it?" he asked.

"You'll have to wait and see."

As we talked, the collies' eyes seemed to grow a little brighter. I'd swear they knew what 'turkey' meant. Well, they'd been smelling something delicious all afternoon and knew there'd be leftovers for them.

I'd save a generous handful for poor little Sky and one for the howler as well. Nobody, human or canine, would go hungry in our house.

~ * ~

On Christmas Eve, I baked our ham—straight from West Virginia to our oven. This gave the collies another reason to keep a vigil in the kitchen. Sky had emerged from her sanctuary, but her eyes were wary. She would never have survived in the wild.

Last night Sue had taken Sparkle with her, and peace reigned in our household again. Still, it wasn't until Brent arrived around five that Sky regained her previous confidence.

He made his usual fuss over her, and little-by-little, she came out of her shell. "Sky should get along with my little blue girl, Larkspur," Brent said. "Both of them are shy and sweet. Let's have a collie get-together when it warms up."

"That sounds like fun," I said. "Eight collies. Ten, if we invite Leonora. I'm surprised you're out and about with the party tonight."

"I hired decorators and caterers, and the sleigh is all hitched up and loaded with presents. I have plenty of time to spare."

It must be nice to be rich, I thought. *Nice to be able to play Santa Claus to Foxglove Corner's needy children.*

Brent handed me an article neatly folded. "Here, Jennet, I wanted you to see this clipping from a Maple Creek paper."

The headline read. *Switching Out Antiques,* and the color picture of a table set with china, crystal and silver was larger than the story.

131

Nestled in the embrace of evergreens and pine cones was the centerpiece. The silver sleigh I'd bought at the antique shop! Or a replica thereof.

"It's my sleigh!" I cried.

Crane came up behind me. "It sure looks like it."

I focused on the eight reindeer. Each one of them was a little different. One head tilted, another turned to the left, a right front paw raised... One of the deer was slightly smaller than the others. And there was the flower-and-scroll pattern.

"It was taken last Christmas in the dining room of the Larkin estate," Brent said. "Supposedly it's one of a kind, dating from the nineteen hundreds. This photo was used as proof that it belonged in the Larkin family. In fact, it was made for someone in the family."

"I assumed Gloria MacBride was the owner."

I recalled her story about the antique being a special possession of the shop, a kind of talisman.

"Here's the story," Brent said. "When old Melinda Larkin died at ninety-three, her heir, Mallory Larkin, arranged an estate sale. A friend of the deceased, looking to buy a memento, noticed a complete set of sterling silver, described as Joan of Arc, an International Silver pattern. The problem was that someone had substituted a much cheaper look-alike pattern in silver plate for it."

"I don't understand," I said.

"Neither do I, not entirely. It appears that someone, apparently a neighbor, David Wallace, who often looked in on Melinda, stole the authentic Joan of Arc silver, every last teaspoon of it. He swore the substitution was the only tableware he found in the house.

"Apparently this wasn't the only substitution. Someone, Wallace probably, had collected cheap figurines that were similar in appearance to the Larkin collection of Royal Doulton's. There was an inexpensive replica of a Duncan Phyfe table. There were lookalike prints in place of original oil paintings. In other words, all the valuable authentic pieces were changed for articles worth a fraction of their value. The picture of the table set with the sleigh was offered as proof by Mallory Larkin's lawyer.

"It's proof that this happened, but not that the neighbor is guilty," I said.

"Wallace had access to the house on a regular basis. Plus he got the items together for the sale. Toward the end of her life, Melinda pretty much stayed in her room upstairs."

"What about a maid or cook or visiting nurse?

"Melinda had them. Wallace says that if anything is missing, one of them must be the guilty party."

"Of course he'd say that. I guess I'm obtuse, but I still don't understand what this has to do with my sleigh."

"Melinda Larkin had a ton of Christmas decorations. One of them was the sleigh you see in the picture. The cheap substitute in the estate sale looked like this…"

Brent reached under the tree and picked up the silver-plated sleigh he'd given me, the one Nicola had found for him after he'd offered her a bribe. I'd never asked him the amount of the bribe; I didn't want to know it now.

"See," Brent said. "The reindeer are all the same. Mallory Larkin claims this version could be bought at Miller's Christmas Station for twenty-five dollars."

Cookie cutter reindeer.

Amid the confusion of silver sleighs and substitutions and estate sales, I floundered, trying to form a clear picture of the truth.

"You're saying that my silver sleigh was stolen from the Larkin estate? How did it end up for sale in the antique shop?"

"That we don't know, but I'd say that Gloria MacBride or one of her cohorts does."

"I always thought she was a thief."

"More a receiver of stolen goods. A fence," he said.

This wasn't good news. It meant that the silver sleigh, wherever it was, would never be mine. If it were recovered sometime in the future, it would belong to Mallory Larkin.

Even when I'd paid a hundred dollars for it. How much, I wondered, was it actually worth?

"I'll bet quite a few of the stolen antiques found their way to The Silver Sleigh," I said.

Most likely, many of them had been purchased, wrapped as gifts, and at present lay under countless Christmas trees. Lost to the Larkin heiress.

Lost to me.

"I'm glad I have this one, then," I said. "Thank you again, Brent. I'll cherish it. By the way, someone should alert whoever's in charge of the estate. Mallory Larkin, maybe?"

"Already done," he said.

"I'm sorry, honey." Crane laid his hands on my shoulders. "I wanted to give you your sleigh back for Christmas."

"I am too, but…"

"But?"

"I can't believe this is the end of the story," I said.

Twenty-two

That evening, the Spirit of Christmas Present smiled on Foxglove Corners. As we headed to Brent's party, a light powdery snow began to fall, ensuring that we'd have a fresh white cover tomorrow, the one day when snow was essential.

I unbuttoned my coat and loosened my long knitted scarf. It was a pleasure to sit back in the passenger's seat and let Crane steer the Taurus through the snow, to know that he'd be on the lookout for leaping deer and dangerous curves. I was looking forward to Brent's party, happy for the opportunity to attend it with my handsome husband, certain that I'd be the envy of all the women present.

I wondered. Would Brent's Hunt Club pal, Alethea Venn, be there? She wasn't one of my favorite people, but this was the season of good will, after all. Wishing her a simple 'Merry Christmas' wouldn't be out of order.

Perhaps Alethea would ignore me or at least not hurl one of her thinly veiled insults at me. The source of her animosity was ridiculous, in my view. Alethea was a life-long foxhunter. Well, practically life-long. When we'd met, I was an ardent animal activist. I'd moved over into collie rescue since then, but I doubted Alethea would know the difference. Her creed was simple: Dogs were for hunting; foxes were the prey.

It could also be that Alethea was jealous. Of me, a happily married woman? Probably not. But Alethea was also delusional. She regarded Brent as her personal property, and Brent was fond of me.

Good will, Jennet, remember. 'Tis the season.

By the time we reached Brent's mansion, I'd started to wonder if my red knit dress and flashy rhinestone jewelry would be appropriate. Alethea and her friends would no doubt be draped in velvet and dripping with diamonds.

Did wealthy, fashionable women still wear velvet to holiday parties? Well, it didn't matter. Just before leaving the house, Crane had told me that I looked beautiful, and I chose to believe him.

I thought I'd left my insecurities behind long ago. It was only that I hadn't been to many parties since my marriage, or to many social occasions, for that matter.

And why was that?

"No one's going to bypass Fowler's house," Crane said, as he pulled into the driveway. "He must have strung a billion lights outside."

"Not Brent," I said. "His decorators."

Crane found a parking place alongside a Jeep. I wrapped my scarf tighter around my neck and navigated the newly-shoveled walkway, holding on to Crane's arm.

Brent's decorating team had transformed the mansion into a winter castle. He must have hired a florist too, judging from the profusion of poinsettias, carnations, roses, ferns, and holly berries that greeted us on the other side of the massive entrance. He must also have hired a band. The version of "Jingle Bell Rock" that filled the hall didn't originate in a CD player.

"Our house looks just as nice," Crane told me as we shed our snowy outer garments and I sat on the bench to unlace my boots and change into black suede heels.

"I think so," I said.

One needed only a beautifully decorated tree and a wreath or two to make the plainest house shine at Christmas. Oh, and a view of falling snow through the windows. We had all of that.

It was ten o'clock, time for most of the guests to have arrived. From my vantage point in the entrance, I could see about fifty people. There would be three times that many in the other rooms, judging from the noise of the revelers.

Brent's dogs, Chance the collie, Napoleon, and his blue merle rescue, Larkspur, wore collars with jingle bells attached. Extremely well behaved, they wandered through the crowd, soliciting pats and treats from the buffet. Attaching bells to a collar was Brent's idea. I might just steal it for our own dogs tomorrow.

Larkspur padded up to me, wagging her tail, her eyes sparkling. She looked neither quiet nor shy, and if ever a collie had a happy smile, this one did. Thanks to Brent.

Looking splendid in a hunter green shirt that set off his dark red hair, the lord of the manor welcomed his guests with a hearty handshake or a kiss, depending on the sex of the guest. I rated both a kiss and a hug, even though we'd seen each other only a few hours ago.

"Jennet, Sheriff!" Brent's booming voice all but drowned out the music. "You're late. Did you run into trouble?"

"Just getting away from the collies," I said. "They wanted to come with us."

"You should have brought them."

"All six? I don't think so."

"The place looks bright, Fowler," Crane said.

Lucy Hazen stood at Brent's side. She had forsaken her traditional black dress and gold jewelry in favor of deep cobalt blue with silver chains and bangles.

"Did you deliver all the Christmas toys?" I asked.

Lucy's eyes sparkled. Every time I saw her, she looked prettier. "It was so much fun playing Santa and Mrs. Claus. We had more than enough presents. Brent dropped some off at the hospital for the children."

"Let's check out the buffet," Crane said.

My man of few words.

We'd had sandwiches and coffee earlier, which couldn't compete with roast beef, turkey, and goose. Also I wanted to see what desserts the caterers had brought. And I could have a glass of wine or some fancy holiday drink, a green or red one. After all, I wasn't driving tonight.

We met Annica at the buffet. Crane started to fill his plate with turkey and stuffing and moved along the table while I seized the opportunity for an update.

Annica had one of the drinks I'd envisioned for myself, a tall glass of green something-or-other with ice chips floating on the surface.

"It's punch," she said. "It's minty and chocolaty."

In her short white sheath, her only jewelry a pair of emerald earrings, she stood out, even in this crowd of brightly dressed women.

Emerald earrings! The ones Brent had bought at The Silver Sleigh. That accounted for Annica's radiance. She could have outshone the blinking lights on Brent's massive, heavily decorated white pine.

"Are the earrings a present from Brent?" I said.

She nodded. "Do you know what this means?"

"Emeralds look good with red hair?"

"No, no. *I'm* the pretty lady with the beautiful eyes. Don't you remember what he said at The Silver Sleigh that day? I thought Brent had some other girl in mind. He must care about me a little."

Don't read too much into a gift, Annica.

I wished I could say that. I couldn't, of course, be the one to extinguish the light that was Annica with a dash of practicality.

"I'm sure he does," I said.

To the tune of nine hundred dollars, I thought. But then Brent's generosity wasn't news, and the emerald earrings were the perfect gift for Annica.

"Did you have anything to eat yet?" I asked.

She glanced toward the entrance. Brent had left his post, and I couldn't see Lucy; but was that Alethea Venn? She stood at the door, slipping her fur coat off her shoulders. Real fur, I thought with a sigh. No *faux* fur for Alethea. Maybe she'd skinned the fox herself...

"I'm not hungry," Annica said. "I was dancing a little. The band's good, but I always seem to run into fox hunters at Brent's parties. I don't have a lot in common with them."

"There's more to a man that his sport," I reminded her. "And don't forget. Brent is a hunter."

"Brent's different," she said.

"Well, I intend to take advantage of this spectacular spread."

"Maybe I'll try a slice of goose," she said. "You know, I've never tasted goose before. I wonder if I'll like it?"

"That's what Mrs. Cratchit served," I said.

"No, she served turkey. The biggest one in the city. Scrooge bought it for the family."

"It depends on which vision you're referring to. I'm going to have turkey." Even though we'd had it the night before last. "That's my favorite."

Annica drained her drink, and we moved leisurely along the buffet table. I filled a plate with turkey, stuffing, cranberry sauce, a helping of sweet potato casserole, a dinner roll, and added about a half cup of salad. Just for balance.

Plate in hand, I looked for Crane in the crowd that milled around the room. Glittering women in vibrant holiday colors and dapper men, some of them wearing ties with foxhounds or assorted Hunt themes. I saw Brent circulating like a good host and his dogs spreading their own brand of good cheer. The canine kind.

Swirls of red, green, silver, and gold. Flickering candlelight and Christmas music. The tinny jingle of bells...

Where was my husband?

Annica touched my arm. "Jennet, look over there— by the window."

Crane sat polishing off his dinner with gusto and talking to a woman in a Christmas green dress who held a champagne flute in her hand.

Alethea!

"She's zoomed in your man," Annica whispered.

The predator!

"Not for long," I said.

A young blond man in a tweed jacket, carrying a heaped plate, came up behind Annica. "Care to join me for dinner, Annica? We can get reacquainted."

With a fleeting glance at Crane and Alethea, and another inscrutable one at me, Annica said, "Uh— yes, I guess so."

I crossed the room and slid into the empty chair on the other side of Crane.

Say something significant!

"How's the turkey, Crane?" I asked. "Alethea."

Crane gave me a sideways grin, the kind that romance novel heroes are always bestowing on the heroine. "Good," he said.

"How charming you look tonight, Jennet," Alethea said, with a smile that anyone else would consider warm and sincere. She twirled a strand of her long auburn hair, darker than I remembered. As she did, her rings flashed in the candlelight. They were immense stones set in gold, one a sapphire, the other, a ruby.

"Are you still involved with that subversive animal rights organization?" Alethea asked. "M.A.R.A., I think they called themselves."

Remember. Good will toward men. And women as well.

"When Caroline Meilland was murdered, M.A.R.A. disbanded," I said.

She must know that.

"So you're not going around with a protest sign these days?"

"I'm in collie rescue now," I said.

"How quaint." She rose. "Well, Deputy, it's been nice chatting with you. I see our host over there. If you'll excuse me."

Crane nodded. "Alethea."

"Merry Christmas," I added and lifted a forkful of stuffing to my mouth.

It was cold.

Twenty-three

"She seems nice," Crane said.

Honestly. I thought Crane was a better judge of character. Well, he was also a man, and Alethea was a woman of many faces. I'd forgive him this time.

"Except for that comment about M.A.R.A. being a subversive organization," I said.

And her condescension. Calling collie rescue quaint. What nerve! Did she know the meaning of the word 'quaint'?

Alethea and I lived in different worlds. I was quite comfortable in mine.

"That remark was uncalled for," I said.

The music was louder in this part of the room, which was closer to the dance floor, and the melody was unfamiliar, a trifle discordant. Hardly a holiday selection. If it was, I didn't recognize it. I had to raise my voice to be heard.

"What were you two talking about?" I asked.

There was that sideways grin again.

"The weather," he said. "We're going to have a white Christmas. No doubt about it."

"What else?"

"Jennet!" Crane's frosty gray eyes sparkled. "You sound like you don't trust me."

"It's Alethea I don't trust. She knows you're my husband."

"Yes, she must know that, and she has to know that M.A.R.A. died with Caroline Meilland. Nobody's come along to take her place."

And the fox hunts continued, undisturbed.

Crane scooped up the last of his stuffing and glanced toward the buffet table. "We also talked about The Silver Sleigh. Turns out Alethea and Mallory Larkin are old school friends. Alethea wanted to know what the chances were that Mallory would have her stolen possessions returned to her. The real ones. She has no use for the shoddy imposters."

Alethea and Mallory Larkin. Now that was a surprise— and a connection.

"What did you tell her?" I asked.

"That her friend had probably seen the last of them."

"If she'd asked me, I'd have sent her to Gloria MacBride's shop."

"Alethea says Brent told them about Mrs. MacBride, and they visited the shop. Mallory Larkin didn't see anything she recognized. Of course, Mallory didn't live with her aunt. Anyway, they sold all the good stuff."

"All of it?" I thought about the expensive doll in the red dress that Annica had admired and the exquisite antique jewelry. How could it all have disappeared in a few day? More strangeness.

"The good stuff. The Larkin antiques are long gone, I'm afraid," Crane said.

"There must be a way of tracing them," I said. "Wouldn't they have kept records?"

"Not of stolen goods."

I recalled my first trip to the shop. Holly had been uncertain of the sleigh's cost. She'd consulted a notebook, which was where, presumably, she'd come up with the ninety-nine dollar price tag.

"Something strange is going on at that place," I said. "I thought so when they tried to convince me to sell the sleigh back to them. Then there are those women with the made-up Christmas names."

The music had stopped, and a merry buzz and spurts of laughter filled the gap. Crane's plate was empty. I'd been nibbling at my dinner, more interested in our conversation than food.

"I'm going back for more turkey," Crane said. "When the band's break is over, will you save a dance for me?"

I smiled. "More than one."

"Remember that," he said.

While he was gone, I finished my dinner. Even though it had grown cold while I'd quizzed him about Alethea, everything was tasty, especially the stuffing which was almost as good as mine. Now for one of those fancy desserts I'd seen on my first trip through the buffet.

~ * ~

Before I had a chance to explore the dessert assortment, Brent materialized out of the crowd and dropped into the chair Annica had recently vacated. Larkspur flopped down at his feet and licked her chops. I gave her the last piece of turkey on my plate.

"The dogs are making out like bandits tonight," he said.

"This little blue girl deserves some happiness. Kind words and petting and treats galore."

I followed this speech with gentle pats on Larkspur's soft head.

"She's really come around," Brent said. "She was scrawny and shy when I adopted her."

"I love a rescue story with a happy ending." I couldn't help thinking of Sparkle who might have a long wait for her forever home.

"Your house looks beautiful." I added. "Sort of like a palace."

"I think so, too. Where's the sheriff?"

"At the buffet."

But I didn't see him there. Where was he?

Alethea!

"This is my favorite night of the year," Brent was saying. "When the toys are all delivered. When all my best friends get together. Great food, presents, surprises in the most unlikely places... "

"And music," I said. "I'm enjoying the band. You *do* know how to keep Christmas well, Brent."

His hearty laugh rang out. Larkspur gave a start and stared at him.

"Isn't that what they said about Scrooge?" he demanded.

"I guess it is."

"What are you going to do tomorrow?" he asked.

"We're having a quiet day at home, opening presents, having company. You're welcome to stop over," I added. "There's a gift for you under our tree, and I have a good ham. Nothing as elaborate as your spread, though."

"Speaking of food, did you have enough to eat?"

"I did. I was just going to get some dessert..."

I could see them from my seat, rows on rows of delectable colorful, once-in-a-year confections.

"Did you see my train and Christmas village?" Brent asked.

I glanced at the luminous white pine. It stood in a surround of brightly wrapped presents, all of them presumably for Brent. None of them had been opened, and no train circled the tree.

"It has a room of its own," he said. "Follow the signs on the walls. 'To Brentsville.' Better still, I'll show you." He took my plate and started to rise.

A vision in bright green floated up to us. "Are you still here, Jennet?" it asked.

I looked into Alethea's ice-cold eyes. "At the party?"

"In this chair, I meant. By the wall."

Was she implying that I was a wallflower?

"I'm just leaving," I said. "If you'll excuse me, Brent, I'm going to…"

Check out your train? See if it's still snowing? Listen to the music? Choose one.

"Mingle," I said.

"See you later, Jennet," Brent said. "Save me a dance."

Okay, calm down. You handled that like an expert.

I spied Lucy across the room. She stood in front of the tree, seeming to delight in each individual ornament.

"What have you been up to, Jennet?" she asked as I approached her. "We haven't had a visit in ages."

"I'm trying to solve a couple of new mysteries," I said. "There's the case of Rosalyn Everett. Her disappearance appears to be a murder. And I haven't given up on the silver sleigh antique that was stolen from our house. Crane thinks it's hopeless," I added.

"The murder or the theft?"

"Probably both."

"I read about the Larkin antiques," Lucy said. "There was a similar incident last year at an estate sale up north. All the valuable pieces went missing and cheap imitations popped up in their place. They never did find the original ones."

"Maybe the same crooks are responsible."

"Whatever you do, don't take unnecessary chances," Lucy said. "Both situations are fraught with peril."

"Do you see danger hovering above me?" I asked.

"Not at the moment. Everything in your life is bright and clear."

"Let me know if you do," I said. "Recently a clue practically fell into my lap." I told her about Rosalyn's letter, begging me to solve her murder. "As soon as Christmas is over, Sue Appleton and I are going to pursue it."

"I'll keep my antennae polished," Lucy promised with a sly smile. "Right now I see a silver sleigh."

"Really? My antique? Can you tell me where it is?"

"Here on this branch." She pointed to a tiny silver sleigh enclosed in a snow globe, the most unusual decoration I'd ever seen. She tapped it with her finger, and the snow began to fly.

"Everybody has a silver sleigh except me," I said. Then I remembered Brent's gift and chided myself for being childish.

"I'm going to grab a bite to eat now," Lucy said.

Visions of desserts danced in my head. Yule log, plum pudding, creme caramel, cakes topped with green and red frosting.

"I'll join you," I said. "Oh, wait..."

Across the room I saw Crane deep in conversation with his friend, Lieutenant Mac Dalby, and a pretty woman who must be Joanna, the wife Mac described as perfect. I didn't know Mac was one of Brent's friends.

"I'd better grab my husband before that shameless fox hunter friend of Brent's sees him," I said.

~ * ~

The rest of the evening passed in a pleasant blur of dancing and games and scintillating conversation, everything Brent loved about Christmas. I finally got my dessert, a thick slice of Yule log which was worth waiting for. The band stepped aside to make way for a three-piece orchestra that favored classical Christmas music.

Pastime with Good Company I love and shall until I die...

I didn't see Althea, which was a gift in itself.

Brent had a present for each of his guests, an ornament from the antique shop. Was there no end to his generosity and financial resources?

At last the clock struck midnight, twelve loud bell-like chimes. At two o'clock the party wound down, the band and orchestra packed up and took their departures, and the snow continued to fall.

Christmas day was finally here.

Twenty-four

I woke to a sparkling Christmas wonderland. In the absence of the wind that more often than not blew through Foxglove Corners, snow still clung to the bare branches. The part of the world from my bedroom window was blanketed in an expanse of luminous white.

It was later than I'd planned to sleep, almost nine-thirty.

Crane slept on, but downstairs the dogs were restless. Soon they would wake him. Halley stole into the bedroom and nudged me with her nose. Behind her, Misty stood in the doorway, wagging her tail.

"Quiet," I said as Misty whimpered.

The dogs wanted to go out and play in the snow. They wanted breakfast. They wanted to tear open the toys that, somehow, they knew were for them. What I wanted—to go back to bed—was immaterial.

I suddenly knew the answer to the question I'd pondered last night. This was why I didn't attend more parties or social events—this feeling of not having had enough sleep, of being half awake and adrift in churning waters. Make that pooling snowmelt.

You're getting old, I told myself. *Partying is for the Annicas of the world.*

It was going to be another long day, but a wonderful one.

I slipped into the red velour robe I only wore during the holiday season and went downstairs, following a tail-wagging Misty and trailed by Halley.

First on the agenda was a special Christmas breakfast. French toast, grapefruit with cherries, and fresh squeezed orange juice. Next came playtime with the collies, after I dressed, of course, then opening presents and finally company. My sister, Julia, was coming over around two, and Camille and Gilbert planned to join us for a late supper. In the afternoon, I expected Brent and Lucy, not necessarily together. Annica intended to spend the day with her relatives, and Leonora was skiing at a resort up north.

I gazed out the kitchen window at the pristine vista, the snowswept woods, and the yellow Victorian across the lane with its soft yellow color and evergreen roping draped around the wraparound porch.

Christmas is here again, Oh, Christmas is here again, that wondrous day of joy and gladness...

I fed the dogs and began to gather the ingredients for breakfast: eggs, white bread, and salt.

Candy wolfed down her breakfast and started barking. On the other side of the kitchen door, Raven answered her, for once wanting to come into the house.

"Hush, you'll wake Crane," I said.

"He's awake."

Looking much brighter than he should, for we'd gone to bed at the same time, Crane entered the kitchen. He was already dressed for the day, wearing a festive red shirt in honor of the season.

"Merry Christmas, honey," he said, wrapping his arms around me. "What can I do to help?"

"Take the dogs out while I fix breakfast."

They all trooped out into the fresh snow while I soaked bread in a bowl of beaten eggs and arranged the slices in the frying pan. Soon the table was set, the grapefruits were ready, and the rich fragrance of the balsam tree in the living room drifted in the kitchen, awaking memories of past Christmas mornings.

I was pouring coffee when Crane opened the door. My entire collie family came in, snow on their toes and mischief in their eyes. They shook themselves vigorously and crowded around the water pail.

Let the day begin with good food and drink for man and beast, I thought. This wondrous day.

~ * ~

Happy hours are the shortest known to mankind. We had waited for this day, forever it seemed, busy with shopping and frenetic preparation. Then it was late afternoon; the day was winding down. Prints made by boots, deer, and dogs marred the unbroken snow cover outside.

Inside tree lights and candlelight wrapped us in a magical glow.

I reminded myself to cherish every fleeting moment as I touched my new necklace, a faceted crystal heart on a long silver chain. Crane had also given me a small crystal collie. This was the year of crystal. I found that I didn't miss silver.

As I poured cups of hot chocolate for my guests, I thought how fortunate I was to have my family and good friends around me. Camille and Gilbert, Crane's uncle who resembled him so closely; Lucy and Brent; my sister, Julia, whose English courses at the university kept her busy throughout the year; and last but never least, the collies. They lay engrossed with their new toys and bones. I'd found a replacement plush goat for Misty, this one an improbable green with pink horns, but she showed more interest in her Nylabone.

Some things can't be replaced.

As I settled back and sipped chocolate, I marveled that my life had gone from satisfactory to perfect in a few brief years.

Don't do anything to jeopardize it.

That sounded like something Lucy would say, but she was engaged in lighthearted banter with Brent about last night's sleigh ride and the snowman Brent had almost collided with.

The warning had come from deep within myself, no doubt inspired by my resolve to pursue the mystery handed to me by Rosalyn Everett, that dark Christmas gift. Sue Appleton and I were going to River Rose tomorrow. And where would that lead? Not to danger. I felt certain of that. I was only going to retrieve Rosalyn's journal and follow a few clues. Sue would be with me every step of the way.

"This will be my last family Christmas for a while," Julia said. "I'm going to miss all of you so much."

The sentiment was sad, but her smile was radiant, as golden as her hair. Julia's dream of living and studying in England was finally coming true. She'd be leaving after the first of the year. I was going to miss her, but this was what she had wanted for a long time.

"You'll have to keep us posted," Lucy said. "Write about every little thing you do and all the places you visit."

"I'll keep a travel diary." One of my presents to Julia, a blank book with a picture of the Tower of London on the cover, lay in her lap waiting to be filled.

"I wish I were young enough to take a trip to Europe," Camille said.

"Who says you aren't?" Gilbert demanded. "We can plan a trip anytime. Maybe a cruise."

"Well, I love my home."

Enough said. I did too.

"When I first came to Foxglove Corners and saw that old yellow Victorian in desperate need of renovation, I knew it was what I'd been searching for," Camille said. "This was where I'd be happy again." She laid her hand on Gilbert's arm. "And I have been."

Strange. I'd had the same feeling, and on my first full day in Foxglove Corners, I'd met Crane.

In the midst of Christmas joy, surrounded by my husband and those I loved, I was conscious of an odd drop in my spirits. A sudden coldness, although the flames in the fireplace sent their warmth throughout the room.

I'd felt like this the moment I stepped on the haunted tiles in my classroom at Marston High School and been overwhelmed by sorrow, when the floor begin to move underneath my feet.

Someday all of this perfection might be snatched away from me. The tree, so beautiful, would turn dry and yellow, the ornaments would go back to their box, and the Spirit of Christmas would melt with the snow...

It was nature's way.

"Hey, Jennet!" Brent's booming voice brought me back to the present. "Why so gloomy? Didn't Santa bring you everything you wanted this year?"

Unconsciously my hand strayed to the crystal heart.

"Santa was very generous."

"What's the matter then?

"Nothing at all," I said. "I was just wishing we could have Christmas every day."

Twenty-five

Viewed at close range, the wreath on Rosalyn Everett's door looked as fresh as if the branches had just been cut. It had lost none of its potent fragrance or glossy green color, and the red ribbon looked crisp and new. I breathed in the scent of balsam that hung in the air and for once didn't associate it with Christmas.

A thought swept through my consciousness, moving too fast to be caught.

"I feel like an intruder," Sue said.

She inserted the key in the lock, turned the knob, and pushed the door open.

"We're here with Rosalyn's blessing," I reminded her. "This is what she wanted us to do."

Still, I had approached the yellow ranch house warily, searching the shadows for a ghostly lady in white or the elusive blue merle collie. A light wind stirred the branches, and it was easy to imagine a shape flitting across the snow.

"Let's just find the journal and get out," Sue said.

We stepped inside to a rush of stale air. I took a moment to allow the atmosphere that permeated the dim rooms to wash over me. There is something unworldly about entering a house that has been uninhabited for months. Something alien and soundless. It didn't want us here, and it stopped just short of being threatening.

And it was cold, the bone-chilling cold of a house in which the furnace has been shut off for months.

Once before I'd stood on the porch, looked through the window into this very room and surmised that the woman who dwelled within hadn't gone away, that she'd merely moved to another part of the house. Like a ghost.

That was my fancy. Wherever Rosalyn had gone, she'd probably not spent any time preparing for a trip or even thinking about it.

It appeared that no one had been here since that time. Here was the throw draped over the sofa, the pillow on the floor, the book and the mug, its inside brown with old stains. I hadn't noticed the vase on the side table before. The flowers were dried, pink and white larkspur mixed with baby's breath. Dried flowers seemed a fitting accessory for this strange house.

"That wreath out there is one more mystery," Sue said. "If Rosalyn came home long enough to hang it, why didn't she pick up the pillow and wash the mug?"

"Because she wasn't the one who brought the wreath?"

Rosalyn picked up the book and set it next to the vase. "So long ago. Rosalyn, what happened to you?"

"But there's a flaw in that theory," she said. "Who else would have done it? And why?"

I'd been thinking about that. "It could have been one of the neighbors who wanted it to look like the house was occupied. Could you ask that woman who saw the ghost if she knows anything about it?"

"I'll call Cecily when I get home," Sue said. "Now where is the desk?"

We found it in a corner of the dining room placed kitty corner to face the windows. On top a green desk lamp sat next to a framed photograph of Rosalyn with four of her adult collies in a wooded setting. No bills or correspondence or loose papers. Nothing to tell a tale of a serious problem.

It looked as if the owner had cleared everything off the top prior to leaving on a long journey— which contradicted the lived-in look of the other room.

"Top right drawer," I repeated.

And there was the book, lying on an unopened package of white copier paper.

"That's it," Rosalyn said.

I opened the journal, to make sure. The first half of it was filled, the pages covered with paragraphs and lists written in a neat hand; the second half was blank.

"The first entry is dated last June," I said. "Listen to this."

This morning's narrow escape is the last straw. I can't keep lying to myself. Someone wants me dead. I have no idea why. I have crossed a few people in my time. But murder? So I'm going to take a long look into the past at anyone I ever harmed without meaning to. To start, Clara Bell. That was a long time ago, but I don't think she ever forgave me.

"This should make our task easier," I said.

"We hope."

"It will. We have a name. Clara Bell and an allusion to a grievance."

On the way to River Rose, Sue had expressed her doubts. Rosalyn's mental state was a massive question mark. Sue believed that Rosalyn was dead, but not that the name of the killer would be found in the pages of her journal.

I admit I had my own doubts. The whole affair— the letter directing me to the journal, the fact that Rosalyn hadn't sought police protection while she was alive but chose an unorthodox way to enlist my aid after (presumably) she was dead— seemed too bizarre to be real.

But real or imaginary, here we were following her instructions breathing the close, unhealthy air of her long closed-up house on the trail of... What? Well, that was what made sleuthing fun.

"I have riding students this afternoon," Sue said as she shut the door. "Will you have time to read the journal and make a list of names? We can start investigating whenever you like."

"I'll do that.

I'd already slipped the journal into my shoulder bag and planned to go through it as soon as I got home and walked the dogs.

Sue ran her hand over the wreath's needles. "Do you think we should take the wreath down?"

"No. Some people leave their wreaths up all through January. Besides it's serving its purpose."

Telling the passerby that the homeowner was inside but didn't want to be disturbed. So don't even think about burglarizing this house.

"Besides," I said "we don't want anyone to know we were here."

Ah, that was the thought that had slipped out of my mind. The possibility that somebody was spying on us from one of the nearby houses. Well, it was too late for stealth now.

A nudge of apprehension compelled me to scan my surroundings as we walked back to the Taurus. The kennel building, so quiet, so empty. The woods that rose behind the house. The snow-covered grounds marked with the hoof prints of hungry deer. A ghostly woman in white...

Nothing.

With a sigh I steered out to the road, passed the kennel sign swinging in a mild wind and turned on the road.

"Do you have time for a quick stop at The Silver Sleigh?" I asked.

"If we make it quick. Say a half hour."

"Not even that long. I hear their inventory is low and want to check it out."

"They may have some good sales."

"That too," I said.

I wasn't sure what I was hoping to find at the antique shop. Annica's doll, maybe. Annica had a January birthday. If the doll was reduced, I could buy it for her. Maybe the sleigh display was still intact and every item discounted. The vintage books... Sellers rarely marked them down.

It was only that we had to pass The Silver Sleigh on the way home, and it seemed a waste of time not to take advantage of the opportunity to stop.

~ * ~

There were no cars in the area that served as a parking lot for the antique shop. The building itself was dark, the windows boarded over. The Christmas tree, stripped of its decorations, lay on its side, trapped by the wind in bare branches of a low hedge. Even the large sleigh was gone, along with all the gaily wrapped boxes. There wasn't even a flyer nailed to the door to apprise the shop's customers of a new location.

And the women with the Christmas names: Holly, Carol, Gloria, Nicola... Those boxes in the back room. Whatever was in them.

Stolen goods?

A deep sense of loss swept over me.

I brought the Taurus to a stop. "They're closed. It looks permanent."

"Just like that?" Sue said. "Overnight?"

"And on Christmas Day. That's when they must have moved out."

It seemed incredible. All that merchandise to relocate, the fragile Christmas ornaments? The lamps, the crystal and china, the heavier antiques?

"It was a nice little shop," Sue said. "Whoever closes down a business without giving the customers at least a few days' notice? Well, that's that."

"Not necessarily," I said. "I don't know how, but I'm going to find them."

Of course that was easier said than done. In truth, I didn't know where to begin. Gloria MacBride had done nothing illegal by closing down her antique shop. Usually, though, such a closure would rate a mention in the *Banner*. As Sue had pointed out, a concerned business owner would have posted a notice on the door. Even a note to thank the customers for their patronage and to wish them a Happy New Year.

Well, I could add The Vanishing Antique Shop to The Case of Rosalyn Everett. Curiously, both mysteries involved disappearances.

~ * ~

That night I had the sleigh dream again. I heard bells and stood at the bedroom window gazing down at a silver sleigh large enough to carry four people up the snowy lane. Except this sleigh wasn't going anywhere. It was made of sterling silver, and the team of reindeer were life-sized silver sculptures, each one slightly different from the other.

I felt as if I were in a Christmas fairy story, watching the snow fall and listening to the jingle of magical bells. At any moment the reindeer would come to life, and the sleigh would move out onto the lane and into the snow.

Suddenly I was aboard, feeling the great cold and the sting of the wind driven snow on my face.

The dream ended abruptly as dreams will, while I lay warm and safe under the covers trying to remember bits and pieces of the unfinished narrative my mind had created.

Where, for instance, was I going? And what would happen once I arrived at my destination?

The dream had ended too soon.

I closed my eyes, and if I dreamed again, I didn't remember.

Twenty-six

The next day I treated the dogs to an extra-long long walk through the sparkling countryside and a rousing game of fetch with snowballs. All too soon I'd be back in school and our walking time would be limited.

Afterward, I felt invigorated. The dogs were exhausted. While they rested, I made a cup of hot chocolate, settled in the rocking chair, and opened Rosalyn Everett's journal.

To my surprise, the story of Clara Bell was an old one involving high school days and a boy named Daniel Dawson, the proverbial captain of the football team and Homecoming King.

Rosalyn was going a long way back. She still felt guilty because she had swooped in and captured Dan's interest when her best friend, Clara, made no secret of her feelings for him. The relationship didn't last beyond a few dates. The girls' friendship died a quick death. Clara felt betrayed and rightly so. After graduation, Rosalyn and Clara went their separate ways and apparently never saw each other again.

Did Rosalyn honestly believe Clara had held a grudge all these years?

I wasn't going to waste time trying to track her down.

Rosalyn's next so-called enemy surfaced at the beginning of her career as a collie breeder. She had purchased a show prospect bred by a woman identified as Mrs. Tiller, but for some reason Rosalyn didn't show the puppy. In retaliation, Mrs. Tiller spread unkind rumors about Rosalyn in collie circles, which Rosalyn countered with accusations of her own. It seemed to be a question of ears set too low on the dog's head.

Wouldn't time have taken the edge off the mutual hostility? I thought so, especially after reading Rosalyn's note that Mrs. Tiller had placed her collies in good homes and retired from breeding.

Rosalyn listed six names of people she called rabid competitors. It seemed that good sportsmanship was a foreign concept among her confederates. Still, I didn't see any motive for murder in the brief instances she recorded.

At one time, she had a brief, disastrous marriage. Robert Lander's name made the list with a cross and a question mark after his name. It was easy to interpret that. Rosalyn thought he had died but wasn't sure.

Consider him dead, I thought, and read on. In truth, I began to skim, fast losing interest in Rosalyn's ramblings. It seemed to me that she was adding names to her list simply to have a list.

Everyone has occasional conflicts with others. Sometimes on the road when driving in front of a hostile driver, sometimes in a work place or a grocery store. Confrontations could take place in any setting. In most cases they were forgotten in a matter of minutes. Rosalyn seemed to remember every person who had ever crossed her.

There were a few instances of puppy transitions gone wrong in recent years. One of Rosalyn's rehomed champions ended up in collie rescue, a fact which she admitted she tried to deny. In all I didn't see anything worth pursuing except for one interesting fact.

Fifteen years ago Rosalyn had inherited the property, now known as River Rose, from her great-aunt. Two of her cousins felt they had more of a right to the inheritance than Rosalyn, but the will was iron clad and never contested. Almost immediately on receiving her legacy, Rosalyn hired a builder and the construction of the ranch house and kennel building began.

The cousins' names were Gloria Collins and Margaret Amy Redford.

Gloria wasn't the most popular name for a girl, neither in past decades nor in present times. Still, I thought immediately of Gloria MacBride. I had to remind myself not to get carried away. I'd thought the Christmas names of the women in the antique shop were made up. No matter. 'Gloria' appeared to be more of a viable clue than a case of schoolgirl jealousy or a disgruntled collie owner.

All right. I had a name. Gloria Collins. Now what was I going to do with it?

~ * ~

Once again Sue Appleton was ill.

"I already had the flu," she complained. "But I don't feel well, Jennet, and don't want to give whatever I have to you. I had to cancel my lessons. Can we postpone our sleuthing date?"

"Of course," I said. "There's nothing that can't wait."

I told her about my single significant discovery in the journal which in all probability wasn't a genuine clue.

"When you're better, we can look for Gloria Collins and see if there's a connection between her and Gloria MacBride."

"If there isn't one, I'm beginning to think that Rosalyn's enemy list is a work of fiction," Sue said.

"It's a strange case, and it keeps getting stranger."

"Before I started feeling so horrible, I had a chance to talk to Rosalyn's neighbors," Sue said. "Everybody is wondering who hung the wreath on Rosalyn's door."

"So it's still a mystery."

"And..." She paused for dramatic effect, or possibly to get control of a cough. "Cecily saw the ghost again. The lady in white. I don't know why we didn't see her when we were there."

"Ghosts don't appear at our bidding," I said. "Where was the lady when Cecily saw her?"

"It happened the same way. Cecily was at her kitchen window. She saw the lady walking through the snow wearing that fancy white dress with no coat over it. There wasn't any fog that day, but when she approached the house, she just seemed to dissolve. Once again, the ghost seemed to be walking toward the house."

"Rosalyn wants to go home," I said.

What was stopping her?

"I wonder if she had snow boots on under that dress," Sue said.

"I guess spirit feet don't get wet. This means we'll have to go back to River Rose. We still have to find Icy."

"Maybe that's why the ghost is restless," Sue said. "When Rosalyn died— *if* she died— she left her collies alone. All are in homes now except one. She has unfinished business."

It was something to think about.

On the other hand, if Rosalyn wasn't dead, who was the ghost?

~ * ~

A visit to Lucy Hazen at Dark Gables always involved tea and Lucy's offer to read tea leaves. I was counting on this today. Coming across the name of Rosalyn's cousin led me to thoughts of the silver sleigh and from there to my dream. I thought I'd dreamed about the sleigh again last night but wasn't sure. This time I hadn't been able to catch the dissipating strands.

I wanted to discuss the dream with Lucy, who had an understanding of otherworldly matters, which would include dreams, I imagined.

163

So that afternoon I found myself at Dark Gables drinking tea in Lucy's sunroom. It always seemed like continually blossoming summer in this room with its patio furniture and plants, even though the French doors offered a view of a winter garden and cold reality.

I twirled the spoon through the plain white teacup, setting the loose leaves into motion. Lucy Hazen's blue merle collie, Sky, who shared a name with my gentle rescue, kept her eyes fixed on the plate of gingersnap cookies on the wicker coffee table in front of me.

"I don't believe that dreams carry particular messages," I said. "But when I have the same dream three times, I begin to wonder what it means."

"I rarely remember dreams." Lucy took a sip of tea. "Your experience is unusual, but not unheard of. You haven't given up hope of finding your silver sleigh."

"Even if I do, it won't be mine."

"Don't be so sure. You paid for it."

"It's still considered stolen property," I said.

"Even if you don't get the sleigh, you should get back your hundred dollars."

"I agree, but who would reimburse me?"

Lucy passed me the plate of cookies. On the way it came perilously close to Sky's nose. Unlike Candy, she didn't grab one but watched its progress longingly. Good dog! Her eyes brightened as Lucy offered her one. It disappeared in a heartbeat to the familiar sound of crunching. A few crumbs landed in my lap.

I added, "I just wish I knew where the sleigh ended up. I have two others, one left by the thief and the one Brent bribed Nicola to give me. They're both silver-plated."

"In your mind, you've magnified the sleigh," Lucy said. "That's why it's grown from a mantel-sized decoration to life-sized. Just think how valuable a real sleigh made of sterling silver would have to be. Think how much it would weigh."

"Not to mention large silver reindeer." I smiled. "And what would you feed them?"

Lucy laughed softly. "Silver coins."

"You can say it, Lucy. The silver sleigh has become my obsession. If only Gloria MacBride had kept a journal and left it lying around."

"If she were dealing in stolen goods, that isn't likely," Lucy said. "But there must be a record somewhere. It wouldn't be just lying around."

"Sue and I are going to try to find this Gloria Collins I told you about. And on my own I'm going to see if I can find out where the antique shop went."

I sealed my intentions with a long swallow of tea. It was excellent. Red Rose, steaming hot.

Unfortunately with the swallow, I became aware of a vaguely scratchy sensation.

No!

I was *not* going to get sick. I had too much to do, and besides, this was my winter vacation.

Tell that to that insidious germ floating through the air.

Don't think about it. It'll go away.

I finished my tea and went through the familiar motions of preparing it for a reading: Drain the excess liquid into the saucer; turn the cup toward yourself three times, making a wish, while the leaves formed their patterns.

I helped myself to another gingersnap and handed the cup to Lucy who studied the patterns thoughtfully.

"You'll get your wish," she murmured. "I see an initial 'C' or maybe it's a 'G' and look…"

Her gold bangles jingled, a startling merry sound in the quiet room. She pointed to a leaf that even I could interpret.

"A sleigh. But where are the reindeer?"

"You're asking too much of a mere tea leaf," Lucy said. "But I can tell you this. The sleigh is close to your home, moving along in dark clouds."

"Which means?"

"I'd say trouble. Storm clouds. A dark and dangerous time awaits you."

She took the cup back, scanned it for a moment, and set it down on the coffee table.

"And that's all I see," she said.

Twenty-seven

Leave it to Lucy.

Without her gloom and doom rhetoric, I would have left Dark Gables with the hope that someday soon I'd find the silver sleigh. Now, according to Lucy, it was traveling toward my house in a convoy of clouds, bringing darkness and danger to my doorstep.

If my symptoms hadn't distracted me, I would have continued to dwell on the nature of that impending disaster. As it happened, the scratching in my throat proved to be only the beginning of a depressing downswing. I didn't know whether I'd caught Sue's flu or some other winter disorder. The nature of the malady didn't matter. I was miserable.

Overnight my appetite and my energy vanished. My head ached, and swallowing was a chore. For two days Crane brought take-out dinners home, and I ate what I could, which wasn't much. Mashed potatoes. A roll. A thin slice of banana-nut bread from my freezer.

Suddenly another holiday loomed. Crane would be patrolling the roads and by-roads of Foxglove Corners on New Year's Day. Heavy snow was in the forecast. Leonora was home from her Christmas ski trip bursting with news of the handsome new man she had met at the lodge. I didn't want to give her whatever I had so we agreed to communicate by phone.

"You have to be completely recovered before school starts," she said.

"I'm pretty sure I will be," I said.

Once I was back at Marston, there would be the rush to cover the semester's remaining material and review for final exams. Then I'd have to correct those exams and figure out final grades. Then change. New classes to teach. New students. The stress of the unknown. Just thinking about January added to my exhaustion.

"I brought you a souvenir from up north," Leonora said.

"What is it?"

"Something silver."

"A sleigh?"

"Something else.

"I can't wait to see it," I said. What are you doing tonight?"

"Jake is taking me out to dinner and dancing in Canada."

"That'll be nice. I'll be lying on the sofa."

"Turn the television on. Watch the ball drop."

"TV makes me nervous."

"Then read."

"Maybe I'll read the old year out."

I had a new Gothic on my Kindle that should keep me entertained, and I'd given Crane a biography of an obscure Confederate soldier for Christmas. We could toast the New Year and read our books. I'd have sparkling water.

"Well, happy New Year and have fun with Jake," I said.

I lay on the sofa and thought how hard it was to be incapacitated with six collies to care for. Fortunately I had a caring husband and Camille for a neighbor. She hadn't let a fear of sickness stop her from delivering homemade chicken soup and noodles to me as soon as she learned I was ill. Surprisingly, the dogs were good, even the still-mischievous Misty and her mentor, Candy.

Instead of feeling sorry for myself, I decided to take advantage of the opportunity to rest and think. Wouldn't it be strange if my two mysteries merged into one? If Gloria MacBride, suspected silver thief, were responsible for the murder or disappearance of Rosalyn Everett?

On the surface, that connection seemed unlikely. Rosalyn's whereabouts had been a mystery since last summer, the silver sleigh only since before Christmas.

Well, for the moment, I'd take them one at a time.

For the moment you're not taking anything but headache pills, I told myself.

Darn. Double darn. I hated being sick on a holiday. What a dismal beginning for a new year.

Later that afternoon, Camille brought over a huge pot of spaghetti and meatballs and a devil's food cake.

"So you won't have to cook," she said.

"I wasn't planning to, but thanks. You're the best friend ever."

"I didn't think you'd seen today's *Banner*. I found something you'll be interested in. Look on page three."

It was a page of ads with an article about Maple Creek's annual Ice Sculpture Show next weekend. The accompanying photograph depicted a unicorn made of ice.

"I'd love to go," I said.

"Oh, so would I, but I meant the ad. There's a new antique shop in town."

I saw it then.

GRAND OPENING

THE TIME MACHINE

Genuine antiques and replicas~antique toys~ china, crystal, and silver~art and lighting~vintage clothing and jewelry.

"Everything but the kitchen sink," I said. "I wonder if they have a silver sleigh."

"Well, Christmas is over."

"But winter isn't. I wish I felt better."

"If The Time Machine is just opening, they'll be there for a while."

"That's an interesting name. Much more intriguing than something like Grandma's Attic."

I read the rest of the copy:

Step into The Time Machine and see how your ancestors lived. Take souvenirs and keepsakes back with you to the twenty-first century.

Maybe the owners would know Gloria MacBride. They might know why she'd closed her shop so suddenly and where she'd gone. They might even have purchased some of The Silver Sleigh's inventory.

If it weren't New Year's Eve... If I felt just a little bit better...

"I'll make us some tea," Camille said. "Would you like a piece of cake now? Or would you rather wait for dinner?"

"Now," I said, "but just a sliver."

My appetite was returning and my enthusiasm, if not my energy. In my mind I was already roaming the aisles of The Time Machine searching for antique novelties and old time books—not to mention clues.

~ * ~

"Happy New Year, honey."

Crane handed me a champagne flute filled with ginger ale. Neither one of us planned to stay up until midnight. We'd sit by the fire and read until we grew sleepy, then we'd go to bed.

I'd had livelier holidays but with Crane by my side and the dogs in their favorite napping places, I was happy.

"What are you thinking about?" Crane asked.

"Past times." I showed him the *Banner* ad. "I've found a new shop to haunt."

He studied it and gave me a teasing frown. "I hope you won't step into The Time Machine and vanish into the past."

"I'll try not to," I said.

"I thought you were missing a good old New Year's Eve celebration."

"I'm fine staying home," I assured him. "And tomorrow I'll be in good shape. We both will."

I remembered a saying I'd read once. "The day with its possibilities lay before me." Change 'day' to 'year' and I had a motto for the next twelve months.

Instead of reading *Shadows on Spirit Castle*, I found a New Year's story by Charles Dickens titled *The Chimes, a goblin story about some bells that rang a new year in and old year out.* What could be more appropriate?

Outside the snow began to fall. Lost in Dickens' Victorian England, I let my mysteries slide away with the old year. Tomorrow was soon enough to tackle them.

Twenty-eight

Back to school on a snowy January morning. I had ten minutes to summon a modicum of enthusiasm for the day. Who will set an example if not the teacher? Fortunately I felt a hundred percent better, so setting an example shouldn't be a problem.

We were beginning a new unit in World Literature— poetry— with a few brief weeks to cover the material until the semester ended. That was poor planning on my part. I should have chosen the most student-pleasing short stories I could find to hold my students' interest during these last few days.

Was it too late to change plans?

Probably. Poetry it was, then. *Whose woods these are I think I know...* We'd studied that poem in American Literature last month.

Now I had nine minutes.

I unlocked the door and stepped inside. The room looked different. Dark and chilly and unwelcoming.

Well, sure. It had been empty for two weeks.

Turn on the lights.

There. That was better. Brightness and a hint, just a hint, of heat. With luck we'd have some sunshine later.

The snow view through the windows was spectacular...white, glistening, and for the most part unmarred. I deposited my shoulder bag and lunch on the desk and hung up my coat. Then I exchanged my boots for black heels. In the interest of communicating cheer, I'd worn a yellow knit dress with a sparkly snowman pin. Snowmen, after all, are winter symbols.

The bulletin board looked tired and outdated with its bells and various Yuletide cut-outs. In Journalism class we were working on the February issue of the *Courier*. I'd have the circulation managers tear down the old, dusty decorations and replace them with red, pink, and white construction paper. Hearts and Cupids.

I glanced at the haunted place.

Did you think you could escape me?

No one would have tread on those accursed tiles for two long lonely weeks.

Because you can't, you know. I'm here. Waiting.

The first bell rang. A shuffle in the hall ended in an indignant screech. There was a snatch of laughter. Someone was happy.

Suzanne came through the door followed by Nancy and April, three girls bursting with youth and energy. All three wore what appeared to be bright new sweaters.

"What are we going to do today, Mrs. Ferguson?" asked Nancy.

The day had officially begun.

~ * ~

One half day down. Lunch time. It seemed as if I'd never left the school.

Leonora opened a container of fried chicken and a smaller one of strawberries. They must have been frozen but were still strawberries. I'd have to bring more creative lunches. Today's sandwich contained the last thin slices of the Christmas ham. For dessert I had my old stand-by, an apple.

"I wish I were still at the lodge," Leonora said. "That was the best winter vacation ever. But alas! All vacations come to an end."

On the way to school that morning, she had regaled me with tales of her date with Jake. Dinner at a German restaurant, dancing, a kiss at the stroke of midnight to welcome the New Year, and more, which she declared was private. It sounded wonderful, but she never mentioned the new man from the ski lodge.

"Jake seems different," Leonora said.

"How?"

"More romantic. More serious."

"Isn't that what you want?"

"I think so, but it's fun to travel and meet new men."

"Then you're probably not ready to settle down," I said.

She sliced her chicken breast with a plastic knife, a difficult feat but she managed. "I like my life. I have a gorgeous house in the country, two beautiful dogs, a profession I love, except on the day after a vacation."

"All that's important."

"But I love Jake, too."

Well, that was Leonora's conundrum, not to be solved in Marston's ridiculously short lunch period.

Thinking it would be wise to change the subject, I said, "I'm going to test the haunted place."

"I'd leave well enough alone, if I were you."

"I have to know if *It* is still here."

I glanced at the clock. Ten more minutes. Time to start eating my apple. I suspected I'd need fortification for the coming experiment.

~ * ~

In Journalism I assigned our artist, Gwendolyn, to draw Valentine artwork for the February paper. Remembering her unhappy elf, I said, "Why don't you work at the layout table?"

That was as far from the haunted space as she could sit and still be in the room.

"I already did some sketches at home," she said. "I have a teddy bear. It turned out real well."

She retrieved her supplies from the closet and started drawing hearts and flowers. Everyone else had a specific task: a story to write or feature to create. The editors checked on the status of their assignments. In the background the ripping and rustling of paper spelled the end of the Christmas board.

The area around Gwendolyn's desk was empty. It seemed to call to me.

I watched the clock and at the correct time, I strolled over to the space and stood...and felt a sudden nausea grip me. The floor beneath my feet began to dissolve, and a sense of desolation and bereavement enveloped me, obliterating the sights and sounds of the busy familiar classroom.

All is lost.

Hastily I stepped back into a safe zone. The tiles solidified. The alien feelings evaporated.

"Hey, Mrs. Ferguson? Come read this."

I was myself again.

"Mrs. Ferguson!"

And *It*—the monstrous unknown—was still present.

~ * ~

At home I found myself remembering the moment I fell under the spell of the haunted place in my classroom. Technically I hadn't fallen. I had walked up to it, stepped on it, well aware of the possible consequences. So I had nobody but myself to blame for the way I felt now, which was unsettled and frightened.

Just as I had before Christmas break.

I can't think of any situation in which desolation and bereavement would be desirable. As for that strange thought, *All is lost*, in what far recess of my mind had that originated?

I needed a walk with my three gentle dogs, Halley, Sky, and Misty. Fresh crisp air and the familiar scenery of home would go far toward chasing unwanted fancies.

With Raven dashing ahead of us, we set out. At Sagramore Lake Road, we turned and spied a familiar pair, Jennifer and Molly, walking toward us with their Christmas collie. What was her name? Something spicy. Nutmeg? No, Ginger.

My three collies flew into welcoming, tail-wagging mode, while Raven circled the puppy yipping merrily. We all came to a stop.

"Hi, Jennet." Molly held Ginger's leash with both hands as if afraid her treasure would take flight. Like collie babies the world over, Ginger fairly bristled with excitement and love for mankind.

"You said you'd come see her at Christmas," Jennifer said, the faintest hint of reproach in her voice.

"Christmas, well that was a busy time. Then I was sick."

In truth, I'd forgotten about my promise.

The puppy sat and offered her tiny paw to whoever would shake it.

"I taught her that," Molly said proudly. "She can fetch, too. We play in the house."

"I forgot. Whose dog is she?"

"Mine," Jennifer said, "but we share her."

I grabbed the puppy's paw and shook it.

"Did you girls have a nice Christmas?" I asked.

They had and were back in school, happy to be there, happy with Ginger, happy that tomorrow it was supposed to snow again. Just happy with their world. Oh to be that young and optimistic.

I listened to a catalog of Ginger's antics and countered with tales of Misty's exploits and we went on our way, promising to meet again soon.

Sagramore Lake had a dull hard sheen under clouds that did indeed look as if they were harbingers of more snow.

Great. A slow, snowy commute in the morning, and the classroom where something inexplicable, something terrible, was going on. All the fresh air and exercise in the world couldn't banish *It* for long.

Twenty-nine

We chose Saturday at noon to visit the unknown E. J. Lancaster in Maple Creek, hoping that he or she wasn't one of those people who go shopping at that time. Although it is often counter-productive to arrive unannounced on a stranger's doorstep, in this case we had no choice. Sue hadn't been able to find a phone number, not even on the Internet.

"We won't be complete strangers," Sue pointed out. "After all, this person just sent mail to us."

Still, I was a bit apprehensive at the coming meeting.

We found 632 Crescent Boulevard with no trouble. It was an attractive gray brick ranch surrounded by a white picket fence. Icicle lights outlined the façade, and a pathetic fir tree, stripped of its Yuletide finery, lay at the curb.

As we walked up to the porch, we heard the melodious sound of piano playing mixed with loud barking. The music stopped abruptly, cut through by the shrill of the doorbell.

"Here goes," Sue said.

The door opened, and a petite woman with short blond hair appeared. She wore a garish sweater, a hodgepodge of sequined Christmas trees, interspersed with candy canes and bells, some of them sideways, some upside down. A lovely tricolor collie with a silver muzzle stood placidly at her side. Both woman and dog looked slightly annoyed at being interrupted.

Still, the woman greeted us with a smile, although her eyes held a sliver of wariness. One hand rested lightly on the collie's collar, the other on the doorknob. "It's all right, Roxy," she murmured to the dog.

To us she said, "If you're selling something or handing out religious pamphlets…"

"Neither," Sue said quickly. "We're friends of Rosalyn Everett. I'm Sue Appleton, and this is Jennet Ferguson. We're also members of the Lakeville Collie Rescue League."

At the mention of Rosalyn and the League, the woman's wariness vanished.

"Oh… Yes. I thought I might hear from you one day. I'm Ellen." She stepped aside to allow us to enter and ushered us into a small living room, most of which was taken up by an elegant mahogany piano. The rest of the furniture was arranged close together which created a claustrophobic effect—at least for me.

"Can I take your coats?" she asked.

"Thanks," I said. "I'll keep mine."

Ellen kept her house colder than mine, and I was still shivering from the frigid air outside. But I pushed my hood back and took off my gloves.

Sue said, "I think I will, too."

When we were all seated Ellen said, "I was devastated to read about Rosalyn's disappearance, and I was worried about her collies. Did you find homes for them?"

"Most of them," Sue said, not mentioning the few who had perished. "I adopted a blue and a tri myself."

"I was so afraid they'd be put down when I heard Rosalyn had gone missing. All those beautiful collies."

Coming to the point, Sue said, "In the letter, Rosalyn asked Jennet to find her killer. We're trying to learn as much as possible about Rosalyn's life and her friends."

Ellen gasped. "Her killer? Rosalyn was murdered? My God. I didn't read anything about it in the paper."

"We don't know for sure that she's dead, but it looks that way," I said. "Obviously she expected to be dead by the time I received her letter."

"I had no idea." Ellen had turned pale. Clearly this news was unexpected.

"I suspected Rosalyn was in trouble but never dreamed it was that serious," she said. "I didn't know what was in the letter." Ellen ruffled the fur on Roxy's chest, a gesture of mutual comfort, one any dog lover would understand.

"What was in your package, Ms. Appleton?" she asked.

"The River Rose papers. The collies' pedigrees, pictures, and some material pertaining to the operation of the kennel. There was no letter inside, no instructions."

Ellen shook her head. "Rosalyn would never have given those up if she were alive."

"Can you tell us about the last time you saw her?" I asked. "Any detail. Anything at all would be helpful."

Ellen leaned back in her chair. "I remember it like it was yesterday because it was all so peculiar. Rosalyn seemed unlike herself that day, really edgy. All the time she was here she kept looking out the front window."

"Like she was afraid she'd been followed?" I asked.

"Exactly. When I asked her if anything was wrong, she said she had a little problem. Being afraid for your life isn't what I'd call little."

"Did you consider her a close friend?"

"Not really. I met her when I bought Roxy, but we didn't see each other often. Usually it was at the shows. Rosalyn was so knowledgeable about collies, so proud of her dogs, and they loved her. I couldn't believe it when I read that she'd abandoned them. The Rosalyn I know would never do that."

"Why did she want you to wait for six months before sending out the mail?" I asked.

"All she said was by that time she'd know. I asked what that meant, but she said she'd tell me later. There was no later. I never saw her again."

A strange request, but then everything about the Rosalyn Everett affair was strange. Especially her choice of someone who wasn't a good friend to do her this unusual favor.

"I was surprised by Rosalyn's request," Ellen said. "Before that visit, we hadn't seen each other in months."

"And I was surprised when I read her letter. I'd only just met her." I paused, suspecting that this interview was going to be a rehash of familiar information. "Do you know any of her other friends, people she might have confided in?"

"She used to talk a lot about a Mrs. Greer. Mia Greer. You might want to contact her."

Finally, an interesting turn. A new name. Mia Greer wasn't on Rosalyn's enemy list.

"Do you know where Mrs. Greer lives?" I asked.

"She's here in Maple Creek, I believe. I don't have her address or phone number, but you can look in the phone directory."

"Thank you, Ellen. You've been very helpful." I rose. "We'll do that."

Ellen hesitated, her hand on Roxy's head. "Do you know if any of the River Rose collies are up for adoption? I'd loved to have one, and my Roxy needs a friend."

"There might be a collie who needs a forever home in foster care," Sue said. "If you give me your phone number, I'll let you know and we can arrange a meeting. That'll give Roxy a chance to meet the new dog."

As Ellen jotted the number down, she said, "Please, call me if you find out what happened to Rosalyn. Until I hear otherwise, I'm going to believe she's still alive."

~ * ~

"We have two names now," I said as we drove away from Ellen's house. "Mia Greer and Rosalyn's cousin, Gloria Collins. Maybe one of them is the killer."

"Well we can eliminate Ellen. If she's telling the truth."

"I think we can trust her. Apparently Rosalyn did."

Sue checked her watch. "I have lessons this afternoon, Jennet. We'll have to continue our sleuthing another day."

"That's all right. I'm going to try to trace Gloria Collins."

Although it was still early, I was a little tired, and I had dinner to prepare. Unless...

"Would you like to stop for a cup of coffee at Clovers? I'd like to take home dinner for tonight."

I would cook tomorrow, a roast with potatoes and carrots. Crane would love that, and I'd have leftovers for sandwiches.

"I may do that, too, if they have something good," Sue said. "I never know what to fix anymore. Cooking for one is a pain."

"I remember. We'll head for Clovers then."

A half hour later we arrived at the restaurant in that quiet time after lunch and before dinner. We could have our choice of seats and all of Annica's attention, which was a bonus as I wanted to ask her if she'd go with me to The Time Machine.

The Christmas poinsettias were still in place, looking fresh and bright, but the fanciful centerpieces on the tables were gone. Annica wore a vintage floral apron over her red dress and earrings I hadn't seen before, tiny gold baskets filled with pearls.

Settled in my favorite booth with its view of the woods across from Crispian Road, we ordered coffee and beef stew dinners to go. Annica joined us, declaring she'd been too busy to take her morning break. She had seen The Time Machine's ad in the *Banner* and was eager to visit the new shop.

"If we can go on Thursday," she said. "It's my one evening free."

"That'll work. After school."

She stirred sugar into her coffee and added cream. "I was wondering if The Time Machine was the old Silver Sleigh with a different name."

"I hadn't thought of that," I said. "Could it be?"

"Well, one place closes down without any warning, and this new one opens at an odd time. I mean, you'd think people would be all shopped out after the holidays."

"We'll be able to tell if the Christmas ladies are there," I said.

And if even one of them was... Well, that would be interesting indeed.

Thirty

"Wow!"

Annica and I stood in front of The Time Machine, transfixed by the unique window display. A mammoth object resembling an old hollowed-out television console took center stage. It was twice as large as any set I'd ever seen in history books or museums with an amazing array of gadgets, buttons, and accessories I couldn't identify. On a dashboard-sized clock, a gleaming silver arrow pointed to 1893.

It stood on a large wooden platform, marked with red and blue lines, presumably where the time traveler would stand in order to be transported back into the past.

Surrounding the machine in no particular order were the antiques. Vintage toys and old-time books, a set of china with a busy pink floral pattern, a 1920's radio, and small furniture like end tables and a handsome mahogany magazine stand with graceful scrolled sides.

The décor reminded me of props arranged on a stage. Heavy dark green curtains tied back with gold chains completed the illusion.

"I'm speechless," I said, swiping snowflakes off my face.

"It makes you think you could really go back in time," Annica said.

"No, Annica. If anyone invents a time machine, I doubt it'll look like this. This…" I gazed at all the gears and levers and pseudo-scientific ornamentation. "This looks like the cover of a pulp science-fiction magazine from the nineteen fifties."

"Whatever," Annica said. "I like it."

"So do I. It's different and clever." I couldn't suppress a shiver. "Let's get in out of the cold."

Brass bells rang as we crossed the threshold into a large crowded space that looked like every other antique shop I'd ever been in. There was, however, one exception. Everything in my view had been dusted or polished or washed. Wood surfaces shone, glass and crystal sparkled, and the colors of the antique clothing had an appealing brightness. A scent of lavender hovered lightly in the air.

This was, I remembered myself, a new shop.

"What'll we do now?" Annica asked in a whisper.

"Look around," I said. "We have a new place to haunt."

We were the only customers. The proprietor, a tall, handsome woman all in gray hastily whisked her can of pop out of sight behind the counter and greeted us. She had a heavy application of eye makeup and ash-brown hair twisted into a loose bun at the top of her head.

"Welcome to The Time Machine," she said. "Were you looking for something in particular?"

I couldn't resist. "A sterling silver sleigh with eight reindeer."

My reply had obviously taken her aback. "That sounds like a Christmas item. We don't have any sleighs, but we *do* have a nice assortment of gifts suitable for Valentine's Day giving. There's a pretty Cupid lamp, for example. It's perfect for a lady's nightstand."

"I really like silver," I said, "and old time series books."

"I'd like to see the Valentine antiques," Annica said. "Would you have any Valentine jewelry? Earrings, maybe?"

"We certainly do. Follow me."

She led Annica to the back of the shop while I searched for books. At first I thought they were scattered on coffee tables and other handy surfaces rather than arranged in a group. Then I found a charming mahogany bookcase crammed with enticing old volumes:

My Lady of the North, My Lady of the South, The Girl from the Bighorn Country, Spurs for Antonia, the Idylls of the King, and books in *The Wizard of Oz series.*

No series books. No Judy Bolton's or Beverly Gray's. Oh, well. I picked up a paperback, *The Lute and the Glove.* Its tattered cover depicted a woman in a graveyard wearing a long dress and bonnet. Closer examination revealed yellow pages and print so small I hoped I could read it.

It was a genuine old Gothic. I'd make the effort.

"What do you think, Jennet? The hearts or the pink roses?"

Annica held two pairs of earrings in her hand.

I considered. The hearts were pretty—red and enameled— but the roses were exquisite. They were pale pink and delicate with tiny crystals sparkling like dew on green leaves. They would look lovely with Annica's red-gold hair.

"Definitely the roses," I said.

"That's what I think. Stella says they look like me."

"Stella?"

"The owner. It isn't a Christmas name," she added.

"Mmm." But Stella meant star. I decided not to make an issue of it.

"Let's look at that Cupid lamp she mentioned," Annica said. "The one I have now is ugly."

The bells on the door rang, and four people entered, all female, all middle aged and bundled up against the cold. They didn't appear to be together and soon fanned out through the shop.

Annica found the Cupid lamp and fell in love with it. I had to admit it was a charmer, a coy Cupid in *faux* marble surrounded by roses beneath a lavender shade. She declared that she must have it, no matter the price.

It was, I supposed, her silver sleigh.

"I can keep it forever," she said, "even when I get married."

"This is proving to be an expensive afternoon for you," I said.

"That's okay. I have a new credit card."

En route to the cash register, we passed a display of vintage storybook dolls. I recognized Snow White, Little Red Riding Hood., and a maiden with golden hair that fell to her ankles, obviously Rapunzel. They were small, exquisite, still in their original boxes and outrageously priced. Intended for a serious collector, I imagined.

"Jennet!" Annica grabbed my arm. "There's the doll! The one they had at The Silver Sleigh."

"Are you sure?" I asked.

With its red dress, glossy dark curls, and blue eyes that opened and shut, it *did* look similar to the one we'd seen in the other antique shop. On the other hand, there were probably a billion other dolls out there that looked exactly like this one, in other outfits.

"I'm positive," Annica said, checking the price tag attached to the doll's wrist. "Two hundred and ninety-nine dollars. That's the same price."

That meant, if Annica were right, at least one item formerly in The Silver Sleigh's inventory had found its way to The Time Machine.

It was a connection between the two shops, however fragile.

"Let's see if we can find anything else from there," I said.

We discovered six extremely ornate place settings of sterling silver on a table set with elegant china and a crocheted tablecloth.

Remembering the stolen Larkin silverware, I wished I knew what the Joan of Arc pattern looked like. That would have to wait until I had access to the Internet.

Annica spied some earrings that looked familiar, but she couldn't be certain.

"I'm going to ask Stella a few questions," I said.

But she had left the floor. A young girl with long blond hair and bangs had taken her place, ringing up a set of champagne flutes. In her blue jumper and white blouse, she looked like a character from a storybook...Alice-in-Wonderland, perhaps.

"You have a wonderful little shop," I said as I set my well-worn Gothic and a ten dollar bill on the counter. "We'll be back."

Thirty-one

Sue Appleton's twice-postponed meeting of the Lakeville Collie Rescue League took place on a cold, dreary Thursday afternoon when I'd have preferred to stay at home in front of my own fireplace.

Only six people, not counting Leonora and myself, had ventured out. All of us declined to be separated from our coats, although Sue's family room was warm and cozy, with plates of cookies and pitchers of cider set out on every available surface.

"I'm happy to report that some of last year's rescues have found loving forever homes," Sue said.

This announcement met with a murmur of approval from her audience.

"Unfortunately, not all of them," she added.

"Let's hear about the successes first," Emma Brock suggested, pouring cider into a tall glass.

"Well, there's Silver. You remember her. As we speak, she's on a road trip out west with her new owner. Sandy is a lovely young lady. She's crazy about Silver."

Sue passed around pictures of the travelers at the Grand Canyon. They did indeed look happy and comfortable with each other.

"I wish I were on a road trip," Emma said. "Anything for a break from this dismal weather."

"Didn't you say that all of Rosalyn Everett's collies are in homes now?" Ronda May asked.

She was an enthusiastic new member who had known Rosalyn from the shows.

"We still have one in a foster home, but Jennet and I just met a lady who would love to adopt a River Rose collie. All we need is to arrange a meeting between two dogs. There are others still waiting though."

"How is our Sparkle doing?" Leonora asked.

"She's still in foster care and behaving, but then she's the only dog in the house. She doesn't have to share. Her temporary mom may keep her."

"What's the bad news?" I asked, helping myself to an oatmeal cookie. I hadn't had dinner yet and figured oatmeal was a good substitute.

Sue sighed. "Where to begin? It's the same old story. We're desperately in need of foster homes and funds. We've brought seven collies into Rescue just since Christmas. All of them needed vet care. Then we lost a member. She moved to Florida."

But we'd also gained one. Still we were a small group. With more people, we would be more effective. If nothing else, rescues wouldn't be crowded in temporary homes.

"Don't forget Icemaker at River Rose," I said.

"Didn't you say all but one of Rosalyn's collies were in forever homes?" Ronda asked.

"This dog hasn't been rescued yet. He seems to have made his home in the woods behind Rosalyn's house. He's very elusive," I added.

"Technically Icy isn't the League's responsibility," Sue said.

Occasionally she allowed practically to overrule her sentimental side. Practicality was, I supposed, a necessary quality in the president of the Rescue League.

"No," I said, "but he's a collie without a home, and it's winter."

"Remember," Emma said, "Icemaker is one of Rosalyn's dogs, and he's still young and super intelligent. She had such high hopes for him."

I couldn't banish Icy from my mind. A few minutes' exposure to the winter chills had been enough for me. Still, he had a collie's thick coat. So far he had survived.

On the other hand, he didn't have meals prepared for him by a loving hand. He didn't have a comfortable bed, not even a blanket, and no human interaction.

I said, "If we were to find him…"

Sue cut me off. "That would be different, of course. But do you honestly think that's going to happen, Jennet?"

"It could," I said.

If I made more of an effort to draw him out of hiding. If I paid an occasional visit to River Rose armed with treats as I'd once planned to do before every other matter pushed my good intentions out of the way.

I really should make time for a trip to the abandoned kennel. My mysteries appeared to be coming together in a still-puzzling fashion. There was the ghost of Rosalyn, said to be haunting her own property. There were Gloria and Mia, one of whom might hold the key to the Rosalyn Everett mystery. There was, finally, a collie born and raised in domesticity who might perish in the wild or survive. It might be up to me to determine his fate.

All roads lead to River Rose, I thought.

Sue had launched into her fund-raising plans for the first half of the year. A spring yard sale and a 'Picture with the Easter Bunny' event with Ronda, a professional photographer who had volunteered her services. An auction of collie books, figurines, and memorabilia would take place in the summer at Sue's horse farm.

A heavy pelting at the windows suggested that the snow had turned to sleet. As I reached for another cookie, I could see in my mind a collie curling up into a pathetic ball against the onslaught in a nest of fallen branches.

Finding him would require a miracle. At least.

~ * ~

"It's no fit night out for woman nor beast," Leonora misquoted as we dodged icy shards on our way to the Taurus.

She was going to have dinner with us before heading home.

"Nor for wandering spirits," I said. "We should make a stop at River Rose sometime, Leonora. Maybe tomorrow after school?"

"Not tomorrow. It's going to be a long day."

I remembered then. Principal Grimsley had called a morning meeting before classes started which meant that everything would be an hour earlier.

"The next day then."

"Only if it isn't snowing or sleeting."

"Naturally," I said. "I'd like to explore the woods."

With tasty dog treats and maybe chunks of the pot roast that had been cooking in the crock pot all day.

We each grabbed an ice scraper and set to work clearing the windows.

"If we came more often, Icy might get used to the sound of a car and get curious," I said when we were on our way.

"Or he might retreat further into the woods."

"We have to take the chance," I said. "Besides, there's the ghost. The Winter Ghost. I've never yet let a ghost story go uninvestigated."

"It's no fit night for spirits to walk either."

"Well we'll hope for a January thaw."

"Where I'd really like to go is The Time Machine," Leonora said. "I agree with Annica. Maybe those nebulous thieves are still in business in a different location."

"We can go anytime. Are you free this weekend?"

"During the day."

"When I was there I took a picture of sterling silver with my cell phone," I said. "Then I found a picture on the Internet. They're the same. The pattern is Joan of Arc by International Silver, the one stolen from the Melinda Larkin estate."

"I think that was a popular pattern at one time."

"I realize that, with hundreds of sets here in Michigan alone. But then there's Annica's doll, and she thinks she recognized some jewelry. We need more evidence."

"But they didn't have your silver sleigh?"

"No. Or so they said."

As we neared the house, the dogs began to bark. Raven emerged from her house and stood at the lane's edge, wagging her tail in welcome.

Crane would have fed and walked the dogs. The roast would be done and waiting for us.

"I'm afraid I'll have to eat and run," Leonora said. "Or maybe I'll just run. This sleet makes me nervous."

"Think ice day tomorrow," I said, thinking I'd send a plate of beef, potatoes, and carrots home with Leonora if she decided not to stay for dinner.

"With our luck, it'll be a slow, slippery commute and a morning meeting with coffee and doughnuts and Grimsley smiling from ear to ear. He lives near the school."

I brought the car to a stop behind Crane's Jeep. "Let's hope for the best."

Any mention of school these days brought to mind the haunted floor in my classroom. That was one of the mysteries in my life that had no connection to the Rosalyn Everett affair, and it was the one most likely to affect my life.

If I let it.

One day soon I'd have to test it again. Now, however, it was time for home and food.

Thirty-two

Every time I stepped on River Rose land, the snowswept expanse seemed more bizarre.

Or was 'bizarre' the best word to describe it? Haunted would be better; forbidding better yet. Once before I'd had the feeling that Rosalyn's abandoned house didn't want us invading its rooms.

Now *that* was bizarre.

This afternoon the usual otherworldly silence greeted me. Scattered animal prints and fallen branches marred the snow. The festive Christmas wreath still adorned the front door in mid-January, its ribbon crisp and bright. A discernible pall hung over the deserted kennel buildings, and the dark woods behind the house rose to meet a sullen sky. They appeared to issue a voiceless warning:

Don't come any closer.

Leaving the Taurus idling, I grabbed a bag of beef chunks and made my way up to the house calling Icy's name loudly.

An echo flung it back to me, an echo followed by a deep bark. Then another. I'd hoped for a response but hadn't expected one.

I called again. "Icy! Treat!"

He emerged from the side of the house near the blue spruce where I'd first seen him. And oh, he was magnificent! Large and majestic with a silvery-blue coat that shone in the last of the afternoon light as if it had been freshly bathed and brushed. Impossible, of course.

The Quicksliver Collie.

I held my breath, hoping he wouldn't move.

A piece of light green material dangled from his mouth. A rag?

"Are you hungry?" I rattled the bag, a sound that unfailingly drew my dogs from all corners of the house.

He tilted his head, licked his chops.

I tossed a chunk of beef into the snow. He lounged for it, swallowed it in one gulp, and stared at the bag in my hand.

"Poor hungry baby."

I tossed two more pieces and eyed the material that had fallen into the snow.

Focused on devouring the beef, the collie didn't object when I bent down to pick it up. Wet and torn, definitely the worse for wear, it was still recognizable as a woman's blouse or shirt, probably silk.

Whose?

The leap was inevitable. Who but Rosalyn Everett would have worn this blouse found on her property?

From somewhere a snippet of information floated into my mind. Sue Appleton saying, "Rosalyn often wore green. It was her favorite color."

Icy had apparently brought the blouse from the woods. If I could find the place… There might be other garments there. There might be a grave.

I showed Icy the empty bag. "No more. Sorry."

He sniffed at it warily, then dashed off back to the yard, up the incline, and into the woods.

Still carrying the blouse, I followed him, followed his imprints in the snow, crossing treacherous roots that reached out of the ground cover to entrap me. Soon I'd lost sight of the dog but not his tracks.

He must have come and gone this way often enough to create a path of sorts.

The trees grew close together. Hungry branches reached out for me, snagging my sleeves. In an alarmingly short time, my breath grew ragged and my heartbeat raced. Just when I thought I could go no farther, I caught sight of Icy. He had come to a stop in a clearing at a large nest of branches. His makeshift home or…

Something had disarranged the neat order of the branches, scratched or clawed them aside to expose more green material.

I stopped quickly and grabbed onto the trunk of a slender tree for support, still breathing heavily as the significance of the discovery caught up with me. This was Rosalyn's grave. I had found her.

The collie lay down close to the nest, panting, waiting with the air of one who has completed his mission.

Rosalyn's grave. At last. But shouldn't I make certain her body lay beneath the branches?

Yes, but I didn't want to touch a corpse unless there was no alternative. Not when I was alone in the woods except for a dog who wasn't mine. Not when I had my cell phone in my pocket and access to an officer of the Foxglove Corners Police Department.

Just move the branches aside with your boot, I told myself. *You won't have to touch anything.*

No. I couldn't be that disrespectful.

Keeping my eye on the gravesite and the guardian collie, I called Lieutenant Mac Dalby.

~ * ~

"It's just clothes," Mac said. His deep blue eyes held a glint of humor. "Not what you expected, I'll bet."

Not a body then. Not Rosalyn.

"They don't look like somebody's old clothes they threw away," Mac said. "They're pretty nice. Or they were once till they were exposed to the elements."

An entire outfit lay entangled in branches. A green cardigan that looked like cashmere in a shade that complemented the blouse. A long gray skirt. Lacy undergarments, pantyhose, and even shoes, gray suede heels.

For a moment a grotesque image danced in my mind: a body shedding its attire and wandering the earth in spirit form. The "Winter Ghost crossing the snow fields in an old-fashioned white dress, appropriate for a bride?

The discovery was gruesome enough. Why embroider it?

The point was the woman who had owned this outfit. Could Rosalyn have buried the clothes in the woods herself? Why on earth would she do something so macabre?

'Curiouser and curiouser,' as Alice would say.

"Could the body be under the ground?" I asked.

"The ground is frozen now. Depends on when it was buried." Mac stamped at the ground as if to prove his point. "We'll check it out. How did you come to get mixed up in the Rosalyn Everett case?"

"Through my work with the Rescue League," I said. "We've been trying to catch this collie. He wasn't with the rest of the River Rose dogs when they were rounded up. Today for some reason, he showed up with a blouse in his mouth and led me here. I could have sworn it was Rosalyn's grave."

"I had a collie when I was a kid," Mac said. "He was brown. I've never seen a dog this color."

"Icy is a blue merle."

"Whatever he is, he's sure smart. We should have him on the Force."

Icy lay watching us. Not for the first time I wished dogs could talk. Maybe he knew what had happened to Rosalyn. I'd been so certain he was guarding her grave. Maybe he was, but now I doubted it. Clothing should be on a body, not lying on the ground above it.

"This is a police matter now," Mac said. "I trust you'll let us handle it."

"Of course, but I wasn't aware you were still investigating the case. Rosalyn disappeared last summer."

"So far there haven't been any clues."

"If this is a clue, it's a mighty confusing one," I said. "Will you be able to tell if these were Rosalyn Everett's clothes? With DNA?"

"Probably."

At that moment a thought dropped into my mind, a memory really. In the photograph of Rosalyn and Icy, now in Sue's possession, Rosalyn was wearing a long gray skirt and a green blouse.

"They belong to her. I just remembered..." I told Mac about the packet Ellen Lancaster had sent to Sue which led to the letter I'd received.

"Rosalyn thought someone was out to kill her. She wanted me to solve the crime."

"I thought you were trying to rescue her dog," Mac said.

"Well, that, too."

"If there's a killer in the mix, don't take this a step further. I don't want to have to extricate you from a killer's trap again."

"When did you ever do that?" I demanded.

"You get my drift," he said. "It looks like you found your rescue collie. Do you have a collar and leash with you?"

"In my trunk. I always carry spares and a box of biscuits."

"I'll walk you back to your car, then come back and take care of this." He gestured toward the clothing in the branches. "Will the dog go with you?"

"I doubt it," I said. "I'll have to come back, too."

But it was worth a try.

"Icy," I said softly, "you're a good dog. The best. Everyone should have a wonderful collie like you. Will you come with me?"

No one was more surprised than I when he rose, shook vigorously, and walked up to me, wagging his tail.

"Good dog," I repeated, stroking his silvery head. I didn't even let him sniff my hand first; there was no need.

We left the woods, Mac in the lead, and when we reached the Taurus, Icy jumped into the back seat.

I fed him three milk bone biscuits and poured bottled water into a collapsible bowl.

Mac observed the proceedings, a rare look of admiration in his blue eyes.

"You have a magic touch, Jennet."

"That's it," I said. "There's something uncanny about this place. I wouldn't call it magic, though."

"Just the same. Leave this new development to me. You take your dog home and feed him."

He tapped on the glass, and Icy pressed his nose against it.

That, I decided, was a good idea, so good that for once I didn't even mind the trace of condescension in Mac's voice.

Thirty-three

Although Icy had seemed comfortable in my car, his demeanor changed once I took him to Sue Appleton's horse farm. He accepted a drink of water, then began to pace. Finding the windows in Sue's family room, he stared longingly at the snowswept world outside.

He'd left his bowl of kibble untouched and ignored Dahlia and Bluebell who gave him a wide berth. So much for the affection of kennel mates.

"I wonder if Icy will ever be able to live in a house," Sue said.

"I'm sure he will. Only an hour ago he was running free at River Rose. This is a tough transition for him."

"I don't believe he was one of Rosalyn's house dogs," Sue said. "She kept the older collies inside."

To my relief, Sue had welcomed him whole-heartedly, albeit with understandable surprise. After what she had said at our meeting, I thought she would rather we didn't continue to look for him. However, she'd already made his vet and grooming appointments. In the light of the family room lamps, I could see that his magnificent coat had suffered from constant exposure to the elements.

"Once I'm sure he won't try to escape, he can have the run of the farm," she said. "As for Bluebell and Dahlia, they'll come around.

At least they aren't fighting. I'm going to foster him myself," she added.

Icy whined and deserted his post at the window momentarily to continue his pacing in the living room. Back and forth and back again, looking for the way out. I felt a momentary pang. Should I have left him in the woods guarding his strange grave?

No. I reminded myself of the reasons for bringing him into Rescue. Below freezing temperatures, predators both human and non-human, and scarcity of food, among others.

Icy would fare better with Sue, and eventually he would find his forever home.

Sue glanced at the photograph of Rosalyn and Icy that had been in the packet. I was right about the clothes. The long gray skirt and green blouse Rosalyn had worn that day had somehow found their way to the woods.

"I can't understand why Rosalyn would throw away her clothes," Sue said. "And if she wanted to get rid of them, why leave them in the woods? It makes as much sense as everything else she's done."

"They weren't exactly discarded. In fact, I've been thinking about their arrangement. It's as if they were laid out, like she was about to put them on. Allowing for the interference of forest creatures, that is, or maybe Icy."

"Like a ritual?" Sue asked.

"Sort of. Like she planned on getting dressed right there in the woods."

Sue smiled. "After dancing naked by the side of the creek? Ah, sorry. I couldn't resist. I know this situation doesn't call for levity."

"I didn't see the creek," I said. "What's remarkable is that Icy brought the blouse to me. That was strange, too. Anyway, we don't know for certain that Rosalyn did it."

"Who then?"

"The killer, of course."

"But why?"

"That's part of the mystery."

Sue offered me more coffee, but I was anxious to go home. It was late. I was hungry and more than a little tired.

"Well," Sue said, "we have Icy but once again no clue to what happened. Shall we try to locate Mia Greer next?

"Yes, then Gloria Collins. The more impossible this mystery becomes, the more I want to solve it."

I called Icy over to say goodbye. Wagging his tail, he followed me to the door. His dark eyes held a mute appeal.

Take me back!

A tiny piece of my heart broke off.

I said goodbye to Sue and left quickly.

~ * ~

Neither Sue nor I had adequate blocks of time for sleuthing. At Marston, the semester's end was approaching. My final exams were ready to pass out, at present in the closet under lock and key. Next week I'd have a new schedule, although many of my current students were returning for the second parts of the literature courses and journalism.

Next week I'd copy class lists into my grade book, draw up new seating charts, and write lesson plans. Everything new except for the haunted section of the floor. This would be an ideal time to experiment with a different desk arrangement. Could I keep the Twilight Zone free of furniture and traffic?

I could try, but sooner or later I'd forget and take a few unplanned steps. Or some unwitting boy or girl would open his notebook and wonder why life suddenly became unbearable. Someday the room might see another tragedy, and I felt powerless to prevent it.

Leonora and I discussed the haunting in my classroom over lunch. Because neither of us knew what to do about it, the talk soon turned to Rosalyn Everett and my discovery in the woods.

"I'm dying to know what happened to her," Leonora said.

I took a bite of my meatloaf sandwich. Lunch tasted good for a change, and Leonora had brought cookies for us.

"Be careful about using that word 'dying,'" I said.

"Okay. I really, really want to know what happened."

"So do I."

"Let's make definite plans to go to The Time Machine."

"We can leave early on Friday if our grades are in," I said. "How about then?"

"Sounds good. What are we looking for exactly besides those women with the Christmas names?"

"Antiques from The Silver Sleigh and any sign of something 'off' in the shop."

"That's awfully vague," Leonora said.

"True, but it's something, and I never pass up a chance to look at vintage books."

"I still have spaces in my house to furnish," Leonora said, "if I can convince myself to move beyond antique jewelry."

"I think talking to Rosalyn's friend and her cousin will be more profitable."

I still wondered about a connection between the two Glorias but hadn't located either one yet.

"I'll go with you if Sue can't." Leonora handed me a cookie. "I'm glad it wasn't Rosalyn's body in the woods," she added. "Now we can hope she's still alive."

"It's over five acres of woodland," I said. "But Mac and his men must have searched the area thoroughly. And why would Icy have guarded his owner's clothes if her body lay nearby?"

The hour hand on the clock had a perverse way of moving faster during lunch. A quick glance told me I had six minutes to finish my cookie and drink my tea.

"So it's a date?" Leonora asked. "Friday after school?"

"Yes, and we'll have to buy something special to celebrate another successful semester winding up."

~ * ~

I dreamed about Rosalyn Everett that night. It was the kind of dream that remains with you long after awakening. While Crane slept and Halley uttered a soft bark from her station in the doorway, I lay still and relived the dream.

I was on River Rose land, following the Winter Ghost. She was ahead of me, strolling gracefully across the fields of snow, clad only in her long, old-fashioned white dress with its three-quarter length sleeves. As if it weren't so bitterly cold that a few moments' exposure could result in a case of frostbite. As if winter had turned into summer.

Ghosts don't feel cold or wetness seeping into their slippers. I did, even though I knew I was dreaming.

It began to snow, and I couldn't see her. But I kept walking, knowing that the yellow ranch house—the spirit's perpetual destination—couldn't be too far.

Suddenly I was somewhere else, in an unknown place, where the house and the kennel didn't exist. Where there was no incline, no wood, and only the faintest of light emanating from an unknown source.

In the distance I heard Rosalyn's voice:

"Take me back."

Thirty-four

The window of The Time Machine had undergone a glittery transformation since my last visit with Annica. A shower of old-time Valentine cards sparkled among the sedate antiques. Winged Cupids winked at us from nests of white lace and pink ribbons. Towering over them the time machine appeared to have come alive with blinking lights on its control panel.

The arrow pointed to 1900.

"I'd like to buy a Valentine present for Jake," Leonora said. "Something masculine."

"Good luck."

Most of the antiques in my view appeared to be collected with a female buyer in mind. Delicate jewelry, hand mirrors, sequined evening bags. red and pink accessories, and hearts in many different forms.

"Jake might appreciate a heart-shaped chocolate cake more or cupcakes," I said.

"You have a point. Well, I can do that and still buy him something."

She opened the door and brass bells announced our arrival. About a dozen people were browsing in aisles, and there was a sedate buzz of conversation. The atmosphere seemed appropriate in an antique shop, but at the same time mysterious. Perhaps that was true in every shop that dealt with relics from a bygone age.

"Now that Christmas is over, are you still interested in finding your sleigh?" Leonora asked.

"Sure. There's always next year. But I'm really here to find out what's going on with the stolen antiques."

The saleswoman who had introduced herself to Annica as Stella emerged from the shadows at the back of the shop.

Why do all these places have to look so mysterious?

"Welcome back," she said with a pleasant smile.

I gave her a puzzled look. Was I that memorable?"

"I remember," she said. "You were here with another lady last week. You bought a book. A paperback. Your friend bought that precious little Cupid lamp. I was sorry to see it go."

With Stella's powers of observation, I hoped she hadn't noticed me taking a picture of the Joan of Arc silverware. I'd planned to take more today. Now I wasn't sure that would be a good idea—unless Leonora or another customer distracted her.

"I'd like to look at furniture," Leonora said. "I have a Victorian house with a lot of rooms to furnish. Do you have delivery service?"

"I'm afraid not. Maybe someday."

"Look for small items," I said. "I'll see if I can find some good books."

"Big spender." Leonora rolled her eyes. "I'd love to have that armoire." She wandered off to examine an ivory giant with ornate carving. It was about eight inches taller than she was.

"Remember," I called after her. "A Taurus trunk is only so big."

I found the table set with the Joan of Arc silver. The dishes were different, garlands of roses on a pale pink background, perfect for a romantic Valentine's Day dinner. I noticed a prodigious amount of silver scattered on various surfaces throughout the shop. There were coffee and tea services, candleholders, and ornate trays. Any one of these items could have been pilfered or not. How could anyone tell?

The basket of vintage Gothics novels was almost empty. Still I discovered two that intrigued me: *Moura* and *Haldane Station,* the latter seeming to be a time travel. I added a World War II-era Nancy Drew, *The Secret in the Old Attic,* and looked for Leonora.

She had moved past the armoire to a maple coffee table. Its mirrored top was decorated with a graceful flower-and-scroll pattern similar to the one on the side of the silver sleigh. I'd never seen a table quite like it.

"Isn't it gorgeous?" she asked.

"It's unusual, but it has a few scratches."

I ran my hand over one of them in the right corner, about two inches in length. The table smelled faintly of lemon furniture polish.

"That's known as a distressed finish," Leonora said.

"Don't you already have a coffee table?"

"Not like this one. And it can't be heavy. We could carry it out to the car ourselves, and I'm sure it would fit in the trunk. It's three hundred and seventy-five dollars," she added.

I could tell she'd made up her mind. It had been like that for me when I'd first seen the silver sleigh.

"Let's find out how old it is," I said.

When we caught Stella's attention again, she was happy to oblige us with the table's history. "It was built in nineteen thirty right here in Michigan and only had one owner in all that time. You won't see a gem like this for sale in any furniture store today."

"The owner put a few dents in it," I said.

"That's unavoidable when a table is loved and used over the years, as this one was. A lightly marred surface is part of the vintage charm."

I couldn't argue with that.

"I want it, scratches and all," Leonora said. "But that's all I can afford today. I guess Jake will get a cake. Did you find what you were looking for, Jen?"

She could see the books in my hand. I imagined she meant the 'something off.'

"I saw a lovely silver teapot I wouldn't mind having," I said, "but it would be impractical. I like to make tea in a china pot."

"Nothing deserving of more attention?"

"No."

That changed when I saw the young woman at the cash register. It was Nicola, looking slightly older and more sophisticated in a scoop-necked black dress with an empire waist. Her hair was different, too. Shorter and sleeker. There was no doubt in my mind. She was the girl I'd dealt with last month in The Silver Sleigh.

I had found my connection.

Leonora saw her in the same instant. "Hey, isn't that…?"

"Let's get the table paid for and out to the car," I said.

I planned to question Nicola, but at present I didn't want to arouse Stella's suspicions in case she was another link.

I helped Leonora carry the coffee table to the counter, and we set it on the floor while she fumbled in her wallet for her credit card.

"Hello, Nicola," I said.

Nicola gave me a furtive look. Perhaps she wasn't as observant as Stella, or she might just have arrived at the shop and failed to see me earlier. In any event, she looked puzzled. Was it an act?

"You may not remember me, but I saw you at The Silver Sleigh around Christmastime," I said.

"The Silver Sleigh?"

"Yes. The antique shop that closed down."

"Oh yes. I worked there for a short time. I don't remember you. Sorry."

"Did they move to another location?" I asked.

"I don't think so," Nicola said. "The owners felt they'd made a mistake. It was too far out in the country. They couldn't afford to keep it open."

"What did they do with all the merchandise?" Leonora asked.

"Oh, there was a sale. Right after Christmas."

"I didn't know that," I said. "I'm sorry I missed it."

Nicola busied herself ringing up Leonora's coffee table and then my books.

"I see you like those old mysteries," she murmured.

"Gothics, yes. They're one of my passions."

"This one is in great condition." She touched *Moura* gently. "The cover isn't even creased. It looks like it came straight from the warehouse."

I smiled. "That isn't likely. It probably belonged to a reader who cherished her books and took good care of them."

It was obvious to me that Nicola was trying to deflect attention from the fate of the old antique shop.

"I wish I'd known about the sale," Leonora said.

"Well it was a quick decision to close. Once the owners made up their minds, they moved quickly."

And The Time Machine had opened a few weeks later.

I felt certain that Nicola wasn't going to say anything more about her former place of employment and equally certain that the entire inventory, all the antiques, hadn't been disposed of in a quick sale. What if they were in the shop all this time, stored in a boarded up building that appeared to be abandoned?

I'd always believed the silver sleigh was hidden somewhere on the premises.

Well, it was still lost to me. But I was forgetting. My intention in returning to The Time Machine was to determine whether thieves were operating in Foxglove Corners and the nearby towns, lifting valuable antiques from estate sales and replacing them with cheap substitutes, then selling the originals for a profit.

I felt like a real-life Nancy Drew pursuing a mystery with the flimsiest of clues.

But my clues weren't flimsy. Just sparse and mystifying.

As Leonora and I carried the coffee table out to my Taurus, I consoled myself. I had pictures on my cell phone, and I had a connection.

I would be back.

Thirty-five

"I have a pale pink cake stand," Leonora said. "On Valentine's Day I'm going to bake a heart cake for Jake and set it on my new coffee table. How does that sound?"

"Romantic. And you'll invite Jake over for a steak and champagne dinner?"

"Dinner, yes, but maybe pot roast and potatoes and beer. I should have bought a pair of candlesticks like yours and light pink candles."

"That sounds lovely, but we're not that close to Valentine's Day. What if Jake is on duty?"

Or—God forbid—suppose he balked at this intimate invitation? In the past, Jake had been changeable, apt to vanish from Leonora's life for long stretches of time.

"Then I'll do it the next day or the next," Leonora said. "I can use the extra time to experiment with recipes. I'm glad I found this coffee table. It'll bring me luck. I know it."

I let Leonora wander around in her dream world and, when we reached her house, helped her carry the new purchase inside. Wafer growled at it and Lassie viewed it from a safe distance.

It might have been an instrument of torture.

"What on earth is the matter with them?" Leonora asked.

"It's something new in the house," I said. "They'll get used to it. Maybe they don't like the smell of the furniture polish."

The odor was rather strong; it should have evaporated.

She pushed the old coffee table out of the way and replaced it with the antique, setting it in front of the lavender sofa.

"This one has character," she said. "It suits the house."

"Sit down or stand beside it, and I'll take a few pictures." I reached for my cell phone.

Leonora called Wafer and Lassie over to her. Incredibly neither one moved.

"They're afraid of the Coffee Table Monster," I said, and took three pictures of Leonora alone at her good luck antique. "Cheer up, Leonora. Now you can leave all the baked goods you like out, and they won't disturb them."

Before I left, we viewed the pictures on the Camera Roll. All were good and showed the mirrored top of the table clearly.

For a moment I wondered why the collies refused to go near the coffee table, but in the end dismissed their behavior as a strange collie quirk. Because they both loved to lie on the sofa, they were bound to make their peace with the new addition sooner or later.

~ * ~

Mia Greer was as eager for a meeting as Sue Appleton and I were. However, it turned out that she was hoping we had information about Rosalyn Everett. A striking auburn-haired woman with a flair for making gaudy prints look classy, Mia met us for lunch at a steakhouse in Maple Creek.

"I can't imagine what happened to Rosalyn," Mia said. "But after all this time, she must be dead. Somebody will stumble over her body one day when they're not looking for it."

The cheery tropical flower pattern of her silky top clashed with this gloomy pronouncement.

"Let's hope they don't stumble over it," I said, not liking the picture forming in my mind.

Sue, who had whispered to me that she didn't like to eat dinner food for lunch, toyed with her salad, while I asked one of my rehearsed questions:

"Do you have any idea where Rosalyn might have gone?"

"None," Mia said. "She didn't say anything to me about leaving town, and I saw her a week before I read about her disappearance."

I sighed. Another dead end. "Do you know anyone she might have confided in?"

"Only Ellen Lancaster, but I never met Ellen. Rosalyn mentioned her from time to time. She called Ellen her collie friend. Why don't you talk to her?"

Sue glanced at me. "We already did. She's as much in the dark as everybody else."

"Mark my words," Mia said. "She was abducted. Then her kidnapper buried her in the woods somewhere. We're surrounded by a lot of good places to hide a body."

"So," I said, "did she happen to mention anyone who wanted to harm her? Maybe to get even with her for some reason?"

Mia looked up from her steak. She appeared to be genuinely shocked. "An enemy, you mean?"

"Somebody who didn't wish her well."

"I always assumed Rosalyn was a random victim. It happens all the time. You know, you're in the wrong place at the wrong time, and just like that it's over."

"But if her assailant was someone she knew…"

Mia frowned, cutting a small piece of her steak with unnecessary force.

"Then it was a collie person. Breeding and showing were Rosalyn's life."

"Can you think of a motive?" I asked.

"Sure. Jealousy. I always thought the dog show game was all politics. Every woman out for herself. Her dog, I mean. If she had the prettiest, most promising puppy, no one would say anything nice about her. It's all about winning. The judges had their favorites..."

"It can't be that bad," Sue said.

But Sue was involved in competition with her riding students and had often shared similar sentiments with me about the horse trade.

"That's the impression Rosalyn gave me," Mia said. "If she made any enemies, it would have been at the shows."

I couldn't see myself seeking out every exhibitor in Michigan who had ever shown a collie. There must be hundreds of them.

"I still think it was random," Mia said. "I guess all we can do is wait, but it doesn't look good."

~ * ~

"We're doing everything wrong," I said, after we parted with Mia, promising to let her know if we learned anything new.

Sue nodded and slid into the passenger's seat of the Taurus. "With your letter from Rosalyn and the diary, you know more about her than her friends."

"Not enough, though. I don't know where to go with this investigation."

"Mia said it best. All we can do is wait. Just think of all the woods in and around Foxglove Corners. It's possible no one will ever come across her body."

"We don't have to let unending wilderness overwhelm us," I said, remembering the clothes buried in the woods behind Rosalyn's house. "There may be a well-hidden grave at River Rose."

"Didn't you say Lieutenant Dalby planned to search the woods?" she asked.

"True. That doesn't mean there isn't a grave there. Something he missed."

We'd reached the outskirts of Maple Creek and the sky looked ominous. I remembered there'd been a possibility of snow in the morning's weather forecast. We hadn't accomplished anything, and I was anxious to get home, as was Sue who had a riding lesson later this afternoon.

"What can we do next?" Sue asked.

"Find the cousin, Gloria Collins, and hope she's still in Michigan. I tried but didn't come up with an address for her. I'll keep looking."

I hoped we didn't find ourselves at another dead end. At least we were moving, even though it seemed at times as if we were standing still.

~ * ~

Whenever I'm troubled, I tend to dream more than usual, brief vivid fragments, distortions of real-life situations. I would wake up and know I'd been dreaming, but the attendant emotions stayed with me for a few seconds after the dream ended. Frustration, fear, an all-enveloping sense of hopelessness. They refused to die with the dream.

That night I dreamed I was in my classroom at Marston with a particularly rowdy group of students, none of whom were familiar. I was trying to keep them in the room. There was some dire situation in the school, a lockdown perhaps, but one or two girls kept escaping while others forced their way in.

I was powerless to prevent it. Hence the frustration. But why the fear? Why the hopelessness?

It was all so murky which is, after all, the nature of a dream. And as one does in a dream, I moved to other parts of the building—to the front office to collect my mail, to deliver a package to another teacher, to the woods outside my room.

I was looking for Rosalyn's body and at the same time running from some inconceivable horror.

The dream ended there, or if it continued, I couldn't remember anymore.

I was where I belonged, lying in bed beside Crane with Halley in the doorway.

Safe home where no dream could hurt me.

Thirty-six

Sometimes the smallest things make the greatest difference. If Brent hadn't come to dinner that evening, if the talk hadn't turned to the new antique shop in town... Well, what happened afterward might not have happened in quite the same way.

I guess I sounded like one of those Gothic heroines, always on the lookout for foreshadowing.

Anyway, I showed Brent the pictures I'd taken of the Joan of Arc silverware and of Leonora's new coffee table.

He lingered over the Camera Roll, holding my I-Phone up to the lamp and frowning.

"What's wrong?" I asked.

"It's this table. I think I've seen one like it."

"Where?"

"Not in real life. In a picture. Mallory Larkin showed me one of her family albums. She had a photo of her Aunt Melinda sitting in front of a table like this with Christmas candles on it. The table had a glass top with a scroll pattern. Very unusual."

He enlarged the view. Looking over his shoulder, I said, "Leonora's pattern has flowers in with the scrolling. They look like lilies."

"Do you think Leonora would let me take a picture of my own? Then I can show it to Mallory and know for sure."

"Of course she will. She's as vested in solving this mystery as we are."

My thoughts leapt to the silver sleigh and our suspicions about the antique thefts. "Then it follows that the real coffee table was whisked away and a cheap one put in its place for the estate sale? And Leonora bought the original?"

"Convoluted but probably accurate," Brent said.

"It's worth investigating," Crane added. "I mean *you* should investigate, Fowler. Not Jennet. I don't want her buying hot antiques."

"I'm still in the room," I reminded him. "And so far all I've bought are hot Gothics."

Forgive me, Virginia Coffman, I thought. *Your books are eminently tasteful.*

"Let's zero in on The Time Machine," I said. "It can't be a coincidence that Nicola used to work at The Silver Sleigh and is now in the new place. She's part of the gang."

"Whoa!" Crane flew into official mode. "That's ninety-nine percent conjecture."

"I'd like to agree with you, Jennet," Brent said. "But maybe Nicola just likes being around antiques and jumped at the chance to work at the new shop."

It occurred to me that there might be more than one maple coffee table with a decorative glass top in Michigan, especially if the furniture was made in our state. But something told me Leonora's coffee table had originally belonged in the Larkin family. The one sold at the estate sale was an inexpensive substitution. Maybe it didn't even have a glass top.

"I intend to keep my eye on that place," Brent said. "I'll take Mallory along to check it out with me. She should be able to recognize some of her aunt's property if it's there."

"Meanwhile I'm going to keep looking for a way to contact Rosalyn's cousin, Gloria Collins. I'm more and more convinced that she's the woman who called herself Gloria MacBride."

"If you discover anything relevant, do *not* proceed on your own." Crane directed his order to both of us. "It's my job to chase down felons. Keep me in the loop."

I agreed to do as he wished and passed around the plate of banana-nut bread, everyone's favorite. Feeling energized at the prospect of more sleuthing, I relented and fed each one of the hovering collies a piece.

"I'll be perfectly safe at my computer," I said. "If I go shopping at The Time Machine again, it'll be for more hot Gothics."

My attempt at humor passed over their heads.

~ * ~

Searching for Gloria Collins proved more difficult than I'd thought. If it weren't for the allusion to the disgruntled relative in Rosalyn Everett's journal, I would have doubted her existence.

Not that my search engine didn't lead me to dozens of people named Gloria Collins, but most of them lived in other states. The few who resided in Michigan were either too young or too old to be Rosalyn's cousin.

I did find an online antique shop with the fanciful name of Rainbow's End. The owner of the site was G. A. Collins. Browsing through the offerings, I found antiques similar to those sold at The Time Machine and before that at The Silver Sleigh. Among them was a decades-old Royal Doulton, a small lady in green with a small brown bird. I ordered it and sent a message to the proprietor asking if she had a rough collie figurine in her inventory. I wanted to add to my collie collection but also hoped to find a way to connect with G. A. Collins.

Now all I could do was wait.

~ * ~

The rapidly approaching end of the semester at Marston was more than sufficient to occupy my mind. On the first day of final exams, I was testing a section of World Literature and one of American Literature survey. Periods had been lengthened to an hour and a half. Then in the afternoon, I'd have a chance to get a head start on grading the tests and figuring out final grades.

It was going to be a good day, one capped with the satisfaction of two courses neatly wrapped up.

I didn't anticipate any problems. I'd made the tests long enough so the average student would have only five or ten minutes at the end of the session to unwind. Translation...to grow restless and begin to whisper, which would gradually lead to talking.

Principal Grimsley himself patrolled the halls during testing. He expected absolute silence in the building and no students roaming the halls, barring a natural disaster. I couldn't afford any disruptions.

Midway through the essay section of the American Lit exam, I wandered over to the windows to watch the snow fall. Everyone was working quietly, but this period seemed to go on forever. Ninety minutes was too long to keep students focused on an exam, in my opinion. Also, this was the time we usually ate lunch. Thinking of lunch, I had a sudden, overwhelming desire for a cold soft drink or even water.

The water fountain was outside the room, across the hall, as I'd been frequently informed by thirsty students, but of course I couldn't leave my class.

I turned away from the window and noticed that Jeanie had raised her hand. How long ago? While I stood and contemplated falling snow.

I hurried to her side and inadvertently treaded on the one small section of the room I had resolved to avoid.

You should never hurry in this room. Never take a careless step. Never...

Nothing happened. The floor remained stable under my feet. No devastating thoughts bombarded me. Nothing changed. And since I wasn't frozen in place, I quickly closed the gap between us.

Jeanie whispered her question. "Does spelling count?"

"Not if I can recognize the word," I whispered back.

"Okay."

Even though my world hadn't turned itself inside out, I felt a trifle weak. *With relief*, I told myself.

Was it only relief?

What else?

With one glance at the clock and another at my class, I sank into the chair at my desk, still vigilant.

On a regular day I'd be eating my sandwich. If I was feeling weak, it must be from hunger.

Realization struck like winter lightning, unexpected, unwanted. A delayed reaction.

I couldn't stay in this classroom at Marston High School another day longer than necessary. The room, in spite of the careful makeover, provided a rich field to nourish evil. The walls, the ceiling, the floor—all had absorbed the blood and horror of that day.

It could happen again. Any day, in any way, to any one of us. The only question remaining was: When?

I had to get away.

Of course I couldn't. Not for another half hour. I didn't trust myself to stand, so I sat and alternately watched my class and the snow fall. Time passed. One-by-one, students finished their tests and brought them to my desk.

I had judged correctly. With ten minutes left, a whisper here and there led to talking which lead to noise.

It didn't matter. I had all the tests in a neat stack on my desk and Grimsley was nowhere in sight. In any event, a rowdy testing session was the least of my worries.

Thirty-seven

"There must be something I can do," I said to Leonora over lunch.

I was still shaken, still thirsty. I'd brought a can of ginger ale from the teachers' lounge and could have drunk more. In the short interval between the testing session and lunch, I had considered my options, which weren't many.

An exorcism? No, of course not. But I had a vial of water from the grotto of Lourdes at home. It had belonged to my mother. Perhaps a drop of the holy water and a prayer...maybe. Obviously trying to avoid the haunted tiles wasn't going to work. I foresaw dozens of incidents like the one I'd just lived through. A moment's distraction, one false step...

"We'll think of something," Leonora said.

"I'm afraid of what it may mean."

I was eating a turkey sandwich but might as well have been eating cardboard. On the other hand, I was still thirsty. Fortunately the vending machine in the lounge had soft drinks of all kinds, and there was always water.

"The last time, when I kept hearing gunshots in the school, they were a warning of the real gunshot that wounded me," I said. "What if something similar happens?"

"We can't know what the future has in store for us," Leonora reminded me. "How involved are you in this antique business?"

"Marginally. I promised Crane to lie low. Brent is going to investigate as soon as he takes a picture of your table."

That would be this evening.

"Then there's the search for Rosalyn Everett," she added.

"Well that's going nowhere fast, and I don't see how there could be any danger involved in what I'm doing."

"You never heard gunfire at the school again. Or did you?"

"No. We moved back into our rooms this fall, and the haunting or whatever it is took this ghastly new form. Maybe it's best for me to leave Marston for good or at least ask for a leave of absence."

"Too drastic." Leonora gazed out the window into the falling snow for a few silent minutes. Suddenly her eyes took on a familiar sparkle. "I have it, Jen! We'll switch rooms."

"I can't inflict my problem on you."

"You won't be. Don't you remember? I stepped on that section of the floor myself at the right time and nothing happened. Not even delayed action. In fact, my life couldn't be happier."

"Well..."

It was a possible solution, but there were problems. We couldn't just move into each other's rooms. Assignments were made, presumably, by the principal. Or the counselors, which meant the computer. On the other hand, those room assignments were arbitrary, and our rooms were in reality one very long room separated by a divider. They were intended to enable team teaching or allow us to show a movie to a large group.

"Grimsley will have to okay it," Leonora said. "If he does, it shouldn't be that hard to change the room number on the kids' schedules."

"He'll never do it."

"Don't be so sure. He likes me. I'll ask him, and this is the perfect time to make a change. We have to come up with a good reason, though."

"Like wanting a fresh start for the new semester," I said.

"That might work."

"I wish there was something in my room I could be allergic to," she added

"The weeds growing outside the window?" I suggested. "You could tell Grimsley you had to take allergy pills all last spring."

"It's winter."

"But it'll be spring before the second semester is over. By then we'll be established in our different rooms."

"I'll work on it," Leonora said. "Our reason will have to be strong and make sense. Not be just a whim."

Now that we had a plan I felt a little better. But in the meantime, as soon as I got home, I intended to look for that vial of water from Lourdes.

~ * ~

Annica was out of sorts. Her long crystal earrings looked like teardrops.

"Brent is seeing someone else," she said as she moved a cloth languidly over the table. "He brought her here for lunch today. She had a salad."

"Well, he has lots of girlfriends. We always knew that."

"She's gorgeous, and she has money. You can tell by the way she dresses."

"Did he introduce her to you?" I asked

"Yes. I waited on them. Her name is Mallory."

"Oh well, if her last name is Larkin, then she's helping Brent investigate the antique thefts."

"She's still gorgeous."

I told her about Leonora's coffee table Brent thought he'd recognized in one of Mallory's pictures. "We may be getting closer."

"Then you'll get your sleigh back?"

"Maybe. Technically it belongs to Mallory."

"If she has a sense of fair play, she'll let you have it."

"We'll see."

I wasn't thinking about the silver sleigh at the moment, only about buying a dessert for tonight and looking for the relic from Lourdes.

Of course I couldn't tell Annica about the incident at school, but perhaps Lucy would have some advice for me. We'd been able to leave school earlier today, and I'd already dropped Leonora off at home.

Planning to make a quick detour to Lucy's house, Dark Gables, I chose a chocolate meringue pie and tossed a few words of encouragement to Annica.

"Don't worry about Mallory Larkin, Annica. She isn't the competition."

~ * ~

"I can still see the sleigh." Lucy held my teacup up to the light. "It hasn't moved since the last reading."

"That's good, isn't it?"

"It would be better if I didn't see it at all."

She pointed to the tealeaf that indeed resembled a sleigh. It was close to my home. Too close. I was glad Brent had taken over the investigation of the antique thefts.

Lucy set the cup on the wicker coffee table. "Now about this other matter…"

She passed me a plate of oatmeal cookies, then gave one to her blue collie, Sky. Anything to delay the inevitable.

"It's so strange," she said. "An eerie phenomenon apparently meant for you alone."

"No, a few of my students were affected by it, too."

"Stranger and stranger. I don't see anything in your cup that could even remotely relate to what's happening in your classroom."

"If the principal will allow us to change rooms, I'll never have to set foot on those accursed tiles again."

And unlike the ghost of gunfire, the tiles couldn't follow me. As for the tragic happening it might herald, I would have to take my chances on the future as did every other person on the planet.

"When does your new semester start?" Lucy asked.

"Monday morning. We're hoping Grimsley will okay the switch before then. We'll both have a lot of books and material to move."

I sat back and finished my cookie. Store-bought as were most of Lucy's baked goods, it was still delicious. Maybe it was the soothing effect of Lucy's hot tea, but I felt hungry for the first time since my step onto danger. Lucy hadn't really offered me any useful advice, but somehow just talking to her had put my school problem in perspective.

"If Grimsley goes along with our idea, I think this will be a clever way to outwit *It*," I said.

"Oh, my dear. You may never be able to outwit *It*."

"Never say 'never.'"

I didn't really feel brave, not at all. Especially since Lucy hadn't seen my wish in the teacup, which was for solutions to the mysteries with no casualties along the way. "I'm going to try," I said.

I glanced at the teacup with the leaves arranged into the special patterns created by my movements.

Not that I was superstitious, but...

I always said that.

In truth, I believed the tealeaf-sleigh was a harbinger of some unhappy event to come. I believed the horror that haunted the classroom at Marston High School would live on as long as the building stood.

Even if I were gone.

Besides, forewarned is forearmed.

Thirty-eight

Brent had been busy. He and Mallory Larkin had visited Leonora to look at the coffee table, then gone on to The Time Machine where they'd wiled away an hour or so examining the antiques. While there, they had learned of the existence of another new antique shop in nearby Spearmint Lake known as Past and Present.

Brent had taken on the antiques thefts as his personal project. I was glad. He was physically able to take care of himself better than I could, had plenty of free time, and wasn't about to give up until he'd hauled in the guilty parties, making a citizen's arrest, if necessary.

And Crane approved.

I'll have to admit that I was the tiniest bit jealous. The antique thefts were originally my mystery. However, I realized I had other mysteries to solve and should learn to share, as I always tried to teach my dogs.

"Leonora's coffee table definitely belonged to Melinda Larkin," Brent said as he settled into the rocking chair with Misty on his lap. "Mallory recognized a scratch on the leg. She made it when she was a kid."

I was incredulous. "She identified a scratch?"

"She remembered trying to cover it up with one of those furniture sticks. Her aunt was fussy about her furnishings."

I thought of Leonora's Valentine's Day plans for the coffee table. A heart-shaped cake, candles, and Jake.

"Will Leonora have to give it back to Mallory?" I asked

"Of course not. Mallory just wants to find out who ripped off the estate. When we went to The Time Machine, she thought she recognized one of her aunt's sapphire brooches and a mahogany what-not shelf."

If Mallory's generosity continued, maybe I might be able to keep my silver sleigh. If I found it, that is.

"Were there only two items? I asked.

"There could be more. It's hard to tell what was in your relative's house without pictures. Fortunately Mallory had that Christmas album."

Crane said, "We should take pictures of everything valuable in the house, Jennet. Everyone should have that kind of record."

"I wish I'd taken one of the silver sleigh. I was waiting till I finished decorating. Then it was stolen."

"I found out that sleigh was made especially for Melinda Larkin by an artisan who later became famous," Brent said. "She had it since she was a little kid."

"Did Mallory mention its worth?" I asked.

Brent nodded. "Priceless."

As I absorbed Brent's information, a few questions occurred to me. I should have thought of them earlier. There were a lot of unknowns in this affair. A lot of strangeness. And on my part a lot of distraction.

"Why was the silver sleigh part of the estate sale then?" I asked.

"Mallory was out of the country when her aunt died. She asked her friend to handle everything. This friend set aside a few of her aunt's personal things for Mallory to keep as a remembrance."

"Was this somebody she trusted?" I asked.

"I assume so."

"Did anyone ever question the people who arranged the sale?"

"That," Brent said, "is part of the mystery. Infinity Inspired has gone out of business. They can't be traced."

"Ah! They're working with the thieves."

"That would be my guess."

"The name sounds weird," I said. "If this wasn't a one-time heist, they may be operating under different names. I could research them…"

"I'll do it," Brent cut in. "In fact, our next stop is the Past and Present shop. If Mallory sees anything familiar, we'll ask where they bought it."

"So you and Mallory make a good team," I said.

"She's a great gal. Always up for a bit of adventure."

Misty squirmed on Brent's lap, signaling her intent to get down. She was beginning to realize she wasn't a lap dog, hadn't been for months.

"We'll go back to The Time Machine, too," Brent said. "They're always getting new stuff in."

"I will too. I think they have stolen articles stashed somewhere. They bring them out a few at a time to sell."

But how would we ever locate this place? Well, Brent was on the case now.

"I'm almost out of reading material," I said. "By the way, does Past and Present carry books?"

"I didn't notice."

He wouldn't. But I decided at that moment to put visiting the two antique shops on my 'to do' list. It looked as if Brent and Mallory were having all the fun. Brent and Mallory… Maybe I'd been too hasty in telling Annica that Mallory Larkin wasn't the competition.

~ * ~

To my surprise— but not Leonora's— Principal Grimsley okayed our request to change rooms and even praised us for forward thinking.

"That's what I like," he'd said. "For my teachers to be innovative and think outside the box."

Leonora repeated the conversation to me as we drove to Marston on the first day of the new semester. Classes were shortened, a kind of run-through, giving us a half day to make the move. We planned to stay after school but hoped it wouldn't be necessary. Two students of mine and one of Leonora's had volunteered to help us.

"So we'll be all set for tomorrow," Leonora said.

Last night, I'd had a sudden negative thought about the switch. True, I wasn't endangering Leonora's mental health, but what if she had a student who was susceptible to *Its* power? Like the school paper's artist, Gwendolyn, and the girl who had begun crying for no apparent reason. How could I have been so self-centered?

"Suppose one of the kids has an unfortunate experience in that place?" I asked.

Leonora glanced behind her and merged smoothly onto the southbound freeway. "I thought of that when I saw a picture of a kitchen island in *Michigan Domiciles*. I'm going to establish an island in the middle of the room. I'll cover the space with a file cabinet or bookcase or something. Smother it. No noxious vapors will be able to escape. Then I'll arrange rows of desks around it."

"That's inspired. No one will be able to step on it, ever. I wish I'd thought of that."

"Do you want your room back?" she asked with a soft laugh. "Because I can't approach Grimsley again."

"No. He's right. It's good to do something different. It'll be good for both of us and our new classes. And you won't have to take allergy pills."

"Fate is going to punish me for lying," she said. "I'll probably develop allergies this spring."

"You won't because what we did is for a good cause."

Mentally I crossed 'the haunted classroom' off my list. Brent was in charge of Operation Antique Heist. What was left?

~ * ~

Sue Appleton said, "Icy is gone."

"Gone where? Not gone as in dead?"

"I hope not. One of my riding students left the door ajar, and he slipped out. We tried to catch him, but... Did you ever try to catch a dog?"

I sighed and took my phone into the living room, away from the play growling of the collies who were engaged in a mock battle over a plush dragon.

"I thought he was settling in."

"So did I, at times. Then he'd start to pace. He wouldn't socialize with the other dogs. He lost interest in eating..." Her voice trailed off. "I did the best I could, Jennet. His heart was elsewhere."

"He's grieving for Rosalyn," I said.

"Icy is so different from Dahlia and Bluebell."

"He was closer to Rosalyn. He's gone back to River Rose."

"It's going down below zero tonight," Sue said. "He didn't touch his kibble. Not even the beef I cut up for him. Dahlia ate it."

"I'll just have to bring him back," I said. "But not tonight."

"I'll go with you. Give me a call when you're ready."

I tapped the 'end call' button on the phone, wondering why I'd ever thought the quicksilver collie's story had reached the end.

Thirty-nine

The snowstorm came out of nowhere, with no warning except for an imperceptible darkening of the sky. Large flakes spattered the Taurus' windshield, first a few, then many. I turned on the windshield wipers.

Darn. I hadn't expected this drastic weather change when I'd set out from Marston an hour ago. For a moment I considered turning around and heading home while the roads were passable, but River Rose was close, only minutes away; and I'd come this far.

I drove on.

Today's detour was the result of an impulse. Jake Brown had picked Leonora up at Marston after school. They were off on a mid-week date to have dinner and attend a winter festival. Driving home alone, I'd been thinking about Icy and my plan to visit River Rose with Sue. Who knew when she'd be free?

I wanted to see if there were any canine prints around the house or leading to the woods. I thought there would be. I'd call Icy and if we were lucky, he would remember my voice and come.

Wind whipped the kennel sign wildly back and forth as I turned on the long driveway to Rosalyn's house. I parked in front of the kennel building. The snow fell more heavily, but I could still see the wreath on the door. Nothing hinted at life except for the ever-present deer tracks. No prints meant no dog.

All right, you've seen enough. Go home.

I made a slow U turn in the drive and turned the windshield wipers a notch faster.

The howl came out of nowhere, like the snowstorm, a mournful, heart-rending cry like no other sound in the world.

"Icy!"

Letting the car idle, I grabbed a bag of treats and stepped out into the swirling snow. It stung my eyes as I made my way to the blue spruce, around the house, and to the back. I stood in knee-high snow, gazing up the incline into the dark woods that rose up to meet the sky, barely able to see through the snowfall.

The howl had originated in those woods. It could be a wild animal. The coy wolf? Or the quicksilver collie.

Whatever it was howled again.

Icy or coywolf? There was only one way to find out.

Swiping impatiently at my face, I cried, "Icy! Come!"

Several yards ahead of me, halfway up the incline, a figure materialized. It seemed as if the snow obligingly quit falling in that one unhallowed space where she walked.

The Winter Ghost, clad in a fancy white dress with long folds lost in drifts, glided away from me toward the woods. Her dark upswept hair remained unblown in the wind gusts.

And what does that tell you?

I could see that she wore a large ornamental comb, studded with glittery stones and around her neck a pearl choker.

"Rosalyn!" I called. "Stop! It's Jennet."

The figure kept walking.

I followed, moving slowly and awkwardly because my boots kept sinking in the highly drifted snow behind the house.

The next howl became one with the wail of the wind.

What was I doing? Could I possibly catch a ghost?

About as easily as I could overtake a running collie.

I squinted into the whipping curtain of snow, still able to see the woman in white. But for how long?

A rock or root protruding out of the snow tripped me. I fell to the ground, landing heavily on my left side and face. There I lay stunned, while the wind whipped my hair into my face and my thoughts froze.

In the distance, I heard another sound carried on the wind. The sound of bells.

Ring silver bells, ring, joyful ring...

Get up! Now.

I pushed myself up and stood shakily, dripping snow on snow.

In a lull between the wind gusts, I couldn't hear anything; I could see only an unending world of white. There was no gliding spirit, and I didn't hear howling, nor even the ringing of bells. Only the wind.

That's okay. You imagined the bells. Snow and sleigh bells go together.

Could the spirit have entered the woods in the few minutes I'd lain stunned on the ground.

Of course. Spirits aren't bound by distance or time.

Anyway, how did I know it had only been a few minutes?

I was dangerously close to tears. I'd dealt my body a painful blow, and worse, I'd lost both ghost and collie.

~ * ~

All I could do was stumble painfully back to the car and get myself home while I was still able to.

Thank heavens I'd left the door open and the motor running. I brushed snow from the windows and the front seat and returned to the road. It was beginning to get slick, and I drove slowly, berating myself for my incredible stupidity.

I could have lost consciousness in the fall, might have frozen to death because nobody knew where I was. They would be waiting for me at home…Crane and the collies.

And I would be the next Winter Ghost to roam the desolate acres of River Rose.

But that didn't happen, and I'd seen the spirit, not from a distance through a kitchen window but up close. That was good. I'd seen details Sue hadn't mentioned because the neighbor obviously hadn't seen them. The glittering comb in the ghost's hair, the choker around her neck.

I wasn't so sure that the woman in white was the spirit of Rosalyn Everett. When had she worn a long white dress suitable for a bride? And she hadn't answered when I called her name.

Honestly, Jennet. Did you expect her to?

I wondered also about her destination. Whether she was Rosalyn or another lost soul, why was she strolling towards the woods, unmindful of the snow and wind?

She'd been at a different point in her walk when Rosalyn's neighbor had seen her.

Rosalyn's clothes, her dog show outfit, had been secreted in the woods. I felt certain that Icy was there now, choosing the cold and dark over Sue's comfortable house.

And what about the clothing hidden under fallen branches? Who could have been responsible for that gruesome burial?

While lost in going-nowhere thoughts, I'd entered the outskirts of Foxglove Corners which gave rise to another concern. What was I going to tell Crane? He wouldn't be happy that I'd placed myself in danger. I could expect another lecture from Crane, the deputy sheriff.

Maybe I wouldn't have to tell him about the fall. Maybe he wouldn't be home yet.

I touched my face again. It felt dry but tender. Fortunately there was no blood. What if I had a bruise, though? There was no hiding a bruise.

I sighed. Why keep the afternoon's excursion a secret? I could have fallen outside my school or in front of my own front door. I wasn't tracking down a gun-toting criminal; I was just going to see if Icy had come home.

Not home to Sue's farm house, of course. Home would always be River Rose to Icy, just as the green Victorian farmhouse on Jonquil Lane was home to me.

I saw it then through falling snow, our house, aglow from inside, warm and secure and inviting.

I couldn't wait to go through the door.

Forty

I slid the beef and potato casserole into the oven, made a simple tomato and lettuce salad, and settled myself in the rocker while Crane built a fire. We had a long evening ahead of us, but I'd begun to feel the effects of my fall and couldn't help wishing it was time for bed.

Crane took one last look at his fire and rose from the hearth. The light turned the gray strands in his hair to silver. "From now on, don't go to River Rose alone, Jennet. You could have been seriously hurt. Even killed."

Halley laid her head in my lap. I saw the same plea in her dark eyes.

"I realized that too late." I touched my face; it was still tender. "I'm going to have to use a lot of makeup to cover the bruise."

No matter how much foundation and powder I applied, I was prepared for an avalanche of questions from my students. Oh, well, winter falls were common. I'd just tell them I lost my balance on the ice. Or ignore the question, but that was never a good idea with inquisitive teenagers.

"It could have been worse," Crane said. "A broken arm or leg—or neck."

Herald the voice of doom. It was time to defuse the situation.

"At least I saw the ghost," I said. "That's good."

How blasé that sounded. I remembered the first time I'd encountered a supernatural phenomenon, the phantom Christmas tree in the old white Victorian on Park Street. I had been puzzled but not really frightened, especially after I heard the poignant story of the tree. Had I ever been frightened when faced with an unearthly being?

I didn't think so. I'd soon realized that Foxglove Corners was hospitable to its supernatural denizens. The ghost dogs of Lost Lake, the phantom skater who had fallen through the ice years ago, and only recently, the murdered girl whose spirit remained in a secret room in the Foxglove Corners Public Library. Don't forget the unhappy ghost who walked the halls of the Spirit Lamp Inn.

Rosalyn's neighbor had seen the woman in white strolling across the snowy field also. We'd have to get together and compare notes.

Crane was unfailingly supportive of my various otherworldly experiences. Tonight, however, he said, "That snowstorm came up so suddenly. Are you sure you didn't see blowing snow and imagine the figure?"

I didn't have to think about it.

"I saw her as clearly as I see you now. I saw the comb in her hair and a pearl choker around her neck. Yes, I'm sure. But I didn't see Icy. I *did* hear howling, though. That's the saddest sound imaginable."

He dropped into a chair near the rocker. "Okay, I believe you. And you think she's the ghost of Rosalyn Everett?"

"Maybe. It seems likely. I have a hard time understanding why she appears in that long white dress, though."

"Tomorrow I want you to come straight home from school," he said.

"I will, as soon as I take Leonora home." I leaned back and luxuriated in the warmth of the fire and of Misty who was leaning against my leg, watching me. Home was so much better than a snowdrift.

"If you have a chance, will you swing by River Rose every now and then to see if Icy is there?" I asked.

"Sure, but this is where we were weeks ago."

"I thought he would adjust to life at Sue's, but he was restless from the first. This means he still has something to protect in the woods."

"Not Rosalyn Everett's clothes. They're gone."

"That leaves her body."

"Stay out of the woods." Crane spoke in his stern deputy sheriff's tone.

I didn't argue with him. As bad as it had been to take a tumble in Rosalyn's front yard, how much worse to fall in the woods? How much more likely with all those exposed roots and encroaching branches? And how much more unlikely that anyone would find me before I froze to death?

I could have lost Crane and everything I loved. I gave Misty a long pat and felt a tiny bit better.

That wouldn't have happened because I knew enough not to go for a winter hike in Rosalyn's forbidding woods with or without a companion.

"I promise, if you'll look for me," I said. "Icy is wearing a blue collar now."

"I'll look, but you may never get him to accept anyone else's home."

"We have to try. He can't live outside all winter."

"Other dogs have. They've survived."

"Maybe, but it isn't ideal."

"He has a thick coat and probably snagged a few wildlife meals already."

What Crane said was true, but I wanted desperately to give Icy a comfortable forever home again. I thought that was what Rosalyn would have wanted for him, and after all, I was a member of the Collie Rescue League.

That's a lofty ambition, my inner voice said, but it can't happen yet. Something else has to happen first.

~ * ~

"Wow, Mrs. Ferguson. How does the other guy look?"

It was first hour in my new classroom, and the cheeky inquiry came from one of my World Literature students, a boy whose name I hadn't memorized yet. Andy? Allen? A name that began with an 'A.'

He was waiting, along with the rest of the class. There were too many unfamiliar faces in front of me. I wished I'd launched into the day's lesson immediately after attendance.

"There's no other guy," I said. "I slipped and fell in the snow yesterday."

Why this statement should elicit a scattering of giggles eluded me. Sophomores could be so immature, and this group was a little bit too lively for the early hour.

"Open your books to page one hundred," I said. "We're going to begin the course with a survey of short stories from around the world."

Not the most colorful or attention-grabbing opening to class, but the story should hold their interest.

And thank heavens I didn't have to worry about taking a single false step and having the floor come apart under my feet.

The class quieted, albeit slowly. I glimpsed Principal Grimsley passing by in the hall. He sent his traditional pasted-on smile my way and walked on. I read the first paragraphs of the story, then asked for a volunteer reader.

The morning passed with a great deal of first-day-of-class confusion but without a single unsettling incident.

At lunchtime, I returned to my previous room to eat with Leonora. She'd arranged the furniture as she'd planned, with a care to covering the haunted space.

"It feels strange being in a different room," she said.

"I hardly noticed. New classes kept me busy. I think I'm going to have a chaotic morning."

"Then your afternoon classes will be easier to work with. It's the law of averages."

That didn't make sense, but it sounded good.

"I'm glad we changed rooms," I said and lifted the paper glass I'd filled with ginger ale. "Here's to a successful new semester."

~ * ~

"Jennet! What on earth happened to you?"

Annica stared at me, coffeepot in hand.

I had stopped at Clovers for take-out dinners, stuffed cabbages, and stayed to have a cup of coffee and a quick conversation with Annica.

"I had a little fall," I said.

"I was afraid you'd met up with the Master Criminal. Glad you didn't."

She poured the coffee and slipped into the seat opposite mine.

"I was looking for Icy at River Rose," I said. "He ran away from Sue's."

I told my story again. Once Annica knew I hadn't broken anything, she wanted to hear about the Winter Ghost again.

"I've never seen one," she said. "Not even a puff of vapor. And you've seen... How many?"

"I don't know. Under a dozen?"

"I think it's my turn now."

"It doesn't work that way." I took a sip of coffee. It was good but still too hot to drink.

"Brent came in for lunch," Annica said. "He came alone this time, and we had a chance to talk."

"What's new?" I asked.

"He and that Mallory person went to Past and Present. They saw some more stuff from the Larkin place. A set of china and a punch bowl. I forget what else."

I imagined Brent would visit us soon with a full report. If he wasn't busy with Mallory Larkin. In the meantime, I wanted to check out Past and Present for myself and go back to The Time Machine.

"When," I asked, "are you free to go antiquing?"

Forty-one

Past and Present was smaller than The Time Machine and had a cluttered, unattractive window display. Old rocking chairs and steamer trunks, antique dressers and toys jumbled together reminded me of a typical grandma's attic.

Squished between a tea shop and a boutique, Past and Present didn't issue an irresistible invitation to the shopper. If Annica and I hadn't been on a mission, I'd have suggested we go to the tea shop instead.

One shining star in the window caught my attention…an ivory chest embellished with a hand-painted green, blue, and yellow spring scene. If it wasn't too pricey, I might buy it for our bedroom.

"I don't understand the name," Annica said. "And it doesn't roll off the tongue. Past and Present. See?"

"I can think of a few meanings. Find a present among treasures from the past. Or use an object from the past in the present."

"Whatever," Annica said. "You shouldn't have to think about a name. "Let's go in."

The requisite brass bells rang out a welcome, and there was Grandma, a petite silver-haired lady in a fussy lavender dress. The interior of the shop was dim and—all right—spooky. Several of the antique lamps were on, and the pervading scent was lilac…from a candle, I imagined.

We were the only customers.

"Good afternoon," the lavender lady said in a soft voice with a trace of an English accent. "I'm Matilda. May I help you?"

"We're just looking at the moment," I said.

"For birthday presents," Annica added. She pushed the hood of her purple jacket back, and her seahorse earrings clinked against a dangle of seashells.

"That's a wonderful pair of earrings," Matilda said, gazing at Annica's seahorses with admiration. "We have lots of sea-inspired jewelry, being so close to Spearmint Lake. Would you like to see our collection?"

"I would, yes. Do you have coral or turquoise?"

"We have both, in abundance."

"I like the ivory chest in the window," I said.

"That *is* lovely, and a steal at nine hundred dollars."

That I considered pricey. Well, I could spare the price of books, but not old furniture, however lovely. "I was wondering," I said. "Where do you buy your antiques?"

Matilda hesitated. Apparently this wasn't a frequently asked question.

"Mostly at estate sales."

I glanced at the nearby aisles, remembering the items that had come from Melinda Larkin's house, according to Mallory. A set of china. A punch bowl. I saw plenty of china and a few glass or crystal bowls. I wished Brent or Annica had been more specific.

Annica said, "Let's split up. I'll look at the earrings. Didn't you want to buy books?"

"Oh, yes, old time books in a series," I said for Mathilda's benefit. "I collect them."

"Like Nancy Drew?" Matilda asked.

"Nancy and her friends."

"We have some. They're displayed throughout the shop. You'll just have to look around."

Good. That would give me an opportunity to examine the inventory. On a marble-topped side table, I found a novel that looked appealing: *Dorothy Dale, A Girl of Today*. Next to it was a stack of Maida books, topped by *Maida's Little Island,* and next to them, a dog story, *Beautiful Joe*. I remembered crying over that one. I also saw about a dozen volumes of the Campfire Girls in various colorful locales.

The bells on the door rang.

I looked up from the books, and Rosalyn Everett looked back at me.

It can't be.

I looked again. She appeared to recognize me and turned quickly as if to go back outside.

Matilda said, "You're late. Did you run into trouble on the road?"

After that, what could she do but enter?

As she walked into the light of a Tiffany lamp, I saw that I was mistaken. My first fleeting impression of her had been strong but false. This woman wasn't Rosalyn Everett, although she resembled her slightly in the shape of her eyes and cheekbones. But the newcomer's face was fuller, and she had applied blush with a heavy hand.

Oddly, she had the same hairdo, held in place by a pearl-studded comb.

I hadn't seen Rosalyn for several months and couldn't be expected to remember her. But my initial impression stayed with me.

"It's in the back," Matilda murmured. "Will you girls excuse me? I won't be long."

So saying, she led the Rosalyn lookalike to a room in the back of the story and shut the door. Another back room.

"I could have sworn that was Rosalyn Everett," I said in a low voice when I was sure Matilda and the newcomer couldn't hear me.

"Honestly, Jennet, how can she be shopping for antiques and haunting River Rose at the same time?" Annica asked.

"She can't. That's obviously not Rosalyn, but she looks so much like her. I thought for a moment..."

The door opened, and Matilda came out alone. "Did you find what you were looking for?" she asked.

Annica held a three-strand bracelet of coral beads in her hand. I was still holding *Beautiful Joe.*

"I'll take this bracelet," Annica said. "Do you have matching earrings— in the back maybe?"

Matilda glanced toward the back room. "Everything we have is on display. As long as the earrings are coral, they don't have to be an exact match."

"Well, I didn't see anything else that grabbed me. Jennet, what do you think?"

"Let's pay for our purchases and have a cup of tea next door."

We could keep browsing and wait for the back door to open again, but it was getting late. Annica had to go home and read another Victorian novel, and I had to make dinner.

That was all right. We would definitely come back. Or I'd return with Brent. If the antiques he and Mallory had seen before had disappeared, we needed to find out why. If they were there, we had to figure out our next step.

I couldn't explain it, but the face of the woman I'd thought was Rosalyn Everett haunted me. She knew me. I was pretty sure of that.

~ * ~

The owner of the Lakeville Tea Room understood the allure of an enticing window display. Hand-painted bone china tea cups interspersed with trays of frosted delicacies, a white wrought iron ice cream table set for two—who could resist a visit on a cold afternoon?

"Do you really want a cup of tea or did you just say that?" Annica asked.

"Well I said it to smooth our quick exit, but it sounds good. Do you have time?"

"Oh, sure. All I have to do is finish reading my novel. It's fast reading."

We went inside, found a small table similar to the one in the window, and ordered individual pots of tea and chocolate fudge cupcakes—and no, this impromptu indulgence wouldn't spoil my dinner. Unlike Past and Present, the tea shop was crowded.

Lucy would love this place. So would Camille. I'd have to bring them here some Saturday. Some day when my mind wasn't overloaded with thoughts of antique robberies.

"What do you think Matilda meant when she said 'it's in the back'?" Annica asked.

"She might have been referring to a stolen antique."

"Or an item ordered especially for her."

"I like my idea better."

Crane would accuse me of building a fabrication based on a single sentence not meant for my ears. He would be right, but my theory seemed feasible to me.

Working with a shadowy company like Infinity Enterprises, the thieves robbed the estate sales they organized and substituted cheap lookalikes for genuine antiques. They then placed them in shops throughout the area at marked up prices, counting on the distraction of the bereaved and heirs. Or, in the case of people like Mallory Larkin, on their absence.

It was clever, when you thought about it, and carried a minimal risk of discovery. Until someone bought an antique mistakenly placed with the rest of the inventory and started to investigate. Until the antique was stolen from a private home and replaced with an inexpensive replica, deepening the mystery. At this point, the thieves might be running scared.

"I have to talk to Brent," I said. "He described Past and Present as a new antique shop. It looks like it's been there for years, barely holding on."

"So, who do you think that woman who looked like Rosalyn Everett was?" Annica asked.

"I wish I knew. Her cousin, Gloria, perhaps? That would account for the resemblance. I wonder if she's still in the back room gloating over the latest haul?

"Maybe it's all innocent. Like Matilda was keeping an item on layaway for her."

"Nothing in this case is innocent," I said.

I ate my cupcake and continued to enhance my theory, all the while keeping my eyes on the sidewalk. No one in my view exited or entered the shop next door. Soon my plate and the teapot were empty.

As it always did when I was far from home, the snow began to fall.

At least I felt that the trip to Past and Present had been a success. In what way remained to be seen.

Forty-two

Brent turned up at our door that evening with a list of antiques which, in all likelihood, had come from Melinda Larkin's estate. Once he greeted the dogs and seated himself in front of the fire, he read from it:

"The dishes had a design of pansies and blue ribbons. It was a service for twelve. The punch bowl came with a ladle and six matching glasses. Mallory said at one time there were eight. They were all decorated with holly berries and bells. She recognized a pair of pink milkglass lamps and a two-tier mahogany Duncan Phyfe table. Also a what-not shelf. I think I have that right."

"I don't recall seeing any of those items at Past and Present," I said.

"You wouldn't have seen the lamps. Mallory bought them. She always liked them as a child."

"I'm surprised she didn't keep more of her aunt's property," I said.

"The time wasn't right. Remember, she was out of the country when her aunt died. Then there was so much of everything. Mallory has her own house, all furnished. Those lamps caught her eye, though. She just wanted them."

"The punch bowl set sounds lovely," I said. "I might have bought it myself."

"It was real pretty. Her aunt brought it out every Christmas. Just like the silver sleigh."

"It's strange that all the items on that list disappeared between the time you and Mallory went to Past and Present and this afternoon. It's almost as if someone suspected you were on to them and hid them away."

In the handy back room. I wondered what secrets it held. I knew I'd never have a chance to find out.

"Matilda sure doesn't look like a criminal," Brent said.

"Looks can be deceiving. Anyway, I'm sure we're dealing with a ring of antique thieves, not just one person."

"Mallory couldn't prove anything she recognized belonged to her aunt without pictures, so we didn't make any accusations. Even if she could, Matilda would claim she didn't know they were stolen."

"We don't need proof to know what's going on," I said. "But we do if we want to capture those responsible and stop them from robbing the dead."

"There is no 'we' in this project," Crane said. "Fowler, keep Jennet out of it."

I bristled at his tone. He had made himself clear on my involvement more than once. "I'm just brainstorming."

"This is getting to sound dangerous. I don't want to lose you, honey," he added.

"I wouldn't either if she were mine," Brent said. "No one else can make ordinary food taste so good."

I gave him a grateful smile. "Flattery will get you an invitation to dinner."

Anticipating his visit, I'd cooked a pot roast with potatoes and carrots. There'd be leftovers for sandwiches and for the dogs. For one collie in particular, the one I hoped to lure out of the woods.

"Mallory is making a list of antique shops in a two or three hour radius of Lakeville," Brent said. "We're going to check out all of them, looking for more of her Aunt Melinda's stuff."

"Be sure to stop at the Green House of Antiques and all the shops on that street. They call it Antique Row."

"That'll be a starting point."

"None of this activity is going to lead to an arrest," I said. "We have to set a trap for the thieves. Think of them as varmints we want to eradicate."

Brent looked interested. This was hunters' talk. "What kind of trap?"

"I've been thinking about it. How about if we have a staged estate sale at your barn? We can all contribute antiques."

"How would that work?" he asked.

"Look around for a company that manages estate sales. Maybe you'll find Infinity Inspired operating under another name. Mark each item in a certain way known only to you. Then you back off and let them handle everything. You can show up later and complain about any substitution you see."

"One problem is I don't have a lot of antiques lying around," Brent said. "I don't think anyone does." He paused, looking from Crane to me. "Do you?"

"There's an ornate mirror in the attic, and a lamp or two. Oh, and a framed seascape. It was expensive but neither one of us like it."

"Toss in that silver sleigh I gave you."

"No, I want to keep it," I said.

I could see he was warming to the idea.

"We'll call it the Napoleon-Fowler sale," he said.

Napoleon was one of Brent's rescues, a gigantic canine who resembled the old cartoon character of the same name. He was one of Brent's best friends and a trusty guard dog.

"The whole idea sounds crazy to me," Crane said.

"It could work."

"I like it," Brent said.

Crane was intent on playing the devil's advocate this evening. "You're counting on attracting this crooked estate sales manager and using antiques that could be substituted for cheap imitations like that silverware with the saint's name."

"That's the idea."

"That mirror you mentioned is one of a kind. You think your thieves could find a cheaper version of it somewhere?"

"Why not? Mirrors like that are fairly common. Anyway, it doesn't have to be an exact duplicate, just a look-alike. They'd take the original to a store like Past and Present and sell it for, say, sixty or seventy dollars?"

"That old mirror? It's tarnished."

"We'll call it distressed. I'm using it as an example."

"I have a scratched up Singer sewing machine," Brent said. "It belonged to my great-grandmother. She used to sew a lot. For sure, I'm never going to use it."

"You'll never find a cheap imitation of that, but it could be filler. What we need are real antiques they could easily duplicate. The seascape, for instance. It's an original, but there must be a thousand pictures just like it."

"I'll look around in the basement," Crane said.

"I'll bet Camille has antiques she could spare, and it's possible that Leonora does. She has some of her parents' furniture. We'll get a tempting collection together and set our trap."

"In the snow?" Crane asked. "Yard sales are in the spring and summer."

"We're not talking about a yard sale," I said. "It'll be in Brent's barn where it's fairly warm. Instead of Brent and Mallory driving all over Michigan, we'll let buyers come to us. Hopefully the people involved in the thefts will show up."

With luck, one of them might be the Rosalyn Everett lookalike. I already planned to be a constant presence at the sale and if Crane left Napoleon on guard, there couldn't possibly be any danger. Crane wouldn't consider that being involved in Brent's investigation.

"We'll advertise it well," I said. "Make it an irresistible event. How about giving flyers to the antique shops in the area?"

"I'll get right on it," Brent said. "We want to have it soon. Now when's dinner and what's for dessert?"

~ * ~

Whenever Sue Appleton called me on a weeknight, I'd learned to anticipate trouble.

"Rosalyn's neighbor has been hearing howling in the woods again," Sue said. "It's disturbing her sleep. What's more, somebody started a rumor that there's a ghost dog in the neighborhood, maybe one of Rosalyn's collies who didn't survive. It's spreading like wildfire."

Although I wasn't one to discard a ghost story, especially in Foxglove Corners, I didn't like the sound of it.

"It has to be Icy," I said. "If folks get riled up, he's liable to get hurt."

"I'm sure you're right. I've been driving over to River Rose almost every day and calling him. He never comes, and I don't see him. It's funny, though. I saw tire tracks in the snow. We're not the only visitors."

"Crane's been looking for Icy, too," I said.

Poor lost collie. Icy must know he was in danger of being taken away from his lair and confined to Sue's house again. His heart was there in the woods with the cold and snow and predators—and

Rosalyn's body. At times I felt certain that Rosalyn was dead and had been buried in the woods before the ground froze. Dead while all of us thought she had merely pulled her famous disappearing act again.

"We have to redouble our efforts to find Icy," I said. "I can't go in the woods alone or even to River Rose after my fall. Is there a time when we can go together?"

"I think the day after tomorrow is free. Late in the day, when you come home from school. I'd bring Dahlia or Bluebell along, but he never paid attention to them when he was here."

"I have a better idea," I said. "Candy is an unofficial search and rescue dog, and Raven lived outside herself once. They're my sharpest collies. With luck, they'll lead us right to Icy. In the meantime, are you doing anything to counteract those rumors?"

"I've told everyone I talked to that the howler has to be River Rose Icemaker. But word has spread about the mysterious woman in white haunting Rosalyn's property. That neighbor turned out to be a first-rate gossip."

"If we're successful in locating Icy and rehoming him, the rumors will die down," I said.

I wasn't forgetting the Winter Ghost. Just not mentioning her.

Forty-three

Something was different today.

I brought the Taurus to a stop and studied the yellow ranch house in its surround of drifted snow.

The Christmas wreath still hung on the door. Well, who would take it down? The yellow house should look picture-postcard beautiful with its backdrop of rising dark woods. Instead, it looked forlorn and forbidding, one of the unhappiest houses I had ever seen.

"Spooky," Sue said, her hand resting on the passenger's door handle. She reached for the treats she always brought to tempt Icy.

"Wait!"

I had it! The difference. From a room inside the house, a faint light glowed where no light should be.

"Someone's in the house," I said. "They turned a lamp on. And look at those prints. They were made by boots."

Sue reached for her cell phone. "We'd better call the police."

"Not yet. There's no other car here."

"Was it the woman in white, do you think?"

I glanced at Sue, surprised at her haste to leap to the supernatural. She'd been associating with me too long. But this case was different.

"Ghosts don't need boots," I said. "And they don't leave prints behind. Do you have the key to the house?"

"It's on my key ring." She fumbled in her purse. "Why?"

"We're going in. Or I am."

"What if he's still there?"

"I don't think anyone's inside."

"But you don't know."

"It stands to reason."

"It could be a vagrant. Anyway we came to call Icy," Sue reminded me. "Not to play Nancy Drew."

Sue had a point, but I wasn't about to be dissuaded. "You stay in the car then. I'll go alone."

"Not on your life." She opened the door, clutching the bag of treats. "I'm staying with you."

As we walked up to the porch, I studied the boot prints. They led to the stairs and straight to the door, then away from it. Our intruder had come and gone. Then there were the tire tracks.

Could he have been careless enough to turn on a light which might be noticed by a passerby, then forget to turn it off when he left?

Sure. Some criminals were stupid.

"You should call Crane at least," Sue said. "Let him know what we're doing."

And he'd tell me to resist the temptation to investigate, but not in those words.

"I'll tell him later."

Sue fitted the key in the lock and turned the doorknob. I stepped inside, with Sue close behind me.

"We're breaking and entering, Jennet. We don't have Rosalyn's permission this time."

"We're doing no such thing. You have a key. Besides, Rosalyn would want us to investigate. What if somebody realized no one was living here and decided to ransack the place?"

"Still. We should report it."

There was no evidence of a burglary. The air was frigid and forbidding. Again I had a strong feeling that the house didn't want us there. It had secrets and was determined to keep them.

We found the source of the light in the family room, the Tiffany-style lamp that reminded me of a multi-colored lantern ornament.

"It doesn't look like anything's been disturbed since we were here for the journal," Sue said.

"Someone broke in for some reason, and it wasn't the ghost."

I turned the lamp off, and the darkness seemed to intensify.

"Ghosts don't have to break in," Sue said with a soft laugh. "It's strange that the electricity is still on, but not the furnace. I think it's warmer outside."

"Who would turn the furnace on? Rosalyn disappeared this last time in the summer. She wouldn't have needed heat. By the way, who's been paying the utility bills and taxes? And what about the mortgage? How long can they be delinquent?"

"In a case like Rosalyn's, I have no idea. She hasn't been declared dead, only missing."

Bills. They kept coming, whether or not you were able to pay them. Why hadn't I thought about that? Maybe the solution to Rosalyn's disappearance was easier than I thought. Find the person who pays the bills, and you'll have the answers.

But what about mail? That kept coming, too, even after months.

Clearly there were several things I hadn't thought of.

"While we're here, let's search the house," I said.

"What are we looking for?"

"Anything that seems off."

"That's nice and vague."

"You go right, and I'll go left," I said.

My route took me to a long hall with four closed doors. Two bedrooms, one larger than the other that appeared to be Rosalyn's room, a bathroom, and one that had been used as a study. All were neat and orderly as if waiting for the person who never came.

At the end of the hall, a door was ajar. I pushed it all the way open and found myself in a room that contained a little bit of everything, the kind in which people keep unused furniture and furnishings that don't have a proper place elsewhere in the house.

And there on top of a mahogany credenza pushed up against a window, a splash of silver caught the last rays of the January light. I blinked, not believing my eyes.

It was a silver sleigh with eight tiny reindeer. *My* sleigh!

Without stopping to wonder about its presence in Rosalyn's storage room, I grabbed it. Particles of dust floated away into the air. It had been here for a while, unattended and undusted.

But how did it come to be in this house that had been shut up for months? And how long had it been here? Ever since it had been stolen?

A sound broke through my thoughts. A creaking? A floorboard protesting a footstep? Something that ceased before I could identify it. Then all was silent again.

It must be Sue.

I found her in the living room looking out the window. "I didn't see anything out of place. We'd better go. It's starting to snow and..." She broke off. "What's that you're holding?"

"My sleigh. The one that was stolen."

"Surely not by Rosalyn? She's been missing since way before Christmas."

"By someone else then. Someone with a key to the house. That would explain the light."

"Rosalyn might have given a spare key to a neighbor for emergencies," Sue said. "I can check. But I don't see why anyone would see the need to get inside the house now."

"Let's go," I said. "We have to think. This sleigh connects Rosalyn to the antique thefts."

"She can't possibly have taken part in them."

"No. Unless... Well, we don't know the whole story."

Just when I'd been certain Rosalyn was dead and buried in the woods, I saw my theory turn itself upside down. Was the whole disappearance a clever act to enable Rosalyn to operate as an invisible thief?

It was possible, but I thought there must be another answer. Never in my life had I encountered a more frustrating mystery.

"You're not planning to take that sleigh with you," I hope," Sue said.

"Why not? It's mine. I paid a hundred dollars for it."

"Yes, but it's evidence now. You can't just remove it from the scene."

I supposed Sue was right. Even though the homeowner was long gone and presumably dead. On the other hand, now that I had the silver sleigh in my possession, I was loath to relinquish it. If I did, the next time I came to River Rose, it would be gone again.

"Put it back," Sue said. "Tell Lieutenant Dalby what you found. Let him handle it."

"I guess I should. When it was stolen, he *did* say he'd try to find it."

As I set the sleigh on the coffee table, a howl cut through the stillness that pervaded the long abandoned house.

An omen, I thought.

"That's Icy," Sue murmured. "He's near."

I nodded. "Let's see if he's outside."

~ * ~

He wasn't.

We walked around the house, plowing through deep drifts, and approached the woods but came to a stop at their edge. I saw deer prints but no indication that a canine had walked there. Not Icy, not the coywolf.

A few snowflakes drifted down. The light was rapidly fading, and the air had the sharp bite of a woodland predator. I pulled my hood up around my head and thought about the silver sleigh I was leaving behind in Rosalyn's house.

I felt like going back to retrieve it.

We hadn't planned on hiking through the woods today. For one, it was too late. Then snow was in the forecast. It had just been a routine stop at River Rose to see if we could entice Icy into the open.

And look how it had turned out.

Sue emptied the beef jerky treats in the snow, we called Icy one last time, and reluctantly turned to go. As I drove out to the road, I remembered Rosalyn's storage room and the mahogany credenza. What else had been in that room?

Breaking and entering or not, I'd have to return.

Forty-four

As it turned out, I didn't go back to River Rose. Lieutenant Mac Dalby found dozens of antiques in Rosalyn's storage room and more in the kennel building. He came to our house to give his report and visit with Crane who was an old friend.

"It's now off limits," Mac said in the tone Crane had used earlier. "I'm taking over from here."

"I can't stay away," I said. "Rosalyn's collie is still there living in the woods. Sue Appleton and I have been trying to coax him out."

"Oh, yes. The howling dog. We've been getting complaints about him."

He hesitated as if looking at the issue from both sides and finally said, "Okay. Just don't go inside the house."

"I won't."

In truth I had no desire to do so. I remembered the unexplained sound in the house. At the time I'd dismissed it, but in the light of later discoveries, I considered a grim possibility. What if the person who was using Rosalyn's house for his own illegal purposes had been hiding in another part of the house?

I hadn't mentioned hearing anything to Sue or Crane. Probably it was half my imagination and half a part of the house settling. Still I continued to wonder.

Crane said, "I'd rather you didn't go to River Rose at all, Jennet. Whoever stashed the antiques in the Everett place can return any time. Then where would you be?"

"In a tight place."

"They have a major operation going. They won't take kindly to anyone trespassing on the property."

"Is there any chance the antiques belonged to Rosalyn?" I asked. "Not the silver sleigh but the other furniture?"

"There's always a chance, but it's unlikely," Mac said. "There's too much stuff and when the Everett woman was living at River Rose, she kept dogs in her kennel. About twenty of them."

"Maybe she was one of those hoarders."

But that didn't fit with Rosalyn's personality as Sue described it, and when Rosalyn had a litter to sell, she welcomed several visitors to the kennels.

"A house left empty for so long is an invitation to crooks," Mac said. "There's a wreath on the door, sure, but most people have long since taken down their Christmas decorations. Its needles are dried and yellow. It's easy to see why our thieves thought the house would be a good place to keep their stolen goods. I'm thinking they took them out and placed them for sale in antique shops, a few at a time."

"They couldn't have known that Sue Appleton had a key."

"Or that you two would let yourselves in and discover the antiques," Crane added.

"I wonder how they got in. I didn't see any sign of a break-in."

One answer occurred to me, but I didn't like it. They could have obtained a key from Rosalyn.

"Thieves have their ways," Mac said. "It was stupid of them to leave a light on, though."

"I'll concentrate on capturing Icy then, and leave the police work to you," I said. "But when this is all over, I want my silver sleigh back."

~ * ~

Brent threw himself into preparations for the fake estate sale with his customary enthusiasm. He contacted Infinity Inspired, set two dates for the sale at the end of January, and collected antiques from far and wide. All of our friends were eager to participate, even—or especially—Annica.

Over coffee at Clovers the next afternoon, she said, "I have an old cuckoo clock from Germany. My grandma gave it to me. Most cuckoo clocks look alike with carved branches and a bird on top. I've seen lots of others just like it, so it would be easy for the thieves to find a substitute."

"Don't you want to keep it?" I asked.

"No. It gets on my nerves. All those bird calls and music. I need it quiet when I read those Victorian novels for my class. They're not exactly page turners."

"Camille, Sue, and Leonora contributed antiques for the sale," I said. "I'm excited about it."

Annica took a sip of her coffee. "You're counting on the thieves working with Infinity Inspired. I thought they were out of business."

"That's what we heard, but Brent found them. They seem legitimate, a husband and wife team, Mark and Robyn Dunaway. Of course, they could be a front."

"I'm confused about what you're hoping will happen. You talked about attracting the thieves with flyers. That doesn't make sense, the way you explained about the estate sale managers making cheap substitutions."

I guess it didn't. Not even to me, now that I thought about it. But the estate sale was the best idea anyone had.

"It's all guesswork," I said. "Who can tell how they operate? We just know that something underhanded is going on and local antique shops are involved. I hope our sale drives them out into the open."

"What if Infinity Inspired is a legitimate company?"

"Then I guess we'll just sell our antiques and make some money."

"Is Mallory Larkin going to be around?" Annica asked after a moment.

"I assume so. After all, she's the one who was affected by the thefts."

"She sure is keeping close to Brent."

"They're visiting antique stores together," I said.

Her hand strayed to her ice cream cone earrings, an odd choice of accessory for a cold winter afternoon.

"I haven't seen Brent lately," she said. "He used to come in for breakfast or lunch every now and then. I guess he spends all his time with her."

"Brent has a lot of interests. You can get your clock, and we'll take it to him at his barn. He's either there or at my dinner table. That'll give you a chance to visit with him."

I wasn't comfortable in the role of matchmaker, but I didn't like to see Annica so vulnerable. As for Brent, he did seem to be spending a lot of time with Mallory Larkin.

Annica brightened at the prospect. "Maybe I'll find something else for the sale."

~ * ~

That night I dreamed about the silver sleigh. Not the antique Christmas decoration I'd left in Rosalyn Everett's house, but the life-sized version from my earlier dream. That impossible vehicle made of sterling silver and drawn by eight silver reindeer as large as horses—and undeniably alive.

Their breath turned to crystal clouds in the cold night air, and the bells on their harnesses jingled wildly.

The sleigh waited for me on the lane, elegant and washed in moonlight. It waited without a driver while the reindeer tossed their heads and stamped their hooves in the snow.

I didn't want to go any closer to it, but the wind pushed me along until I had no choice but to climb aboard.

There's always a choice, a voice said.

Then we were moving into the blowing snow, the deer running with no driver to hold the reins. Snow buffeted my face and blinded me. I couldn't see anything in front of me except for the deer at the end of the team.

That was the way the dream ended, in waves of icy, plummeting snow, and a vague sense of dread.

It was half past midnight. Half past the witching hour.

I relived the dream once and resolved to forget it. It was nothing but a mere distortion of the surprising discovery at River Rose. My longing to find my stolen antique coupled with the jolt of fear I'd felt when I heard the creaking sound which I attributed to Sue.

It means nothing, I told myself, *so don't be afraid.*

But what if I was wrong?

Forty-five

On Saturday morning, Annica and I drove out to Brent's barn with Annica's cuckoo clock packed carefully in a box. I carried another box filled with antique bottles and vases donated by her mother.

Brent came to meet us, followed by his canine contingent, Napoleon, Chance, and his blue merle rescue collie, Larkspur. All of the dogs were in a state of high excitement at the unusual activity at the barn. Brent took the box from Annica and removed the clock carefully from its wrappings.

"I wrapped the weights separately," Annica said. "You might want to put it together and hang it on the wall."

"This is a mighty fine clock, Annica," he said. "Are you sure you want to donate it to the estate sale?"

She repeated her grievance about being disturbed by music and birdcalls while reading her Victorian novels.

"Okay," he said. "If you're sure. Come inside where it's warm."

In the barn a wood-burning stove took the edge off the frosty air. A coffeemaker and a box of doughnuts on a card table held a place of honor. The horses must be wondering why their peaceful home had been invaded.

I set my box of glassware down and gazed at the display. Brent had gathered about a hundred antiques, enough to stock a store of his own. In fact, that part of the barn given over to the estate sale, resembled a window display in an upscale antique shop. It looked like an honest-to-goodness enterprise.

"Are the Infinity Inspired people here yet?" I asked.

"They're due in an hour. I'm off to North Carolina tonight. That's my story." He winked at me. "Come and meet Mallory. She has pictures of everything and a list of the antiques we've marked."

Annica hid her reservations about Mallory Larkin with a brilliant smile and a saucy toss of her head that set her silver bell earrings jingling. She had once described Mallory as gorgeous. That was an understatement. Tall and slender with long, luxuriant chestnut hair and yellow-flecked hazel eyes, Mallory wore casual jeans and a blue turtleneck sweater that looked expensive. Designer jeans and cashmere and stylish riding boots. In a barn. Sure.

"So you're Jennet," she said. "I've heard so much about you. And..." She turned to Annica. "You must be the waitress, Annalise."

"Annica." A touch of frost crept into Annica's voice.

I found myself firmly entrenched in Annica's camp. In a way Mallory reminded me of Brent's longtime fox hunting pal, Alethea Venn. They were friends, cut from the same rare expensive cloth. I wouldn't be surprised if Mallory rode with the Hunt.

But I didn't think Annica had to worry about competition from her. Once the antique thieves were captured, Mallory would drift out of Brent's life like all the other beautiful women he escorted.

At least I hoped so.

Annica nudged my arm. "Hey, Jennet, isn't that the chest we saw at Past and Present?"

I went closer for a better look. Like the chest I'd admired, it was ivory with a hand-painted spring scene in pastels: pink, yellow, blue and green.

"Yes, but this is a nightstand," I said. "It must be part of the same group."

I walked over to Brent, who stood alone throwing a ball for his dogs.

"Do you remember who donated the ivory nightstand, Brent?" I asked.

"That's Mallory's. She had it in a guest room."

"Does she know there's a chest with the same painted scene at Past and Present?"

"Is there? I didn't see it. Let's ask her."

Mallory was at the coffeemaker, looking at home on Brent's property. Looking as she had been a frequent visitor to the barn.

"That's one of our lures," she said when I pointed it out to her. "My aunt had the rest of the set. When I was a kid, I wanted the nightstand, but I never found the right place for it in my bedrooms."

"You didn't see it at Past and Present?"

"No. I would have recognized it in a heartbeat. That's a one of a kind scene painted on the front."

I imagined the thieves would find a cheap pine nightstand and slap some pastel trees and flowers on it. The real one would be quietly removed and priced around a thousand dollars. The estate sale item would net twenty or thirty dollars, if that.

But unknown to them, whoever *they* were, the pretty nightstand was a delectable piece of cheese in our little trap. Brent and Mallory would demand to know where the real antique was. They'd confront them with a picture of the original. Our plan, haphazard as it seemed at first, would work.

I amused myself with a mental image of the criminals falling into our trap, one-by-one. The Infinity Inspired couple, the ladies with the Christmas names, Matilda, and the Rosalyn Everett look-alike. Maybe Rosalyn herself.

In a few days it could all be over.

Meanwhile, Annica had an afternoon shift at Clovers, and I'd promised to accompany Sue to River Rose to see if there was any sign of the elusive blue collie.

~ * ~

Icy lay on the front porch of Rosalyn Everett's ranch house sheltering from the gently falling snow. His front paws were crossed, and his head tilted slightly. His dark eyes were fixed on the car. He seemed to be waiting for me, which was uncanny. I'd never seen him on the porch.

"Quiet," Sue said. "Don't breathe."

I let the engine run and reached for the bag of treats, shortbread cookies mixed with dog biscuits today.

"If he takes off, we can't go chasing after him," she added.

"No, that would be asking for trouble."

Several snowfalls would have made the woods virtually unhikable unless Icy had blazed a trail from his nest to the house. Well of course, he must have. But still the way would be treacherous.

The blue dog rose and stretched, collie style, then began to bark.

"He's going to take off," Sue said. "Do something, Jennet."

Icy moved but not toward the woods. He leaped down the stairs. Skimming across the snow, he approached the car and jumped on the door.

We had almost taken Raven and Candy along but at the last minute decided to leave them at home. In retrospect, that was a good decision. The presence of two exuberant collies might have sent Icy scurrying back into the woods.

"What do we do now?" Sue asked.

A message burned in his dark eyes. *Follow me!*

"Haven't you ever seen a *Lassie* movie?" I asked. "We follow him."

"But what if he goes in to the woods?"

"We still follow him."

"You just said…"

"We'll never have another opportunity like this, Sue. We'll just have to be extra careful."

And we'd be together. If one of us stumbled, the other would be on hand to help or sound the alarm, whichever was needed.

She sighed. "Why does it always have to be snowing?"

Knowing her question was rhetorical, I ignored it. It was, after all, winter.

I turned the engine off. We opened the doors and sank into deep snow. This was what Icy had been waiting for. He dashed back toward the house and turned once to look at us. Assured that we were behind him, he ran into the woods.

And we followed.

Forty-six

A narrow trail snaked through the woods, one created by Icy in countless trips to and from the ranch house. It had so many turns and twists that before long I couldn't tell whether we were heading north or east.

Every now and then, Icy looked back over his shoulder as if to make sure we were still following him. We were, holding our own on the snow-covered terrain, even though the makeshift path was more hospitable to four legs than two. A dog could move beneath branches that reached out to grab and entrap a taller runner.

At times the blowing snow seemed to swallow him whole, and I lost track of him; but there was still the trail to follow, wending its way through close-growing trees.

As I ran, I brushed the snow out of my eyes. It was imperative that my vision be clear.

From the start, Sue had fallen behind me, but for a moment I thought she'd passed me. I assumed the figure in white was her, barely discernible through the swirls of white.

I blinked the sting of snow out of my eyes.

It wasn't.

The woman moving so effortlessly in front of me wore a long white dress with puffy sleeves. Her head was bare and not a single strand of dark hair strayed from its upswept style.

The Winter Ghost! Had the quicksilver collie turned into the woman in white?

No, it had to be an illusion born of the wind-driven snow and fed by my imagination.

All of a sudden, the figure appeared to dissipate. I was looking at a dog again, a blue merle collie who was slowing down.

Icy came to a stop. I grabbed a low tree branch to keep from spinning out to the ground. He flopped down near an enormous fallen tree, panting heavily. We had come to a partially frozen stream edged by blue spruce forest. In places the stream was buried in snow or frozen solid, providing safe access for a creature to cross. If that creature had decided to do so.

In that instant, the snow seemed to taper off.

Sue caught up with me. Finding her breath, she said, "Do you think this is where he stays? Because I don't see a nest or cave or any kind of shelter. Just that old tree."

Don't say anything about the ghost, I told myself. *Don't complicate the issue. You might have just seen whirling, swirling snow.*

I waited for my heartbeat to slow before speaking, becoming aware that wetness had seeped through the leather of my tall boots. Now that I had stopped running, the cold had overtaken me.

Brushing snow from my parka, I said, "You won't see a cave in these thick woods. I had no idea there was such a pretty place on Rosalyn's property."

Perfect for a summertime picnic. Or a grave.

"This is a good place for a dog," I said.

Icy could drink thawed stream water or lap snow. He could snuggle up close to the downed branches for shelter and lie in wait for a small, unwary animal to venture out of the underbrush. A dog could easily cross over to the other side of the stream on ice or hard-packed snow. But Icy showed no signs of going farther. He had reached his destination.

Of the ghost there wasn't a sign. She might have melted into the snowscape.

"Maybe he's just tired of running," Sue said. "I know I am."

Icy whimpered softly and stared at us, willing us to comprehend his message.

"I think Rosalyn was buried somewhere around here," I said. "Probably before the ground froze, sometime last summer when she disappeared. We have to call Mac. He'll be able to find her grave."

"If he'll listen to you," Sue said.

"Mac had a collie when he was a boy. He may doubt me, but he knows the power of a collie."

"Ah, the Lassie Syndrome again. So you think the dog is telling us where the killer buried Rosalyn's body?"

"Yes, I do. She's here."

When I talk to Mac, I would emphasize Icy's role and not breathe a word of a supernatural being running through the woods.

As I gazed at our surroundings—at the stream steeped in silence, this secret hidden place—I was unprepared for the deep sorrow that gripped me. After all, Rosalyn wasn't one of my dear friends like Camille or Lucy. I'd thought Rosalyn was dead often enough. As often as I imagined she must be alive and in league with the antique thieves. She herself had written of her death.

But this was so final. The sorrow was real. Strangely I didn't have a single doubt that the grave of Rosalyn Everett was nearby. We might even be standing on it.

Rest in peace, Rosalyn, I thought. *God blessed you with a remarkable collie.*

"I'm sure Mac will listen," I said.

Sue tossed a cookie into the snow. Icy just looked at it.

"Let's get back to the car and call him then," Sue said. "I'm freezing. Looks like the snow's going to stop."

~ * ~

To my surprise, Icy followed us back to the Taurus without a backward glance. Well, why not? He must sense that he had accomplished his mission. He gobbled down three shortbread cookies and settled in the back seat where he gazed at the snow-blanketed River Rose from a different perspective.

I reached in the back to pet him. He flattened his ears and accepted the attention. This was the first time I had touched him. Had my caress awakened memories of another long-vanished hand?

"You're a good dog, Icy," I told him. "The best."

"I don't understand," Sue said, when we had called Mac and were waiting for him to arrive. "Why now?"

"You're wondering why Icy decided to come with us today when he's been keeping his distance all this time?"

"Exactly. What made today different?"

"Who knows? Maybe he needed to be certain he could trust us. Today, all of a sudden, he was. All those times we drove up to the house and called him paid off."

"And the treats we left for him. Maybe wildlife lunch opportunities have been getting scarce."

"He was afraid we'd take him away from the woods again, and he couldn't let that happen. We had to find the grave first. Today he made a decision."

"But we haven't found the grave," Sue pointed out.

"No, but we will."

That was what I believed. It wasn't the first time a dog had acted like a human. Through summer rain and winter snow, Icy was unfailingly loyal to Rosalyn. He'd evaded the police who had rounded up his kennel mates—except for the little tricolor collie they'd missed. He led us to Rosalyn's buried clothing and ran away from Sue's farmhouse to be with his mistress again.

That carefully hidden clothing in the woods! How on earth could it be explained?

All in good time, I thought.

The mystery wasn't over yet.

Someday I intended to write a story about a gallant dog who stood guard over his mistress' grave. I might add my brief glimpse of the Winter Ghost. I wasn't sure about that yet. But she was part of the story. The woman in white had always been seen walking toward the house in the woods. Toward the grave. If I never saw her again, I'd know that she, too, had accomplished her mission.

"By the way," Sue said, "I hope you're right about Rosalyn being buried out here. It would be anti-climactic to find more of her wardrobe or, worse, nothing at all."

And Mac, the ever-condescending officer, would never ever let me hear the end of it. He had been a good sport about the previous 'grave.' I needed him to take me seriously this time.

"I can't explain it, but I've never been so certain of anything," I said. "Anyway we'll soon know. I just wish Icy could tell us who killed her."

Before long I heard the distinctive wail of a siren. That would either indicate an accident, an actual emergency, or Mac speeding down treacherous country roads to answer our call.

I preferred to think it was Mac.

Forty-seven

Mac listened to my story, made a fuss over Icy, and reacted to my request the way I thought he would. His blue eyes held more than a hint of skepticism and, of course, his trademark condescension.

"Are you asking me to dig up a frozen forest in January on the off chance that Rosalyn Everett is buried there?"

"If possible," I said. "Don't you have back hoes? What do people do when a horse dies?"

Instead of answering he said, "Tell me again why you think we'll find Ms. Everett's body in these woods?"

"Because of the behavior of her collie, Icy. He refuses to leave the property, especially the woods."

"Didn't you capture that dog once when you found the clothes hidden under the branches?"

"Yes, but he ran away from Sue right back to the woods. Today we saw him lying on the front porch, and he led us to a stream on the property. You'd never know it was there unless you stumbled on it."

"A secret stream! How mysterious."

Sue said, "We think he's been guarding that spot because…"

"Because his mistress is buried there," Mac said. "It makes a nice story. Now that I've come all this way, I may as well have a look. Which one of you is going to lead the way?"

"We all will," I said, knowing Sue didn't want to be left alone in the car.

I had given Icy the spare collar and leash I kept on hand in the trunk for emergency rescues.

"Let's go then," Mac said.

"It won't be hard to find," I said. "Icy made a trail."

We set out through the woods again, Mac in the lead, pushing the tenacious branches out of his way. This time it wasn't snowing, but the pristine white landscape all but blinded me. As we neared the stream, I looked for the Winter Ghost, half expecting her to materialize again in the snow.

She didn't. She wouldn't. With Mac's arrival, she had achieved her aim. Well, half of it. If Mac cooperated, her body would soon be discovered. I still had to find out who killed her.

When we reached the stream, Icy wrenched out of my grasp, dragging the leash in the snow. He lapped furiously at thawed spring water and lay down exactly where he had been before, panting and whining.

"See?" I said.

Could anyone fail to interpret that heart-rending sound correctly?

"I see an exhausted collie," Mac said.

"Have faith in this dog's intuition," I said. "After all, this is the best clue you've had. I don't think there have been any others."

Mac stabbed at the snow with the tip of his boot and stared at the ground with such intensity that he might have had X-ray vision.

As for myself, I had my trusty imagination. I visualized Rosalyn in her long white dress lying in a glass coffin, her body preserved, courtesy of the winter's frigid temperatures. A sort of fairy tale figure. Except she wouldn't be brought to life for the requisite happy ending.

I shivered. The snow seemed to have penetrated the thick sleeves of my parka. I needed to have this matter wrapped up, to be home, sitting in front of my own fireside with a plate of comfort food and a cup of hot chocolate.

"They're calling for a brief warm-up next week," Mac said at last.

"In January?"

"The January thaw. Looks like we'll have one this year. There should be some snow melt." He scanned the area, looking beyond the stream to the line of spruces. "It isn't as thickly wooded out here. More sun can get through."

"Does this mean you'll…" I trailed off. I'd been about to say 'dig her up.'"

"I'll investigate," he said. "Come along, Icy."

Icy rose and trotted to Mac's side. Mac gave me the leash. "Hold on tight this time," he said.

As I led Icy back to the Taurus, I glanced at River Rose, at the yellow ranch house with its Christmas wreath on the door and the abandoned kennel building, the whole buried in brilliant snow. Even with all the brightness that assailed my eyes, the scene looked more desolate than ever. Positively God forsaken. I wondered if I would ever see this place again.

~ * ~

Although we didn't know anything definitive yet, I had hope. Icy appeared to be content with Sue at the horse farm, and Mac had part of the solution to the mystery of Rosalyn's disappearance at his fingertips. If he would pursue it. If the weather cooperated.

I had done as Crane asked, left the matter to the police. I certainly couldn't dig through frozen ground to unearth a corpse myself. Nor would I want to. All I could do was wait for that promised warm-up and wonder how I would ever be able to find Rosalyn's killer. It seemed that I'd have to leave my own mission half done.

Fortunately Brent's estate sale distracted me. According to plan, he had absented himself from the scene. As far as the people at Infinity Inspired knew, he was fox hunting in North Carolina, giving his agents freedom to conduct the sale as they pleased—which we were counting on.

Annica and I met at Brent's barn on Saturday morning, planning to pose as customers while monitoring the antiques. Mallory had supplied us with a set of pictures. We'd already selected the ones we considered good candidates for substitution. Foremost among them, in my opinion, was the hand-painted ivory nightstand.

I had theorized that any substitutions would have been made before the first customer arrived, most likely as soon as Brent left the Infinity Inspired people to their own devices.

As Annica and I walked up to the barn, I breathed in the fresh country air. For the first time in days it held a touch of warmth—the merest touch—but the sky was blue and cloudless, and the sun was shining on the snow.

"It feels like spring," Annica said. "January is the longest month of the year. I can't wait for California strawberries and tulips"

I shared her enthusiasm. "For me, it's spring break, but we have a long way to go."

Napoleon lay at the barn entrance, a gigantic guardian seemingly uninterested in the cars and strangers who had invaded his space. I greeted him by name and was rewarded by a wag of his tail.

We might be about to enter a den of thieves, but we had a formidable protector.

Inside about a dozen people milled around, some examining the antiques with an expert's eye, some apparently wiling away a Saturday morning among the eclectic offerings. The agents had rearranged the sale items for no particular reason that I could see, except perhaps to create makeshift rows. I looked for the nightstand but didn't see it.

A lanky red-haired boy greeted us with a shy smile, letting his gaze rest on Annica. I recognized Tim, one of Brent's helpers at the barn.

He gestured to the coffee machine on the card table and the large box of doughnuts alongside it. "Boss says to help yourself."

Annica poured a cup of coffee, and I selected a powdered sugar doughnut. As I did so, Brent's collies, Chance and Larkspur, materialized at my side, fixing me with irresistible dark eyes. I broke off a small piece for each of them, as Annica drifted toward the antiques near the wall.

Suddenly she exclaimed, "My clock!"

It hung on a barn wall with a collection of paintings, including the seascape I had donated. Its pendulum swung languidly back and forth. As I reached Annica's side, the cuckoo emerged from its tiny house to call the hour, ten o'clock, followed by the lilting notes of *Edelweiss*. On top of the clock, a wood-carved bird sat on a swag of branches, its beak pointed upward.

"It's pretty, but I can see what you mean about distracting," I said.

"That isn't my clock, Jennet."

"How can you tell?" I asked.

"I've had it for years and before that it was in my grandma's dining room. My clock has lighter wood, and its carving is more intricate. Besides, my bird has a chipped wing."

I stepped closer. "There's nothing wrong with this bird's wing."

"No, this is one of those cheap imitations. What did they do with my clock?"

"Hush," I said. "Lower your voice. We don't want to tip our hand."

I looked around, but no one appeared to be paying any attention to us. The closest person, a tall woman in jeans and a black sweater, was arranging postcards on a table.

"Let's find the nightstand," I said.

"Excuse me, Miss…"

I moved to one side as two burly men carried a large bookcase out of the barn.

Had the nightstand already been sold? I hoped not. If it was the same piece I'd seen earlier, I wanted to buy it for my bedroom.

When we found it, a ripple of excitement charged through me. The nightstand was white, but the painted scene was an amateurish rendering. Stick-like trees with unrealistic leaves, and multi-colored daisies poking through tall green spikes. One of the blue daisies bled into the grass. It looked as if a child had illustrated the nightstand in a hurry.

Who on earth would buy it?

"Score two," Annica murmured. "Let's look at the silver."

We found other pieces to add to our list. Probably there were more, but I could hardly sift through the pictures I'd tucked into my shoulder bag.

"It's time for Brent to make his entrance," I said. "Let's go find him."

A canine yelp drifted out from the back of the barn. It turned into a piteous drawn-out scream.

Annica stared into the darkness. "What was that?"

Faces turned toward the sound. Then it ended, and the hum of conversation resumed.

"Larkspur or Chance," I said.

I hadn't seen either of them since they'd begged for a piece of my doughnut. What if one of them had been hurt? Kicked by a horse?

The horses are in their stalls. Not free to kick a hapless dog.

"Stay here and keep watch," I said. "I'm going to find out what happened."

Forty-eight

Inquisitive equine eyes followed my progress as I walked between the rows of stalls. Most of them were inhabited, as Brent had horses of his own and also boarders, but all were secured behind their half doors. I didn't see Chance or Larkspur or any other dog who could have made that terrified screaming sound.

Could it have come from one of the horses? I glanced at the intelligent eyes trained on me, wondering.

No. I rejected that idea. Horses don't yelp.

Napoleon, then? I didn't think so, but I didn't see him either, or even one of the ever-present cats. I might have been alone in this part of the barn.

And why, I wondered, was no one else concerned about the cry of an animal in obvious distress? Usually there were one or more owners tending to their horses. And where was Tim? Or one of the other boys? As a rule, Brent didn't allow his helpers to work alone, especially on a day when he expected strangers to troop through the barn.

A black face, beautifully shaped, leaned forward, and the horse greeted me with a soft whinny. Her name was Midnight. I called her Black Beauty. I remembered Brent had wanted me to ride her.

The barn smelled of fresh hay and horse—and I detected another scent in the mix. A too-sweet, cloying odor that wasn't generally associated with a barn.

Something was wrong.

I almost called out to Annica, almost went back to the estate sale, but something urged me on.

The door at the other end of the barn was open. Light streamed in and fresh, cold air—and a soft whimper, the kind of sound Sky had made the other day when I had inadvertently locked her on the porch.

If an animal had been hurt—and what else could have happened?—I had to find it.

I stepped outside into a shoveled area behind the barn and looked to the right. Nothing here either...

A hulking shadow took shape at my side. Before I could react, a sharp pain exploded in my head.

I felt myself fall forward into the snow, and all the light went out of my world.

~ * ~

I was cold. My head hurt. Badly. So did my back and arms and every other part of my body.

I couldn't go to school today. I'd have to call...

Realization struck like another blow.

I wasn't home in bed. I lay on a hard surface. Somewhere. I tried to assemble the fragments of thoughts that skated through my mind.

There was a strong smell of hay. Was I still in Brent's barn?

I had to be. Where else...?

I tried to rise, but the pain pulled me back down. It originated at the top of my head and radiated downward, settling behind my eyes. Separate knife pricks. Agony.

So lie back. Think. Remember.

Annica and I had gone to Brent's estate sale. We had set a trap for the thieves. Then I'd heard a dog scream in pain, heard a weak whimper. What else?

I'd followed the sound into the other part of the barn where I found nothing but the horses in their stalls. Then I went through the door.

Annica!

I tried to say her name, but my mouth was dry. It felt as if I'd swallowed a mouthful of hay.

I'd told her to stay behind and watch.

Dear God. Where am I?

Gradually the images came, in glaring color but out of order. A white nightstand with a spring scene hand-painted by an amateur. The horses. Napoleon. The open door…

We had set a clever trap for the Infinity Inspired people and their confederates. So clever. Practically foolproof.

And I had wandered blithely into it.

But surely I'd be rescued. Annica would know I wouldn't just walk into the shadows beyond the estate sale and vanish.

Why not? This is Foxglove Corners, where it isn't unheard of for a person to disappear. Consider the case of Rosalyn Everett.

Brent would come. We had been going to find him when I heard the siren cry of a dog in pain. Crane… He thought I was on a harmless shopping trip with Annica. He wouldn't worry until he came home to find I wasn't there.

Wait! Crane would know I was missing long before that. When I didn't come back, Annica would follow me. When she couldn't find me, she'd summon help and call Crane.

But how would anyone know where to look for me?

All right. Rescue might not be eminent, but neither was it an impossibility. First, I had to figure out where I was.

Again I tried to rise. Again the pain pulled me back to the hard surface on which I had been lying.

Lord, I prayed. *Help me.*

With that plea I recalled an old saying: *Heaven helps those who help themselves.*

~ * ~

It was cold. So very cold.

So much for Lieutenant Mac Dalby's warm-up.

It was snowing again, a slanting, pounding snow that stung my face.

And there was pain.

I sat in the silver sleigh, letting the eight silver reindeer carry me over the snowbound roads and by-roads of Foxglove Corners.

We were on Jonquil Lane. In the distance I could see my green Victorian farmhouse with its stained glass windows shining like jewels between the twin gables.

Somewhere dogs were barking. My collies.

I was almost home.

Because the snow blinded me, I didn't know when the sleigh became airborne, when the snow ceased. When the team of reindeer took me to the stars.

I didn't know our ultimate destination. All I knew was that I wasn't going home.

~ * ~

I must have dozed. Dozed and dreamed.

The sleigh dream again. Well, it was fitting. This whole affair had begun with a silver sleigh.

It was still cold, and the pain had taken up residence in my head. I felt nauseated but at the same time alert.

I had been struck unconscious and abducted from Brent's barn with Annica and about a dozen people on the premises. My kidnapper had taken me to an unknown location that smelled of hay. But not of horse.

Was I in another barn? An empty one?

The floor was stone-hard, and the area unheated. But there were windows and slashes of light. Pushing up the sleeve of my parka, I squinted at my watch. It was one-thirty.

Of the same day?

Carefully I tried again to rise and this time succeeded. More or less. That hard floor felt unstable under my feet. It felt as if it were moving in slow circles.

Like the haunted tiles in my classroom at Marston before Leonora covered it with furniture.

I needed to take a pain pill, to control the pounding in my head. I reached for my shoulder bag, wondering if I could swallow one without water.

My purse wasn't there. Of course, it wouldn't be.

When Annica saw my abandoned purse, she'd know without a doubt that I'd met with foul play. If she found it. My abductor might have discarded it in the trash.

So I couldn't take anything for the pain, but I still needed water—and food. I'd had a light breakfast and a doughnut at the sale. Nothing else.

Don't worry about food. Try to walk.

Exploring my prison would give me an advantage, albeit slight one. I especially wanted to look through the window.

The window… If I could find something to break it with…

I took a few faltering steps and didn't fall. Encouraged, I made my way slowly to the window and peered out. A wild white world stared back at me. The wind was blowing, whipping snow into monstrous drifts.

Through a moving veil of white I saw the house. A yellow ranch house with a Christmas wreath on the front door and behind it dark woods brooding on their slope. And I knew.

I was in the deserted kennel building at River Rose.

Forty-nine

I couldn't imagine a more isolated location than River Rose. Who would look for me here? Mac planned to investigate my claim that Rosalyn Everett was buried in the woods—when it warmed up. One look outside told me this wouldn't be any time soon.

In the meantime, what could I do?

Remember, Heaven helps those who help themselves. Do something.

A sense of urgency flared beyond the pain that held my head in an unrelenting grip. My abductor might return at any time. Surely he didn't intend to leave me here to starve to death?

What did he hope to accomplish by removing me from the barn? I feared this was only the first step in a diabolical plan.

It might be possible to break through the window, if I could find an implement capable of shattering glass. There must be something I could use, but first I had to rest, just for a while. Breaking a window seemed a Herculean task at the moment. Standing and taking a few short steps had drained the dregs of my energy.

Leaning back against a wall, I let my mind drift back to Brent's barn. I tried to imagine what Annica had done when she realized I wasn't coming back. How long was it before she grew suspicious?

The estate sale was crammed with fascinating objects. I could almost see her looking to see if there was any jewelry among the offerings or returning to the cuckoo clock. Waiting. Having another cup of coffee, another doughnut.

How long?

From Annica, my thoughts traveled to my assailant. It must have been someone at the estate sale who had left the barn and lured me to the back door with the cry of a dog. One of the crooked Infinity Inspired people, no doubt.

Obviously he or she had heard me discussing the antique substitutions with Annica. Why, I wondered, had he chosen me to kidnap? Not that I wanted Annica to share my fate.

Being focused on the antiques, I hadn't noticed anyone who looked suspicious or familiar.

Incidentally, what had happened to the dog? What had my kidnapper done to make it cry out in pain? How did he know I'd respond to the cry?

Back to Annica. Eventually she must have followed me. Maybe she'd found my purse outside the barn, maybe not. She might have returned to the sale, thinking I'd doubled back and she hadn't seen me.

What would she do when she couldn't find me? Look for my car which would be parked in front of the barn where I'd left it.

Call Crane?

Maybe not right away. If I knew Annica, she would follow our original plan to find Brent. In any event, Brent intended to return to the barn and confront the thieves with proof of their dishonesty.

I wouldn't be there or anywhere on Brent's property. I'd be one of those unfortunate denizens of Foxglove Corners who vanish literally between footsteps.

By now, they'd have notified Crane. He'd know that I was officially missing.

In the meantime,

Heaven helps those who help themselves. Those who sit around woolgathering are doomed to... Well, just doomed.

Rising again, I made an attempt to focus beyond the pain and the cold and explore my prison.

No place on earth is more forbidding than a long-abandoned building in the middle of nowhere. Except for a collection of leashes, collars, and crates, nothing was left of the gallant collies who had once inhabited the kennels, neither their scents nor their spirits. I couldn't even count on ghost dogs to come to the rescue this time, and we'd taken the living dog, Icy, away from River Rose.

I shivered, not altogether from dread.

I was thankful that my captor had left me my parka and equally thankful for my tall boots and warm turtleneck sweater. I wouldn't freeze. Well, not immediately.

Hunger and thirst were more likely. If only I had a candy bar in my pocket or life savers. Anything to ease the dryness in my mouth.

I tried to swallow and discovered that my throat hurt, too.

Sue had once mentioned that Rosalyn had installed bathing facilities for the collies in her kennel and a television set because a few of the dogs liked to watch *Lassie* reruns and *Animal Planet*. Bathing facilities meant faucets and running water.

I found the tub and grooming tables in a dark corner, together with a cabinet filled with shampoo, brushes, combs, towels, and the like. At last... Thank God. A drink.

I turned on the faucet and my heart sank. The water had been turned off.

All right. That didn't work. Now, the door.

I tried it. Locked, of course.

What now?

Squinting into the dimness, I became aware of grotesque hulking shapes pushed against one of the walls.

What on earth?

I looked again. The shapes took recognizable forms.

Understanding was swift and jolting. It was furniture. Like the spare room in the ranch house, the kennel had been used to stash stolen goods. A love seat. An armoire. Chests and lamps and small tables and paintings. Boxes and larger items.

The one-time kennel housed a jumble of antiques for which cheap near-duplicates had been found to fill any number of estate sales. Dust covered every surface. Unlike the antiques in the house, apparently these had been here for a long while. Stolen from how many antique shops over how many months and years?

If I looked long enough, I might come across Mallory's ivory nightstand and Annica's cuckoo clock.

But I couldn't waste time in a futile search.

My heart almost stopped as I confronted a pale figure in a white parka. Myself, looking like a haggard spirit, reflected in a tall, ornately framed mirror.

Could that mirror break the glass in the window? If so, I could remove the jagged edges and hoist myself up by standing on one of the tables. Up and over and out...

Then what?

It would be a long, cold, snowy walk to the nearest neighbor who might not even be home.

Anyone seeing me from the road might think he was watching the Winter Ghost gliding along in the snow.

That doesn't matter. Just get out of here. With luck, there'll be a car on the road or a jogger.

I went back for the mirror. It was almost as tall as I was and so heavy with its thick ornate frame that I could scarcely lift it.

I tried, and it slid out of my hands and fell back on the floor with—I could have sworn—a shudder. I could never lift it high enough to send it crashing through the window.

Something else then.

Desperately aware of time running out, I pounced on the stashed antiques looking for a likely implement. Sharp and not too heavy to handle. A hammer would be perfect.

Quickly I rifled through the nearest box, but it was packed with silverware.

Would Rosalyn have needed a hammer in her kennel? Certainly it wouldn't appeal to a thief or potential buyer even if it were an antique model.

Slowly I became aware of an intrusive sound in the tomb-like silence. A sinister scratching that seemed louder than it probably was.

Rats? Not rats. Please!

In my frame of mind, the sound resembled the imagined scratching of fingernails on a coffin lid or the digging of a dog trapped in a closed space.

Pure imagination. Don't let it distract you.

Making a valiant attempt to quell my terror, I sank onto the loveseat.

Did something of the River Rose collies linger in the forsaken kennel after all?

You will get out of here! But you have to get up.

I resumed my search for something, anything, and almost stumbled on a snow shovel lying on the floor, pushed out of the way. Perfect! It was only slightly heavier than the one I used at home.

Only a few minutes now… With luck…

I pounded the glass, kept pounding until I heard a loud crash. Dodging flying shards, I kept pounding.

There! Most of the window had shattered, leaving a body-sized opening framed by lethal jagged edges.

You're halfway there!

Carefully I removed pieces, shoveling them as if they were snow, until I felt I could pass through by stepping on a stool or...

I found a small maple table and stood in front of the space, feeling unsteady now that freedom was at hand.

The light snow I'd observed when I'd first looked out the window and seen the yellow ranch house had intensified, driven by the wind into huge pummeling waves. I'd be exchanging shelter, such as it was, for a blizzard.

There was no choice, not really.

Bracing my arms on the window frame, I stepped out into the swirling snow and freedom.

Fifty

I landed in snow. The impact set my head to pounding again and wrenched my knee, but I hadn't done any serious damage to myself. Only given myself more pain. The snow was a blessing in disguise. I scooped up a handful and shoved it into my mouth. The relief was instantaneous, and there was plenty more where that came from.

Pulling my hood over my head and my gloves out of my pocket, I took the first plodding steps away from the kennel. The wind tried to push me back. It was stronger than any human and had a chilling wail, but no matter. I was free, and even fighting my way through a blizzard was preferable to being locked in an empty kennel waiting for whatever horror came next.

Now... Which direction was the road?

Left, I thought. Yes, left.

I could barely see the lines of the yellow ranch house to my right, and the woods beyond were lost in a swirling white maelstrom. Still visible but rapidly disappearing in the snow were tire tracks and the deep imprint of boots. Left by my kidnapper?

If I could make it to the road...

There's no reason why you can't.

With each step, I seemed to grow stronger, although the simple act of walking was a major production. In places the snow had drifted up to my knees. It was a living entity, a creature from an alien white world. It battered my face and eyes, stealing my vision.

Step down, deep down, pull your leg up. Take another step.

My knee was really hurting.

The creature turned into an inferno of hungry white flames. How could I have thought I could walk to safety in this snowstorm?

Remember, you have no choice.

In moments I lost my sense of direction and time. I couldn't tell if I was headed toward the long driveway that led to the road or wandering blind in the snow.

Just keep going.

I did and, after what seemed like hours, reached the road. The kennel sign swung madly in the wind, threatening to break loose and fly away. At one point I thought I heard a dog barking through the wind's moan. Wishful thinking. There were no dogs left at River Rose.

I turned left. The sound I'd mistaken for barking grew louder, became distinct. It was an engine. A car. Headlights broke through the snow illuminating the brush that grew along the verge.

Would the driver see me? I had to signal. Somehow. This might be my only chance.

As quickly as I could, I stepped back, out of the way. Just in time.

The vehicle burst through the falling snow like a maddened drone and swerved on the road. Headed toward me!

For a moment that froze in time, I saw the driver's face clearly through the arc of cleared snow on the window.

It was Rosalyn Everett!

That swerve was deliberate. She meant to hit me.

I jumped out of the way. Lost my footing on the slick surface. Went down into the thorny embrace of a snow-glazed bush.

The car skidded to a stop. A door slammed. A nightmare figure wrapped in a long dark fur coat advanced on me.

There was no place to run, no way to escape her. Leaving the glow cast by the car's headlights, she moved steadily toward me as if walking in deep snow were no effort for her.

So this is the way it would end for me, murdered in the snow by a woman who was supposed to be lying in her frozen-over grave.

"Rosalyn…"

Even as the name left my mouth, I saw that the driver wasn't Rosalyn Everett. She was the Rosalyn lookalike, the woman I'd seen briefly in the Spearmint Lake antique shop, Past and Present. The elusive cousin Gloria? My abductor.

She extended her hand.

"Let me help you up." Her shout carried over the scream of the wind.

I tried to rise, to back away, but a cutting pain sliced through my knee. Behind me, behind the brush, yawned a deep impression in the snow. A ditch, if I remembered correctly.

"Did your car break down?" the woman demanded.

I ignored her question.

"This is no weather to be stranded. I'll give you a lift to the nearest gas station. Or a hospital. Are you hurt?"

Her attempt to feign compassion fell flat. Not for a moment did I think she was sincere.

I made another effort to stand, clenching my teeth against the pain that streaked through my knee.

"Here. Let me."

The hand moved closer. It wore a long black leather glove that disappeared in the sleeve of her coat.

"I'm all right." The wind was so loud I could hardly hear my own voice. I waved her away. "Just go on your way and leave me alone."

She took hold of my arm, yanking me to my feet. My knee gave out. I almost fell again.

"No, you aren't okay. Into the car with you. You'll freeze to death if you stay out here."

There was no place to run. No way to run. It was all I could do to stand.

She pushed me into the passenger's seat and took her place behind the wheel. My mind registered heat, too much heat, and the hum of the windshield wipers. Snow flew right and left, clearing the windows. A strong, unpleasant scent filled the car. It was the cloying odor I'd smelled in Brent's barn.

Not that I was surprised.

The woman's gloves were off, figuratively and literally. They landed in my lap. Bare handed, the woman gripped the wheel and steered the car back to the road. She turned in at the driveway to River Rose and passed the swinging kennel sign.

"I can't understand," she said, "how you always manage to turn up in the wrong place. Right now you're supposed to be in the kennel under lock and key."

I didn't want to give her the satisfaction of an answer. But to maintain a stony silence was counter-productive. It was obvious she knew what I'd been doing, perhaps even knew about our trap. If I were to have a chance to escape her clutches, I needed information.

"What places?" I asked.

"Every antique shop in town, the estate sale, Rosalyn's locked house, for God's sake. It's like you were following me. For all I know you were."

"My friend, the red-haired girl, doesn't know anything about your—business," I said. "She was just along for the antiques."

"I doubt that."

"Who are you?" I asked.

"We met once. I told you my name. Don't you remember?"

I didn't. "You look like Rosalyn Everett, so I assume you're a relative of hers. Her sister?"

"Close," she said. "Go all the way back to a little shop named The Silver Sleigh. You purchased a valuable antique that shouldn't have been on display and refused to return it."

With that nudge, I remembered. Gloria MacBride, the woman in black, the woman I'd thought looked like a vampire. Something familiar, a resemblance, had tugged at me then but subsequently slipped out of my mind, not to return until this moment.

Oh, yes.

"Do you remember now?" she prompted.

"You stole the silver sleigh and left that cheap imitation in its place. You broke into my house. How did you know...?"

"What?"

I was about to ask her how she knew that my most aggressive collies would be out of the house that day, then remembered a green car Camille had seen cruising up and down the lane. Instead I said, "Since you have my sleigh in your possession, you owe me a hundred dollars."

She laughed. "I love a person with a sense of humor. Too bad we're on opposite sides of the fence."

I wondered if she knew we'd discovered some of the stolen antiques in Rosalyn's spare room. Of course, the sleigh was no longer there. Mac had taken it to the station as evidence.

"Beastly weather," she grumbled, as the car skidded on an icy patch.

"Where are you taking me?" I asked.

"Back to the kennel. Don't worry. It won't be for long. I'm sorry you'll be in no condition to rain on our little parade."

She brought the car to a stop in front of the kennel and reached into an oversized pocketbook that lay on the floor. Out came a gun. I might have anticipated it.

"Get out."

I stepped down into the deep snow again, felt a wind gust barrel into me. In spite of her gun and the prospect of being imprisoned again, I had a fleeting moment of hope.

If she didn't notice the broken window, I'd be no worse off than I'd been earlier. Before that long, punishing walk to the road unless... She intended to kill me now.

No, it would make more sense for her to have dispatched me back on the road and tossed my body into the woods.

She had a plan. I wished I knew what it was without asking her. Well, I didn't have to know details.

"You won't get away with this," I said. "Brent Fowler is on to you, and kidnapping is a serious crime."

"Fowler can suspect all he likes. He needs proof, and he won't have it. We're just antique lovers acquiring and reselling goods. There's nothing dishonest about that."

It was still snowing; the wind still blew. If I could only distract her somehow and run into the snow, I'd have a chance. A small one, but a chance.

A chance to die now? That wasn't what I wanted.

She still held the gun, although it wasn't pointed at me.

You can't walk, let alone run.

Maybe she wasn't going to kill me. But if not, why the gun?

She unlocked the door of the kennel building and shoved me inside, looking around the dim interior.

"How did you get out? Ah, I see."

She saw the shower of glass on the floor and the snow that had blown in.

"Change of plans," she snapped. "We'll let ourselves into the house. I guarantee Rosalyn won't mind."

Fifty-one

In other circumstances, the yellow ranch house would have been an oasis, offering shelter from the snowstorm. Sanctuary.

In this case, with an armed assassin behind me, it was just another prison.

I couldn't let Gloria force me into Rosalyn's house. If I did, it might well be my last stop on the wild, hazardous ride that had begun with my desire to own an antique silver sleigh.

She would kill me there in the house that had never welcomed me.

If she didn't, if I were lucky, I could escape again. There were windows in every room. Almost every room. Closets don't have windows.

Don't think about closets.

Certainly I wouldn't have to search far for implements. What house didn't have a hammer? As soon as Gloria left, I'd start looking for one. Break another window. Begin the long walk to the road.

Assuming she left me free to move.

We were close enough to make out the dark woods that rose behind the house. I could see individual trees, lean and dark, grown so close together that only the thinnest of creatures could travel through them. Except for the few openings like the trail that led to the stream beside Rosalyn's grave. It would be covered with new snow but still passable.

Those forbidding woods.

In my mind I saw myself fleeing down that trail to another destiny, one that would extricate me from this deadly situation.

Yes, but don't forget she has the gun.

We trudged along in the snow up to the porch with its steps drifted over. I willed myself to stop shaking. She couldn't think I was afraid. If I were going to make a move, I had to do it now.

But I needed help.

The Winter Ghost making an unheralded appearance to shock Gloria into immobility. Gloria would drop her gun... I'd grab it.

Mac arriving in a snowstorm with his men and equipment to break through the solid-frozen earth to Rosalyn's grave and finding me in the hands of a killer...

Crane on his white horse galloping through the snow to my rescue...

Heaven helps those who help themselves.

"The police know about the antiques you stored in the house," I said. "They know about you and your friends."

"Those antiques? I always suspected Rosalyn was a hoarder. She had all this stuff in her house and kennel..."

"Yeah, Rosalyn."

"Anyway, we'll soon be on our way. Keep walking."

Seen up close, the Christmas wreath on the door showed signs of age. Its needles were turning yellow and falling in a thin layer under the door. The ribbon, stiff in the frigid air, was the color of blood.

Nothing lasts forever. Not a wreath, not happiness, not life.

Gloria followed me up the stairs, stepping in the depressions I made in the drifted snow. She pulled a key out of her pocket with her free hand and pushed me roughly aside.

Now! Or never.

With a shoosh, a body flew past me, knocking me against the railing. It plowed into Gloria and took her to the floor of the porch. Two bodies slid on the slippery wood porch surface. It looked as if two animals were locked in a to-the-death battle, two bundles of fur, one dark brown, one silvery gray, thrashing in the snow. One of them was winning. One growled ferociously, one screamed the horrible sound of a human being torn apart.

"Icy!"

He had torn the sleeve of Gloria's fur coat in his mouth, shaking it as if it were a tug-of-war toy.

The screaming had stopped. There was blood on the snow. A gaping red wound on Gloria's arm.

Dear Lord, had Icy killed her?

I didn't want that. Not even to save my life.

"Icy," I said again, softly this time.

He left the sleeve and came to me, wagging his tail in an astonishing transformation. He was a collie again, the quicksilver collie with a trace of snow still clinging to his coat and caught in his toes. He had watched over Rosalyn's grave and come to me for treats and apparently been content at Sue's horse farm until something called to him.

He had escaped from Sue again.

At that moment, I remembered the sound of barking I'd heard and later decided was a car engine. So long ago, but probably only ten or fifteen minutes had passed.

How could he have known? How did he know enough to stay with Rosalyn until the police came to her grave? There was nothing supernatural about Icy's feat. He was simply a dog. A magnificent collie, a champion in every way possible.

I ruffled his wet fur and kissed his head.

"But what took you so long?" I asked. "Another minute and it would have been too late."

~ * ~

Gloria wasn't dead. She was, however, severely mauled. I found her cell phone in the purse that had held the gun and called Mac—and Crane, of course; but I had to leave a message on his voice mail.

When Mac and the ambulance arrived to take charge of the scene, the paramedics took her to the hospital. Mac confiscated the gun.

"Don't even think you're going to blame Icy for this," I said. "He isn't vicious. She was going to kill me. He saved my life."

Mac regarded the blue merle who lay on the porch guarding the torn sleeve. I wondered if Gloria's coat had been fake fur or real fur. Mink, I decided, a vintage coat. What else would such a horrible woman wear? And how irrelevant that thought was.

"Every girl needs an Icy," Mac said. "But didn't you and your friend take him back to her farm?"

"He wouldn't stay there. Icy knew I was in trouble. Don't ask me how."

"I won't," Mac said. "I know collies. I had one when I was a kid, if you'll remember. But he sure as hell wasn't as smart as this dog."

"I want to go home," I said. "And Icy can't stay here."

"Good idea." Mac helped me into his patrol car. Icy didn't need any help. He jumped in after me and rested his head in my lap as if he were already home.

"Oh, yes," Mac said. "That reminds me. On to important stuff. We've all been looking for you. Crane and Brent are frantic. Your friend reported you missing. She couldn't figure out how it happened but she kept babbling something about a dog."

That sounded like Annica.

"We heard a dog cry out in pain," I said. "That was part of Gloria MacBride's plan. I guess she knew I couldn't resist finding out what was wrong. What happened to the dog, by the way?"

"That was Brent's Larkspur. She suffered a hard kick in the ribs but will be okay. She's just traumatized."

"Poor baby. She was a rescue. I'm so sorry she had to go through that, but you'll be able to arrest them now, won't you? I don't know how many were in on it…"

"I hate to tell you this, Jennet, but the sale was shut down while Brent was helping Crane look for you. The barn was cleared out. Everything is gone. Everyone is gone. Except Ms. MacBride. She's the only one we have."

"But we have proof," I said. "Mallory took pictures…"

Then I knew what he was saying. With the antiques gone, pictures weren't worth the paper they were printed on.

"What about Infinity Inspired?" I asked.

"Out of business."

"Again?"

"It never was legitimate."

"But there are other people. There's Carol, who co-owned The Silver Sleigh with Gloria. That woman, Matilda, in Past and Present. That's an antique shop in Spearmint Lake. I'm sure she knows Gloria."

"I'm sure she does and just as sure she'll deny it."

There wouldn't be any retribution then unless you counted the wounds Icy had inflicted on Gloria MacBride and her punishment for my attempted murder. The only remaining antiques were the ones stored in the house and kennel. Maybe they could be restored to their owners.

I supposed all that mattered was that we'd broken up the ring of antique thieves, although in a far different way from the one we had planned.

What mattered most were my life and Icy and the future he'd given me.

God bless all good dogs.

"I'm just glad it's over," I said. "And don't forget. The silver sleigh you confiscated belongs to me. Now I really have to go home. It's nice sitting in your patrol car, but I just can't warm up."

And I desperately wanted to be reunited with Crane.

Mac nodded. "Next stop, home."

Fifty-two

I filled the silver sleigh with chocolate Valentine hearts and set it on the mantel amid a collection of burning candles. I intended to keep the sleigh on the mantel all year round with tiny chocolate Easter eggs, summer potpourri, candy corn, and finally miniature candy canes.

Crane had built a fire, a cheery antidote to another snowy January night. I'd never appreciated warmth and fire and my beloved home more. Not to mention my husband.

Brent and Annica were joining us for dinner. We had a lot to celebrate, the most important blessing being my escape from the murder-minded Gloria MacBride.

The antique thieves had scattered, for I didn't believe Gloria was working alone. Mac had been correct in his assumptions. The owners of The Time Machine and Past and Present denied having any dealings with her or any knowledge of antique thefts, for that matter.

"How about those women with the Christmas names?" Annica had asked him. "Carol, Holly, Nicola..."

"With The Silver Sleigh shuttered, try and find them."

It was obvious Mac considered the case closed.

I could have challenged Matilda's claim since I'd observed her talking to Gloria, but without proof, decided to let sleeping dogs lie.

Speaking of dogs, Icy was with Sue again, although I'd hoped he could join my collie family. He was a popular dog. Even Mac had hinted that he would like to adopt him.

But Sue was going to hold on to him.

As for the little blue merle, Larkspur, she was at Brent's side whenever possible. I hoped the vicious kick she'd suffered hadn't set her adjustment back.

On the weather front, the forecast warm-up had been delayed. No one knew for certain that Rosalyn's body was buried by the stream in her woods, but I didn't need final proof. Icy's word was good enough for me.

Once again in my super-adventurous life I could say "All's well that ends well."

Except for the questions. There were so many of them. Undoubtedly some would never be answered. Take the case of Rosalyn Everett, parts of it still enshrouded in mystery.

Gloria was talking from her hospital bed, possibly hoping to evade charges. She claimed that her cousin, Rosalyn, was the one who had come up with the idea of arranging estate sales for the sole purpose of finding substitutes for valuable antiques and pocketing the profits. Gloria herself was a minor player, always easily influenced by her more aggressive cousin.

Rosalyn's disappearance?

Rosalyn was always strange, even as a child. She'd had spells. That time she had left the dogs and for so long, but thought only a few hours had elapsed. That was a good example of her disconnect from reality. Her mother, Gloria's Aunt Rose, had been the same way.

Her killer?

Gloria didn't even know she was dead.

A likely story.

How to reconcile these statements with Rosalyn's fear recorded in her diary that someone was out to murder her?

I couldn't. I believed Rosalyn. That someone had to be Gloria. About Rosalyn's involvement with the antique thefts, I didn't know. Gloria could say anything about Rosalyn, malign her infinitely. A dead woman can't defend herself.

Once Rosalyn was out of the picture, her house and kennel were perfect places to stash stolen antiques. The wreath and perhaps even the clothes in the woods were ploys designed to distract and confuse the curious.

In the midst of the uncertainty, I created a possible version of what may have happened.

Rosalyn discovered Gloria's secret life and threatened to expose her. In doing so, Rosalyn signed her own death warrant.

Outlandish? Maybe. But no one had come up with a better scenario.

I stepped back to admire my display and fell into Crane's arms. He'd moved so silently I hadn't realized he'd come into the living room.

"I'm beginning to think one day you'll disappear in a cloud of smoke," he said.

"That'll never happen."

God willing.

His lips were warm on mine. In his kiss I read a promise that I'd never be cold and alone again.

He had murmured variations of that sentiment ever since our reunion. I never tired of hearing them.

"I don't know how many times I can dodge a bullet," I said.

He kissed me again, a longer, deeper kiss. "I wish we weren't having company."

"They won't stay all night. Now I'd better check on the roast. I don't want to burn it."

He followed me into the kitchen. "Who thought an estate sale could be deadly?" he asked.

"Thank heavens for Icy. I wish we could have kept him."

"Seven collies? We'd have to build another house."

We'd thanked Icy with a porterhouse steak all to himself and a story in the *Banner*, which didn't impress him. It didn't seem like enough.

As if she sensed the status quo was in danger of being altered, Candy nudged me. She'd been keeping a vigil in the kitchen, savoring the enticing smell of prime rib.

"Sue will never give Icy up," I said.

"She'd better keep an eye on him."

"Icy has no reason to run away," I said.

"His mistress is still gone."

"But we know where she is. It's only a matter of time until she's moved to a cemetery. But you may be right. Icy is a remarkable dog."

It wouldn't surprise me if he escaped from the horse farm again, returned to his old home, and followed the trail to lie and mourn once again at the grave in the woods.

That was what remarkable dogs did.

~ * ~

Brent arrived bearing gifts as he usually did. A bottle of wine and a bouquet of hot house roses for me. The roses were gorgeous, mixed rainbow colors with an intoxicating fragrance.

At his side, Annica pushed back her hood, and her earrings, sprays of red Valentine hearts, clinked together.

We were both thinking of the next red holiday.

"Brent is feeling generous today," Annica said. "He bought me a clock. It's not a cuckoo, but that's okay. I don't like chirping and music. Just chimes."

Crane took Brent's snow-covered jacket and Annica's purple parka.

Brent found his favorite seat, the rocker. "I wish you'd let me replace that painting and the other stuff, Sheriff. I'm trying to pay everyone back for their lost antiques. Where they are now is anybody's guess."

"They're probably in another state," I said. "Thank heavens Gloria MacBride won't be traveling with them."

"She'll recover. Then I hope they charge her with attempted murder."

"That's not much incentive for getting well," Annica pointed out.

I said, "What's going to happen to River Rose, I wonder."

"Once Rosalyn's death is confirmed, eventually it'll go to her next of kin."

"Does she have one?" I asked.

"I don't know."

I wasn't even sure if she had made out a will.

I thought of the snowswept acres, the yellow ranch house so attractive if you didn't know its history, and the kennel building. Most of all, of those thick, dark woods that had kept their secret so long.

That haunted place, home of the Winter Ghost. For a time she would have River Rose to herself without even the quicksilver collie for a companion.

That was the way it had to be when you were dead.

"Enough talk," Brent said, rubbing his hands together. "When's dinner, Jennet? I can tell you're cooking beef, but what's for dessert?"

"What would you like?" I asked.

"A pie."

"What kind?"

"Your special chocolate meringue."

"I guess I read your mind," I said. "That's what we're having."

"Talk about coincidences."

A soft missile landed at my leg. I looked down to see Misty wagging her tail proudly, a sweet collie smile on her face. With her long nose, she nudged her toy close to me.

I could hardly believe what I was seeing. Misty's treasured goat had resurfaced. I hadn't seen it in days. Weeks.

"Where did you find it, girl?" Crane asked.

Missy kept wagging her tail and closed her mouth carefully around it.

"It came home, just like the silver sleigh," Crane added.

I had a different thought.

We would never know where the little toy had been and why it reappeared at this particular time. Some mysteries will never be solved.

Meet

Dorothy Bodoin

Dorothy Bodoin lives in Royal Oak, Michigan, with her collie, Kinder. She graduated from Oakland University in Rochester, Michigan, with Bachelor's and Master's degrees in English Literature.

Dorothy worked as a secretary in Italy for Chrysler Missile Corporation for two years. Afterwards, she taught secondary English until leaving education to write full time. She is the author of the Foxglove Corners cozy mystery series, six novels of romantic suspense, and one Gothic romance.

VISIT OUR WEBSITE
FOR THE FULL INVENTORY
OF QUALITY BOOKS:

http://www.wings-press.com

Quality trade paperbacks and downloads
in multiple formats,
in genres ranging from light romantic comedy
to general fiction and horror.
Wings has something for every reader's taste.
Visit the website, then bookmark it.
We add new titles each month!

95702619R00182

Made in the USA
Lexington, KY
11 August 2018